A Child of the Dales

By Diane Allen

DIANE ALLEN

A Child of the Dales

MACMILLAN

First published 2022 by Macmillan
an imprint of Pan Macmillan
The Smithson, 6 Briset Street, London EC1M 5NR
EU representative: Macmillan Publishers Ireland Ltd, 1st Floor,
The Liffey Trust Centre, 117–126 Sheriff Street Upper,
Dublin 1, D01 YC43
Associated companies throughout the world
www.panmacmillan.com

ISBN 978-1-5290-3720-3

1 3 5 7 9 8 6 4 2

A CIP catalogue record for this book is available from the British Library.

Typeset by Palimpsest Book Production Ltd, Falkirk, Stirlingshire
Printed and bound by CPI Group (UK) Ltd, Croydon, CR0 4YY

Visit **www.panmacmillan.com** to read more about all our books
and to buy them. You will also find features, author interviews and
news of any author events, and you can sign up for e-newsletters
so that you're always first to hear about our new releases.

To my brother-in-law Ray Alderson (Aldy)
For the love of Dales ways and horses

Chapter 1

Border of North Yorkshire, 1785

'Put another shovelful of coal on the fire and back it up for the night, lass.' Martha Metcalfe looked at Ruby and sighed as she leaned against the bar of the inn. 'Just look at the bloody weather outside. Lord knows what we'll wake up to in the morning.'

Ruby shovelled a good helping of the locally mined, poor-quality coal onto the large open fire and watched as it dampened down the flames and took away the heat for a while. It would smoulder all night, along with the locally cut peat log, and keep the inn warm in the middle of the worst snowstorm they had experienced in quite a while.

'I think we must need our heads seeing to! Who else would live in a godforsaken hole like this, on top of the world – the highest inn in England, with the nearest village over eight miles away?' Ruby said and stood back with her hands on her hips. The inn stood high and nearly alone on the rough moorland of Tan Hill on the border between the Yorkshire Pennines and the wide Eden Valley, with views up to the Scottish Borders on good days. Once the area had supplied coal to the King at Richmond from the nearby pits, but now the mines were nearly forgotten.

She nodded at a drinker who was worse for wear in the corner of the bar. 'What are you going to do with him then?' Ruby looked at the small, wizened old man, curled up and snoring loudly enough to take the roof off the ancient inn as he slept where he'd finished his night's drinking.

'He'll be right – we'll leave him there until the morning. Old Jake won't hurt anybody. Besides, we can't throw him out on a night like this, he'd never make it home. I wouldn't want anybody to find him frozen to the bone on the road back down to Reeth.' Martha gave a sigh. 'His wife will be turning in her grave if she knows that he's spending all his hard-earned brass drowning his sorrows in the corner of our hostelry. She was such a pious soul, never hardly spoke to anybody.' She smiled and looked at the old man, who was obviously broken-hearted after the death of his wife.

'I'll get a blanket and put it over him. He's had the best part of eight pints tonight. He and Rob Jenkins got carried away playing dominoes, which was alright for Rob as he lives just next door, but Jake should have known better on a night like this.' Ruby picked up the lit candle from the end of the bar and made for the stone

2

stairway. The candle flickered as she climbed the steps – the draughts of wind even penetrating the thick walls of the pub as they howled and growled, with drifting snow as high as the roof against the most exposed side of the seventeenth-century building. She quickly made her way to the bedding box along the narrow hallway, then walked back to the woman she had always known as her mother, since she had been found on the inn's steps on a midsummer morning all those years ago. She carefully unfolded the heavy grey blanket and placed it gently around the faithful old drinker. Since the death of his wife, the Tan Hill Inn had been his second home, and Martha and Ruby felt obliged to give him their care and attention.

'That's right, put it over him, the silly old bugger. He should look after himself a bit better than he does. It is a pity he's no family to care for him.' Martha, the inn's tough-talking owner with a heart of gold, smiled when Jake didn't move a muscle as Ruby placed the blanket around him. 'Right, let's away to our beds – it will be morning all too soon. I must admit I'm not looking forward to undressing. I might go to bed as I am, and nobody will be any the wiser. It will be that cold upstairs.' She smiled as she saw the disgust on Ruby's face. 'It's alright for you, lady, you are young and bonny-looking, but when you get to my age it makes no difference what you dress like. Men would tolerate me, no matter what I appeared or smelt like. They come here for the beer and the whisky, not to gaze and think unmentionable thoughts, like they have been having, looking at you of late.'

3

'I couldn't go to bed in my clothes. I might not wash, because the water in the jug will be freezing, but I'll definitely undress. Anyway you are wrong: many a man flirts with you over that bar, and you are loved by all the miners and travellers who come along this road. They always ask for you, if I serve them.' Ruby grinned at the woman who was as broad as she was tall, with greying hair and a dress that had definitely seen better days; but for all that, she had a loving smile, a bonny face and eyes that twinkled with mischief and entranced many a customer over the bar, when the worse for a drink.

'Pah, it's the drink that talks – and well you know it. They know they are on safe ground when they flirt with old Martha. Now you, my lass, are a different bag of doings. You've got to the age when you are catching men's eyes. I've seen them ogling you of late. You want nowt with any of the locals. I don't know where you came from, but those looks are not from around here. You deserve to court somebody with wealth, not some down-on-his-luck miner or farmer.'

Martha looked at Ruby. She had brought the girl up as her own, but her looks would always belie where her true roots lay. Her skin was olive and smooth, even in the coldest of winters, and her hair was raven-black and she had almond-coloured eyes and high cheekbones. Where she had come from that summer morning, no one knew. There had been no sign of her mother or father as Ruby lay screaming for attention on the step of the Tan Hill Inn, wrapped tightly in only a colourful shawl, in a wooden box with a silver bracelet beside her. Fred,

Martha's husband, had brought Ruby in to her and had stared with dismay at the small, angry form that had been left without name or explanation, and both had wondered what to do with her. Martha had never been able to conceive and looked upon the baby as a gift from the gods, immediately making the small crying bundle her own. Only the locals in the coal miners' cottages next door knew how the baby had been found and they swore not to breathe a word to anyone who showed an interest in how Ruby had appeared.

Now that Ruby had grown into the most beautiful young woman and had reached the age of nineteen, men were queuing up to see her as she poured them a drink and smiled at them, making conversation easily with the local miners. The silver bracelet that she had been left with, which now fitted on her wrist, was Ruby's only link to her true family.

'Shh, what's that – is somebody is knocking on the main door? Who on earth is out on a night like this?' Ruby said quietly and looked at Martha.

'I don't know, but we'd better see. Get the pistol from behind the bar – you can never be too careful – and stand behind me while I open the door. Nobody that's lawful and right in their head will be out on a night like this.'

Martha glanced at Ruby as she reached for the ancient pistol that had never been used by either woman, but which they kept behind the bar for protection.

'Don't hesitate to shoot if you think they are up to no good,' Martha said as she took the candle and walked over the well-worn stone flags to the small, narrow entrance to the pub. 'Who's there? Make yourself known. What are you doing out on a night like tonight on this moorland?' she yelled from behind the door and glanced worriedly at Ruby.

'Open up, woman, before I die this night. I'm Reuben Blake – Black Blake to those who know me in this godforsaken place. The blizzard has caught me on my way to Reeth. For the love of God, woman, open the door. I'm not armed, I'm of no threat to you, but you'll have to bury me if you don't show pity on this soul of mine.' Reuben Blake yelled through the sturdy wooden door and hammered on it as he clung to life, frozen to the bone.

Martha turned to Ruby and whispered, 'Oh, my Lord, it is Reuben Blake; of all the people knocking on the door this night, it is the devil himself.' She glanced at Ruby and shook her head. 'He's a bad lot – we shouldn't let him in.'

'But he'll die, Mother. You can't leave him out there, not in this weather.' Ruby pulled on Martha's arm, urging her to open the bolts on the door.

'Let me in. I'll curse you for the rest of your days if you leave me to die here. There will be no peace for you, Martha Metcalfe. I'll make sure the devil takes your soul as well as mine this night, if you don't let me in.' Reuben leaned against the door, shivering and covered with snow.

'God help us, he will sell my soul to the devil – he's already in league with him, from what I've heard,' Martha whispered to Ruby as she pulled the bolt back from the door. 'Keep your distance from him, my lass. I'll let him in, as we can't let him perish.'

Ruby stood back and watched as Martha opened the door and the frozen form of Reuben Blake tumbled into the bar room, staggering across the bare wooden floor to one of the chairs next to the fire.

'A brandy, woman, I need some warmth in these bones of mine.' Reuben took his cloak, coated with snow, from around him and removed his felt hat to reveal a mop of long black curly hair and a hardened face, with steel-grey eyes that looked at Ruby as she ran behind the bar to do his bidding while Martha warily stoked the fire and gazed at him. 'Don't worry, I've got brass on me. I can pay my way. I thought I was gone from this world for sure. The weather is as wild as hell, and my bloody horse lost a shoe as we climbed the Silver Hill, else I wouldn't be bothering you this night.'

Reuben looked at Martha as he warmed his hands, then stood with his back to the fire, warming each and every bone in his body while swigging back his brandy and demanding another when he placed the empty glass down on the table before him.

'I see this place has not improved since my last visit. It's still a pigsty, and I can see that I'm as welcome as ever to you, Martha. At least your barmaid is easy on the eye,' Reuben said with sarcasm as the colour returned to his cheeks.

'You know why you are not welcome here, Reuben Blake. My Fred would still be alive now if it hadn't been for you and your raggle-taggle band of followers. I will never have it in my heart to forgive you for not saving my Fred from the blow that put him in his coffin.' Martha wailed and sat down heavily in the chair, next to the man she blamed for her husband's death.

'To hear you talk, you'd think it was me who hit your old man. It was an accident that he got in the way of Donald Beattie and the Aldersons. He should never have got involved in the row. The horse wasn't worth that much anyway, and it certainly wasn't worth your old man's death. Besides, old woman, they were not my followers – just horse-dealers like me, but with fewer morals. I've more about me than them lot, and a great deal more sense than your old fella, who should have turned his back on their exploits. He'd have still been alive if he had.'

'If that bastard of a man hadn't stolen the horse in the first place, there would have been no fighting and my Fred would be alive, and your mate would not be rotting in Richmond gaol. I'll never forget you standing back and laughing at Fred's feeble attempts to defend himself. You could have saved him, but you never lifted a bloody finger. It's right what they say about you, Reuben Blake: your heart is black – black as that coal on the fire there.'

Martha stared at the man whom honest people in the Dales and on the moors were fearful of, and who was hated for his thieving ways and his hold over everyday folk.

'It's time you and your brothers – aye, and that old mother of yours – changed your ways. Lived decent lives, like the rest of us.' Martha glared at the man she hated, but whom she feared for his quick temper, and because he was descended from Border reivers, who were well known for their underhand wheeler-dealing as well as their horse skills.

'And you, Martha Metcalfe, should not listen to idle gossip. The horse wasn't stolen, we just happened to come across it on the moorland. And when we came here with it, to find its owner, we were thought the worse of. If you think I was going to take on a fella I knew to be the best in the county with his fists, then you think wrong. Your Fred should have stopped behind the bar, like this bonny creature is doing. By, I'd have been coming here more often if I knew you had her serving.' Reuben grinned and flashed a smile at Ruby.

'You can keep your eyes off her – you are old enough to be her father,' Martha said sharply. 'Besides, she's my daughter, so she's not fair game for you.' She spat and stood up, then looked at Reuben.

'Nay, nowt as bonny as that can have come out of your old withered bones, and she doesn't look a bit like Fred. She's a dark beauty. There must have been a bit of better breeding in her from somewhere.' Reuben grinned again, then went and leaned on the bar and stared at Ruby, who showed no fear of the older man, who obviously thought a lot of himself to be ogling somebody half his age.

'My mother's right – I've no desire to be looked at and talked about by you. I'd forgotten your name until tonight, but I remember now. I was only a child when you and your so-called friends stopped outside and chose to fight the local Alderson family. I watched as I lay in the heather and I saw my father killed. No wonder Mother didn't want to open the door to you tonight. She should have let you freeze.' Ruby glared at Reuben as she went and sat back down at the table; she wasn't going to be scared of this bully, or his family.

'By, she's brave, this 'un. She's got a sharp tongue on her, which she will have learned from you, no doubt.' Reuben turned and looked around him. 'He seems content.' He noticed old Jake still asleep in the corner, oblivious to the night's happenings. 'That reminds me. I could do with putting my head down. A good night's sleep in a decent bed and I'll be out of your way if the weather improves, come morning. I'm sure you'll be glad to see the back of me.' Reuben smiled at both women.

'The less time I have you under my roof, the better. I can't throw you out, so I suppose I will have to put you up for the night. Ruby, you sleep with me tonight, and we'll let him sleep in the back bedroom. Unlike you, Reuben Blake, I'm a God-fearing soul, and I could not live with myself if I threw you out on a night like this,' Martha said and scowled.

Reuben put his hand in his pocket and pulled out a small leather purse, emptying three sovereigns onto the table he was seated at. 'Here, that'll stop your moaning. It'll pay for my stay and, hopefully, you'll fill my belly in the morning. Don't worry, I'll not be braving your bed tonight. I hardly have the strength to climb the stairs, let alone waste energy on seeing to my urges, no matter how bonny that face of yours is.' Reuben smirked and looked at Ruby as she passed him a lit candle. 'My horse is in the stable next to that old nag of yours. I took the liberty of feeding and watering it, before I knocked on your door. It's too fine a beast to let loose in this storm.'

'That's true to form: horses put before folk. You'll never learn, Black Blake, and the hearts you must have broken with your wild ways,' Martha admonished him.

'Hold your whisht, you old crone. Now where's my bed? The brandy's done its work. I'll sleep tonight and then I'll be away at first light.' Reuben took the candle from Ruby's hand and noticed the glint of the silver bracelet on her arm, but couldn't be bothered to examine it more carefully as she led the way to his room, up the stone steps to the back of the ancient inn. 'At least it's a bed – that's the best I can say,' he commented as he looked at Ruby, standing proud and defiant at the bedroom door. He stared around the bare room, with the wind howling and the snow cladding the window outside. 'You'll not be joining me then? I could do with somebody to warm my bones.' Reuben grinned as he sat on the edge of the bed and pulled off his boots.

'It would be a cold day in hell before I'd do that,' Ruby said and pulled the door to behind her.

Reuben smiled, whispering to himself as he pulled the tattered quilt over him. 'You've about got it right, lass. It is a cold day in hell when you have to stay at the Tan Hill on a night like this. It's not out of choice that you have me under this roof – nobody in their right minds

11

would stay here, let alone live here.' He blew out the candle, put his head down and listened to the wind howling. He'd be away in the morning, he thought, as he closed his eyes and recalled the defiant Ruby. She reminded him of somebody – somebody he had loved a long time ago – but that would simply be a coincidence, as she was the daughter of that old crone Martha.

'The sooner he is out of this house, the better,' Martha said to Ruby as they lay in bed together. 'By the sound of the wind, we'll be lucky if we can get rid of him in the morning, as the snow was already drifting up to the eaves and the front door, when I opened it.'

'He's wicked, isn't he, Mother? You can see it in his eyes – they look straight through you. I don't think I'll sleep tonight, knowing he's across the hallway,' Ruby said into the darkness.

'I've got the pistol by my side, and perhaps Jake would hear and come to our rescue if Reuben tried anything.' Martha sighed.

'I wouldn't put any faith in Jake. He never stirred all night, not even when Reuben Blake was hammering on the door.' Ruby closed her eyes as she tried to fight the tiredness that had washed over her.

'Well, if they find us dead in our beds in the morning, he can't go far, not while the weather is like it is. Besides, his horse is shoeless and if he stole our horse, he'd soon realize he'd be better travelling on his own feet. My old Belle is a bit like me: long in the tooth, and with only one speed. No, we are stuck with Reuben tonight, so we are best getting some sleep. We'll see what the day brings tomorrow.' Martha yawned; she'd sleep, even if Ruby didn't. As for Reuben Blake, he could do as he pleased, as long as she got some shut-eye.

It was just breaking light when Ruby crept downstairs. She'd not slept well throughout the night, for thinking about the man who lay in the room across the corridor from her and her mother. She pulled back the wooden shutters from the windows and peered outside. The wind had dropped, but the snow was still falling, and it clung and shone like a million crystals in the dim light of the coming morning's sun. Drifts were whipped up into high peaks, to the height of the inn, where the wind had blown it into fascinating shapes; in other places it was only a few inches deep. There was no way anybody would be leaving the inn this morning, she thought, as she poked the fire back into life and looked at Jake, who was still snoring in his adopted corner. She'd leave him be for a little while longer; after all, he wasn't going anywhere in the current weather. Alas, that also meant she and her mother would be lumbered with Reuben Blake for the day, unless he dared take his life in his hands and continue on his journey to the nearest village of Reeth, or back home to the high fells of Stainmore.

Once the fire had leapt back into life, she went into the stone-flagged kitchen and, grabbing her shawl from behind the kitchen door, opened the back door to the yard outside. It was relatively clear of snow, being protected by the front of the inn. She hoped the water pump would not be frozen, as she stood at the back door next to the pump and the stone trough that was usually filled with water. A bit of snow lay fresh and virginal upon the yard, and Ruby glanced across at the four miners' cottages. The only sign of life within them came from the smoke rising from each chimney. There would be no work done in the open coal mines today – or for a while, if the weather did not lift.

She pulled her shawl tightly around her and hung her bucket over the pump's head as, with both hands, she took the handle and pushed it up and down, in the hope that water would soon fill her bucket. There might be snow on the ground, but it was not freezing as hard as it did some days she had known at the Tan Hill, so she was grateful that after a while her bucket was filled with cold, clear water for the morning's use. Back in the kitchen, she filled the kettle and lit the small fire that she and her mother would cook on and stay close to for the rest of the day, placing the kettle on the hook that hung above the flames. She then went into the larder and cut slices of home-cured bacon from the flitch that hung from hooks in the ceiling. The pig had been killed and butchered in autumn for days just like this, when the inn was dependent on what stores they had laid down for the winter. In the spring a piglet would be bought and fattened and reared for the following winter – it was a cycle that had been that way for as long as anyone could remember. It was a matter of life and death if provision was not made for the northern Dales weather, which could turn so quickly.

She placed the fatty slices into a large frying pan and

then carried it through to the larger fire in the bar, which had quickly jumped into life with the coal that she had placed upon it. The aroma from the frying bacon soon filled the air, tempting Jake to wake and listen to his empty stomach, which had started grumbling at the smell of food that it now longed for.

'Bloody hell, lass, for a minute I wondered where I was. I must have slept here all night. I remember looking out of the door and thinking there was no way I'd face the walk back home because of the weather, but after that, my mind is a blank.' Jake pulled off the blanket that Ruby had placed around him and stood up, stretched and yawned. 'It's no good, I need a pee. I'll be back in a minute. I'll go and relieve myself outside.' The old man looked at Ruby as she fried the spitting bacon. 'Any chance of me having a slice of that, before I make my way back home?'

'That's what I'm cooking it for – there's enough for all of us, including our other guest when he makes his way down the stairs.' Ruby scowled as Jake disappeared quickly out of the front door to relieve himself at the corner of the inn, out of the gaze of anybody in the cottages. She could hear footsteps overhead making the ancient floorboards creek. She had also wakened Reuben Blake with the tempting smell of bacon, but in his case she would not waste her breath on much conversation, she decided, as Jake came back in and stood beside her, warming his hands.

'It's still bloody wild out there, but there is a chink of blue sky showing itself over the fells at Stainmore – it will happen improve in an hour or two. I'll be on my way then, out from under your feet.' Jake smiled at Ruby. 'Is there a chance of a drink of water? I could drink a beck dry.'

'Blue sky over Stainmore? The sun always shines on the righteous. Isn't that right, my bonny lass?' Reuben Blake stood at the bottom of the stairs and grinned at Ruby, and looked at the astonishment on Jake Hartley's face.

'Lord preserve us, I didn't know you were staying here? Bloody hell, I must have been drunk last night. I can't even remember seeing you here.' Jake stood and stared at the man everyone knew, but gave a wide berth to.

'I was a late visitor – you know how it is, Jake.' Reuben grinned and winked as he sat down in the chair next to the fire.

'Oh, I see. Aye, I understand.' Jake looked at Ruby, who seemed angry as she finished frying the bacon.

'His horse lost a shoe and he got stuck in the blizzard – there's nothing more to be read into that, Jake Hartley. So don't you go tittle-tattling down in Reeth. He should have died out there, if I'd had my way.' Ruby walked past both men with her fried bacon and left them looking at one another.

'She's a fair lass, is that one.' Reuben grinned at Jake.

'Aye, she's a good 'un – she's thought a lot of around these parts.' Jake sat down in the adjacent chair and wondered what to say to the dark visitor with a repu-tation from hell.

'Good morning, gents, and I say that tongue-in-cheek.

16

I trust you both slept well?' Martha walked down the stairs and looked at the two guests, neither of whom she had wanted. 'Has my Ruby wakened you up with the smell of bacon? I'm afraid you'll have to have yesterday's bread with it. I'm up late this morning, else I'd have baked it by now. I couldn't sleep a wink because of one thing or another.' Martha gazed at Reuben. She'd lain in her bed thinking only of the man in the next room, frightened that at any time he might come in and have his wicked way with Ruby, and do even worse to her.

'It'll make no difference. I'll be on my way as soon as my horse and I have eaten, although I'll have to walk it, no matter the weather. I've some business in Reeth that I need to get sorted,' Reuben said and looked across at Jake, who was shaking his head.

'You've not seen the drifts out there. They are the height of the inn at the side the wind was blowing. It would take you all day just to walk a mile or two. The snow might be stopping, but the depth of snow in places is too deep to risk going anywhere,' Jake replied.

'You live in Reeth, I've seen you drinking at The Oak. If we go together we'll come to no harm. I'm not stopping another night in this godforsaken place. Besides, my business, as I say, won't wait. Once we get off this moorland and make our way down Arkengarthdale the way will be clearer.' Reuben looked at Jake, knowing that he would not dare argue with him.

'You stay if you want, Jake. I don't mind you staying another night.'

17

Ruby came back into the room and stood with her mother, placing a tankard of water in front of their regular.

'No, I'll not outstay my welcome. I'll go and ask Rob Jenkins if I can stay another day and night with him – they'll have room for me – and then I can come and have a drink here tonight, rather than be on my own, back home,' Jake said quickly. He'd no intention of risking his life with Reuben Blake or in the snowdrifts.

'Well, whatever you both do, Ruby and I will bring you some breakfast and then it's up to you to sort out your own lives. As for us, once we've milked the cow and I've made the bread, the inn will be open as usual, although I can't see many visitors coming this way today. Probably the odd miner for a gill or two, if they can get away from their wives, and that will be that.' Martha peered through the small-paned windows that over-looked the desolate moorland. 'I sometimes think I need my head seeing to, for living in such a desolate place. And then spring will come, and I'll smell the earth coming to life and see the wild pansies in bloom, and I'll realize there is no better place on God's Earth.' She sighed and glanced at Ruby as they made their way into the kitchen to prepare breakfast for their two unwanted guests.

'I'll not rob you or leave you for dead, you old bugger, if that's what you're frightened of.' Reuben looked across at Jake and smiled.

'Nay, it's not that. I'd rather wait here a while until the weather improves. There are worse places to be stranded, and I've nothing to go home for.' Jake hung his head.

'Aye, you might be right. I never knew there was such a bonny lass working here, else I'd have been calling in earlier, and my brothers would never have been away. How old Martha has given birth to her beggars belief,' Reuben said and looked into the fire, warming his hands as he did so.

'She didn't; Ruby might call her "Mother", but Martha's not her real mother. She and old Fred found Ruby on the steps of the inn early one summer's morning. She was wrapped in a shawl, and the only thing with her was the bracelet she wears around her wrist. She looks nothing like Martha, thank God. But whoever Ruby's real mother was, she must have been a beauty, and she must have had a kind heart as well. There are not many nicer lasses than our Ruby – everyone around here takes care of her.' Jake went quiet as Ruby came to the table with two plates of fried bacon and slices of Martha's bread and placed them in front of their guests.

'I'll be back in a minute with some tea, unless you want a pint of ale. But you, Jake, I'd say you had enough last night. Something in your belly this morning is more important.' Ruby looked at both of the men and noticed Reuben glancing at the bracelet that was her only link with her birth mother. 'You can take your eyes off my bracelet – you'd have to kill me first to get it off my wrist,' she said sharply as she walked away from him. 'Happen I shouldn't say that, because that's just what you did to my father,' she added, then made her way quickly back to the safety of the kitchen and Martha.

'Well, she is usually a grand lass,' Jake muttered. 'She has obviously taken a dislike to you.'

'Aye, it seems she blames me for old Fred's death, even though it was not me who felled him. She's got spirit, I'll give her that.' Reuben pondered how to get a better look at the bracelet that had taken his eye.

'I'm not going back in there with the tea – that Reuben Blake keeps looking at me. I wish he'd go back to where he came from,' Ruby said to her mother and sat down at their kitchen table, swearing under her breath.

'I'll take it through. You go and milk the cow; we are short of milk, and no doubt the Lunds, Jenkins, Baxters and Browns will be knocking on our doors for some, seeing as the miners' cottages are cut off from everybody this morning. We can at least sell milk, if nothing else, on days like these.' Martha grabbed the two mugs of tea and looked at Ruby. 'I'll stand for no nonsense from that rogue – he'll soon get short shrift from me.'

'He's dark in his thoughts, Mother, you've only got to look into his eyes. No wonder he gets the nickname "Black Blake".' Ruby took a sip of her tea and then reached for her shawl. 'I'll feed Belle as well as the cow when I milk her, but I'm not feeding his horse – it must go hungry.'

'You feed it; he paid us well last night and, besides, the poor animal can't help who its master is. Reuben will probably see to it himself anyway, as he's known for his horse skills. Folk praise him for his horses, so his heart is good somewhere.' Martha walked out of the kitchen, shaking her head. When Ruby took a dislike to someone, she really did not hold back with her tongue, despite her generally soft nature.

Ruby pulled her shawl tightly around her and battled her way over the yard to the stable and cow house, which northerners called a shippon. The snow was whipped up into peaks at the side of the buildings, into strange and weird shapes, and now that the sun was breaking out, with only the odd fluttering flake coming down from the heavens, they glistened and sparkled in the weak winter sunshine. It was a beautiful sight, she thought, as she looked down Arkengarthdale and over to the north-east, towards the mountains of the Scottish Borders. However, it was too cold to stand about, gazing at the beauty of nature, when she could hear the cow mooing and complaining that it needed milking.

'Alright, alright, Daisy, I'm here. I know I'm late, but we've visitors in the inn and they come first, although I don't know why,' she muttered to herself as she turned the round metal latch into the shippon. 'Are you hungry and all?' She looked at the doe-eyed Jersey cow and ran her head down its back. 'And you are out of water. I'll fill your bucket up with that first, and then I'll fill your hay trough for you to eat while I milk you.' The cow mooed in agreement as Ruby picked up the heavy metal bucket and went to fill it at the pump, before loading the hay rack next to Daisy's head with fresh-smelling summer hay from the loft above. She then pulled up her

21

stool and started to milk, warming her hands by rubbing them together, before gently pulling on Daisy's teats, squirting the fresh milk into the wooden pail under the cow's udders.

The cow chewed contentedly on her breakfast, and Ruby soon got into a rhythm, emptying the udder quickly, with enough milk to supply the inn and the four miners' cottages for that day. The black cat from one of the cottages stretched and slunk from her bed in the shippon. Knowing when there was a free breakfast available, she purred and wrapped her body and tail around Ruby's legs.

'We can't have you going hungry, can we, Lucky? Here, I'll fill this old saucer up as usual, but don't let me mother know, else she'll be charging your mistress for it.' Ruby tipped milk into the saucer that acted as Lucky's breakfast plate most mornings, then watched as the warm milk was lapped up by the adopted cat. She walked back across the yard and placed the pail of milk just inside the inn's back door. Her mother would put it through a sieve to clear it of any impurities, before using it to make butter and sell.

Ruby returned across the yard to the stables. She wondered what sort of horse Reuben Blake owned, as she opened the dry wooden door to reveal the horse that had lost its shoe and landed them with an unwanted visitor.

'By, you are a beauty – you put our Belle to shame.' Ruby looked at the large black horse that stood at least sixteen hands high, and which turned its head and gazed

22

at her as she entered the stable. Its mane was long and silky, and the white blaze that ran down its face made it look the perfect horse, as it pricked up its ears and snorted at her, taking in her unknown scent. 'You have a bit of Arab in you, I bet, with legs like that.' Ruby stroked the horse's withers and went to hold the halter that she was tied up with, as she spoke gently to it. 'Now what's your name? You are as dark as your owner, and no wonder he gets called Black Blake: you and he are well matched.' The horse nudged her gently and snorted as she stroked its muzzle.

'Her name is Midnight. And you are right, she is part Arab, but not too much, else she'd be no good for around here. The old fell pony you've got is more suited to these parts.' Reuben Blake walked over and patted his horse on the flanks and looked at Ruby. He'd been standing in the doorway, unbeknownst to her, and had heard every word she said. 'She's the love of my life – more faithful than any woman can ever be. Aren't you, my sweet, apart from when you lose a shoe in a snowstorm?' Reuben stroked and patted his horse's head and smiled. 'I hope you haven't given her anything to eat; she's particular, is this one. There's some bran mash and oats in a bag that I placed down by the doorway for her. You don't get a horse like this by feeding it any old owt.'

'No, I've not fed her, but I'll go and see to Belle and leave her to you.' Ruby moved her arm away from stroking the black horse and tried to squeeze past Reuben. He grabbed her hand and looked at the bracelet upon it, then grinned as she stood there defiantly.

'That's a bonny bangle. It must be worth a bit of money, looking like that.' He stared at the snake-shaped bracelet, glittering silver, with ruby eyes and silver filigree skin covering it.

Ruby wrenched her arm away from his grasp. 'You'll have to kill me for it. I'll not give it to you while I've breath in my body,' she snapped.

'Aye, lass, you really have got me wrong. I'll not be parting you from your bangle, and you are safe with me in here. I'll not be laying a finger on you, so don't you worry. Get your old nag fed, and I'll be on my way in another hour. I'll brave the snow, now the wind has dropped and the sun is coming out. I have got a man waiting for me down in Reeth and he'll not wait for ever. You and old Martha can breathe safe – I'll not be under your roof another night.' Reuben watched Ruby. She hated him, he could tell, and she had a fire in her eyes and a look that he knew all too well.

'I'm sorry. It's just that for years I've remembered watching the fight, and I recall you standing there as my father lay dead on the ground. You should have helped him.' Ruby stood her ground.

'I couldn't have stopped it; it was simply an unlucky blow. I don't suppose you saw me carrying your father into the inn and placing him on one of the tables. I gave evidence at the trial of Donald Beattie, his killer. I told the judge how it was, and that I wasn't to blame for your father's death. Fred should have kept his nose out. Donald Beattie always did have a quick temper and used his fists before talking, the madman.'

24

'I didn't see that. I ran and hid in the old lime kiln, as I was frightened. It was dark before I went home, to find my mother crying and sobbing, and cursing your name and that of Donald Beattie. All I knew was that my father was dead and my mother was broken-hearted because of you. Your name has never been mentioned since the day we buried my father. It is a wonder you are not cursed, you were hated so much by me and Mother. You should never have darkened our door last night – you were best forgotten.'

Ruby looked at the man who stood in front of her. He was handsome in his own way, and a few years ago she imagined him turning many a woman's eye, with his long dark hair and tanned skin with high cheekbones. He even dressed differently, in a long black coat and white shirt under a purple waistcoat, finished by black moleskin trousers and a pair of substantial black leather boots. Standing more than six feet tall next to his horse, he looked the part of a highway robber or gypsy king. No wonder everyone was frightened of him.

'Aye, well, folk believe what they want to believe; give a dog a bad name and it sticks. I'm no saint, but I've never killed a man. I might play the law at its own game – make a bob or two out of the greedy rich – but I'd never take a man's life, I hope you'll believe that.' Reuben stared earnestly at Ruby; he wanted her to know the truth and not believe what other folk said about him.

'Well, you can live your life as you see fit, it is no concern of mine. Once you have left this place I'll prob-ably not set eyes on you ever again, and you'll be forgotten about.' Ruby walked to where Belle was harnessed and grabbed her water bucket, emptying out the dirty water around Reuben's feet before going to refill the bucket from the pump in the back yard.

Reuben watched her as Ruby pumped the water and walked back across the yard. He knew those looks and that soft nature, with a quick temper if provoked; it was what had attracted him to the love of his life in the first place. He wasn't wrong. When he'd first glimpsed the bracelet he'd known straight away that she was his daughter. He'd got the same matching bracelet at home, and if it was placed on Ruby's arm, the snakes would entwine, just as he and Ruby's mother had all those years ago. Vadoma, her birth mother, had been his reason for living, until she disappeared along with her travelling gypsy family.

When Vadoma had fallen pregnant by him, they had planned to run away together, but then her father had found out and everything went from bad to worse. Her two burly brothers had brayed him to a near-pulp one night, ambushing him on his way home from Kirkby Stephen. They had broken his bones and left him for dead, cursing Reuben and spitting on him as he pleaded for his life. They would not have a non-Romany in their family: he was a 'gorger' and he'd committed the ultimate sin in bedding one of them and getting her pregnant. They had laughed when they had left him to die; and that he would have done, had it not been for an early-morning traveller finding him and taking him home.

Reuben looked now at the young lass whom he knew

26

was his own flesh and blood. What he was going to do about it, he didn't know. He was tempted to tell Ruby as she walked past him to feed the inn's horse.

'Stop staring at me like that. It's not right,' Ruby said as she filled the hay rack up for Belle to eat and offered an armful to Reuben for his horse.

'Sorry, I don't mean to stare, but you remind me of someone from a long time ago.' Reuben took the hay; he'd save the bran for his return trip, he decided, as he saw that the hay was of decent quality.

'I suppose old gossiping Jake told you that I'm not really Martha and Fred's daughter. He takes great delight in telling everyone that I'm a foundling – he makes all sorts of tales up about me. He thinks I don't know, but I do. The folk living in the miners' cottages next door keep it quiet, but old Jake can't help himself; he loves to gossip.' Ruby finished feeding her horse and turned to look at Reuben.

'Aye, he did, although he said no more than that. Do you not have a clue as to who your parents were?' he asked tentatively.

'No, this bracelet and the shawl that I was left in are my only clues. I used to lie on my bed at night and wonder exactly who I was, but then I realized it made no difference. Martha loves me and that's all that matters.' She stood and looked at the handsome but dark man who was showing an interest in her. 'My mother told me to tell you, when I was getting the water, that I'd to make sure you pick up your change from your stay with us – she'd hate to rob you. There are enough thieves about

27

here this morning.' Ruby grinned and then turned her back on Reuben.

'Tell her to keep it. She's earned her money,' Reuben shouted back. Martha had earned that money and more besides, if she had been bringing up his daughter for the last nineteen years, he thought as he lifted his saddle down from the hook on the stone wall and started to place it on his horse. He'd walk the horse down to Reeth; the way would be treacherous and he'd have to take his time with his horse missing a shoe. That would do him good, as he'd a lot on his mind. He couldn't help but wonder if perhaps he should have told the lass that she was his daughter, but when he returned next, he'd bring proof with him.

Because return to the inn he would, once he had told his mother he had found his offspring. There hadn't been a day in his life when he hadn't thought of Vadoma and the child she was carrying. He might not have his Vadoma now, but he could at least have his daughter.

Chapter 2

The way down the steep valley of Arkengarthdale was nearly impassable, and the snow had been whipped up into fantastic sculptures, leaving some parts of the way barely covered and others with drifts five or six feet deep. Reuben looked around him: everything glistened and sparkled in the sun, nearly blinding him with the light as he held onto his horse's reins and picked his way down the well-known track that wove down the dale like a thin grey ribbon.

He had stumbled and slipped a few times, and so had his horse, and now as he passed the snowbound inn called the Charles Bathurst, he was tempted to stay the rest of the day and night there instead of carrying on to the Kings Arms in Reeth, where he had business with his dear friend, the landlord. Reuben looked at the inn; he could just remember Charles Bathurst, after whom the inn was named – he had been a brute of a man, whose great-grandfather John had been the doctor to Oliver

Cromwell. Bathurst himself had stood for Parliament, but had never got elected; instead he had bought the surrounding lands, and he owned the lead mines that covered the neighbouring fells. The power went to Bathurst's head when he threw a waiter at the Kings Arms in Reeth down the stairs and told the poor landlord, when approached about it, to 'put the charge on my bill'. He eventually went insane from drink. He had a lot to answer for, had Charles Bathurst: the fells around him were scarred and tattered all along the valley from his pursuit of riches. The local miners searching for lead made him wealthy, but only just managed to put bread on their own tables.

Reuben shook his head and looked up at the sky. He had better get a move on and reach Reeth before night-fall, as the sky appeared heavy with snow. At least then he could do his business, and drink and eat with his good friend Francis Verity, who knew how to make a fella welcome – unlike the poor setting of Martha's at the Tan Inn.

He stepped out with his horse and thought about the lass, Ruby. She was a real beauty, just like her mother. She'd left him in a quandary, as he wanted her to know that he was her father, and he wanted to take her home where she belonged, away from the wild Tan Hill and the drunken miners who drank there; she would probably end up wedded to one of them and have numerous children around her skirts, and little money in her purse, just like the rest of the local women. He could offer Ruby so much, if she would return home with him. Little did she know that she had a grandmother and two uncles who would welcome her with open arms – especially his mother, who'd always wanted a daughter.

He thought about the look Martha Metcalfe had given him as he walked his horse past the doorway of the inn. She'd shouted at him and said she didn't want to see him back in her inn, when he glanced back at her, hoping to glimpse Ruby. He'd noticed the tatty bedroom curtains move as he put his head down and made a start on the eight-mile walk into Reeth. Martha was a secretive old soul; she kept her thoughts to herself, and with good reason. No wonder, if she had always thought he had played a part in the death of Fred, her husband.

Reuben's thoughts wandered as he walked down into the valley, which was opening out as he moved on towards Reeth, his memory taking him back to the days when he had been young and free of any worries. His thoughts were of dealing in horses, as his family had done for centuries, and of attending Appleby Horse Fair, where he had first met his Vadoma. She'd been riding a dappled grey mare, bareback, with her bright skirts pulled up to her thighs and her long black hair flowing down over her shoulders. She'd nearly knocked him over as she showed off her horse skills in front of the admiring crowds of interested buyers.

Reuben remembered his father grinning at him and saying, 'That's a grand bit of horse-flesh, if ever I saw it. Or is it the rider you are interested in, lad?' He'd smiled at his father and shaken his head at him. 'Don't even think about it, lad, she's not for you. Not unless you want one of her brothers to send you to the good Lord. They are watching you, and they've seen how she's smiled at you. She dances with the devil, does that one, with looks like those.'

His father had been right, but that had not stopped Reuben from speaking to Vadoma after she ran her horse through the River Eden – she was as good at riding a horse as any of her menfolk. She'd stood and smiled and had watched the others run the rigours of the deep pools under the bridge in the centre of Appleby, both of them knowing instantly that they were attracted to one another, no matter what their families thought.

The love affair had blossomed in secret over the following months, until Vadoma's family decided to up-sticks and travel back to Ireland. But it was too late by then; the damage had been done, and Vadoma was taken away carrying Reuben's child. No word had come out of Ireland and he'd searched the Appleby campsite frantically the following summer, but despite her brothers being there, Vadoma and her mother were nowhere to be found.

Reuben sighed and put his head down now. The memories of Vadoma and the baby she had carried still hurt, and now that he had found the child, he couldn't let her not know that he was there for her, and tell her who her true father and mother were. He would return to the Tan Hill Inn, whether Martha Metcalfe wanted him to or not.

It was dusk when Reuben reached the small village of Reeth. Lamps were lit in the windows and smoke curled and danced into the grey winter's sky from the illuminated hearths within the squat stone-built cottages. He and the horse were exhausted as he led Midnight into the yard of the Kings Arms. The three-storey inn overlooked the village green and had a view all the way down Swaledale; it was a popular haunt of the locals, with its home-brewed ale, good food and small rooms, which always had a good blaze going in the hearth all year round. He passed over the reins of his beloved horse to the stable lad, giving him instructions on her care and asking him to go to the blacksmith's at first light. He aimed to return to his home of Banksgill, which lay in the hills of north Stainmore, with the River Belah weaving its way down below, making the meadowland green and luscious in summer.

Reuben ducked his head as he entered the inn. The doorway was not built for someone of his stature, and he took his felt hat off his head and made for where he knew his good friend Francis Verity would be. It would be the bar, and he would be leaning over it, listening to the locals' gossip and joining in with his views; sometimes Reuben thought his friend was more concerned with the gossip than with pouring a good pint or noggin of rum. He tipped his head in acknowledgement to a slip of a lass who curtsied to him and then went on her way, lighting the oil lamps along the walls of the well-worn stone corridors. At least he was more welcome here than at Tan Hill, Reuben thought as he walked into the main bar.

'Bloody hell, look what the north wind has blown in! I'd given you up for dead. I thought somebody had done the world a favour and done you in, you old bugger.'

Francis Verity came from behind the bar and held his hand out for his old friend to shake, and smiled broadly as he gazed at him. He grabbed Reuben's hand warmly and drew him against his body, patting him on the back. 'You look frozen to the bone. It's been wild weather this last day or two and I thought you'd have bunkered down at home. Here, sit down by the fire, I'll bring you a tot to warm those bones.' Francis put his hand on one of his regulars and urged him to move from the seat next to the fire, which he quickly did when he saw it was Reuben Blake needing his seat.

'I thank you, Francis. I thought at one time I wasn't ever going to see these old walls and you, old friend. My horse lost a shoe climbing Silver Hill, and then the snow fell, making me take shelter at Tan Hill. These walls are a lot more welcoming than those of old Martha Metcalfe.'

'You take shelter wherever you can, my friend. Old Martha is a queer old stick, but she'll not let you die on the moors. Besides, she's mother to one of the bonniest lasses for miles around, from what I hear from the folk who have visited there of late. I bet she took your eye.' Francis grinned and then looked over to his barmaid. 'Bring a tot of rum here and then a pint of our best, and tell my Jane to laden a plate with a good portion of that mutton hash that's simmering in the kitchen. This man needs bringing back from the dead. I know he's frozen to the bone as he hasn't shown any interest in a woman I've mentioned.' Francis laughed and pulled up a chair next to Reuben as he warmed his hands on the heat of the fire.

34

'Aye, I saw the lass, and you are right – she is a beauty – but I'm getting too long in the tooth for attracting women nowadays,' Reuben said, not wanting to reveal the real reason behind his lack of interest in Ruby as a woman.

'My God, man, you must be tired and hungry! You are the only one who's seen her and not commented on her. Fill your belly and have an early night. And in the morning, when all is quiet, we will talk of our business. I suppose the plans go well?' Francis asked quietly and winked at his friend.

'Aye, you've no fears there. As you say, we will talk about it in the morning when there are less folk about to eavesdrop on our conversation.' Reuben yawned and spread his legs out under the table. After Jane's plate of mutton hash, all he'd want to do would be to sleep. The business could wait a few more hours. Tonight he needed a good night's sleep to clear his head of his thoughts of Ruby, and to concentrate on the business at hand.

'Aye, that we will. Your bed's made up and the fire's lit in your usual room. Just tell one of my maids if you need anything; they know to give you priority.' Francis pushed back the stool he was sitting on, to go and serve at the bar and listen to that evening's gossip. He was only thankful Reuben Blake had shown his face to him that evening, as his cellar required his attention.

Reuben awoke into the darkness of his room, with a maid knocking on his bedroom door.

'Sir, Master Verity has asked me to check that you are

alright. It's gone ten in the morning and he is concerned,' the maid called from the other side of the door.

'Aye, tell him as soon as I'm dressed I'll be down with him. Has the blacksmith come to my horse yet, or is he as lazy as me?' Reuben shouted back, sitting on the edge of his bed in his nightshirt, with the lure of the warm bed still attracting him as he stretched and yawned.

'The horse is shod and fothered; it wants for nothing, sir. And your breakfast is keeping warm in the kitchen. I've to bring it out for you to eat while you and Master Verity talk in the dining room,' the maid called back and listened for her instructions.

'Right, tell your master I'll be down as soon as I'm dressed. I aim to do our business quickly and be in my own bed by the end of the day, weather permitting.' Reuben pulled on his trousers after relieving himself in the chamberpot, and then pulled back the heavy drapes of the curtains, which had made him believe it was still nightfall. Outside the clouds hung to the hills, the snow had given way to rain and there was now a grey slush on the ground around the inn. As the fells were still white with snow, and would be until spring, getting back home in the day would be hard. He should have been up with the dawn, rather than idling in his bed, he thought as he pulled on his boots and made for downstairs, to talk business with Francis.

'I take it you slept a bit too well, my old friend. You looked knackered, so I hadn't the heart to wake you.' Francis was hanging up the pewter tankards from the night before, after washing them.

36

'It was your Jane's supper, it made me drowsy, and the bed was a whole lot more comfortable than Tan Hill's,' Reuben said as he sat down at a table in the oak-panelled dining room and looked across at Francis.

'Don't you be blaming me, Reuben Blake. I like to keep my men fed – it's no good travelling on an empty stomach.'

Jane Verity came walking into the room with a bowl of steaming porridge, milk and a mug of tea upon a tray. 'I've held you this back. If you had been up earlier, you could have had bacon, eggs and kidneys, but I'm busy now with food for the rest of the day.' She placed the tray down and leaned over in front of Reuben, her ample figure and her rosy cheeks reminding him of the good wife his friend had.

'Thank you, Jane. There's nothing like a good meal, or a good woman, to put life back into a tired body,' Reuben said, winking.

She laughed and then proceeded to remind him that she was a happily married woman and to look at somebody who was free and single.

'That's more like my old mate. Do you know, Jane, he didn't even comment about that lass at Tan Hill last night, he was that jiggered?' Frances laughed and looked at Reuben, as he glowered slightly at Ruby being mentioned again.

'I should think not! He wants nowt with a slip of a lass, when he's got full-grown women like me queuing up for his attentions.' Jane winked at Reuben as she teased her husband's oldest friend.

'Get yourself back into the kitchen and let us men do business – you are putting the poor bugger off his porridge.' Francis slapped his wife's bottom as she left them both; she was best out of earshot, and well she knew it. The less she knew about her husband's dealings with Reuben Blake, the better.

'So, Reuben, what news have you for me? Are plans afoot?' Francis sat across from his friend as he added a touch of salt to his porridge and then continued to eat it.

'Aye, don't be fretting – we have a lugger coming into Saltburn in a fortnight's time. We've come to an arrangement with John Andrews to halve its cargo, if we supply him with some of our men. It's laden with rum, gin, brandy and tobacco and it'll be rich pickings, providing we don't get caught. The Revenue men will not be bothering us, but the local militia might get wind of our dealings. The customs officer is easily quietened with the offer of a free drink in John's Ship Inn. He gets the best of both worlds: a night of drink, his pay from the government and a barrel of the best Geneva, if he says and sees nothing.' Reuben lifted the spoon of porridge to his lips and then looked across at Francis. 'We'll be laden down with stuff, and away across the Pennines following the packhorse trails, long before dawn. Now, what do you want from us? And by God, don't breathe a word of our dealings to any soul. My neck, and the necks of others, are at risk if the militia get wind of our venture.'

'My Jane says I shouldn't be dabbling with you, but she's not got the pressures of running this place. Money is tight and where I can save a ha'penny, then I will, just to keep body and soul together. Drop me a barrel or two of rum and some tobacco; gin doesn't sell as well in these parts, but I'll not say no to a barrel or two, if there is some to be had. Locals like something with colour to drink, around here. Otherwise they think it's watered down. I don't suppose there will be any silk in your cargo, to keep my Jane sweet?' Francis sighed.

'There could be a length of the finest – I'll see to it. Anything to keep your bed warm and your stomach fed, my old friend.' Reuben grinned at his mate, whose wife was a little too extravagant with her meals, and who liked the finer things in life.

'That'll keep her off my back: anything for a quiet life. You don't know how thankful you should be to be single. I'd never wed again.' Francis sat back in his chair. 'There are rumours that the duty and excise are going to be lessened, so perhaps it will not be worth your while in the future for you to do these runs.'

'Aye, well, I'll believe that when I see it. The rich fill their bellies and try to keep us poor in our places. We'll never have the same privileges as those that sit in Parliament, and a few stolen barrels are not going to make them lose any sleep, especially here up north. They've enough to keep themselves busy with down on the south coast – the wreckers and smugglers run riot down there. At least I use a barter system: a boatload of finest Yorkshire sheep for my contraband, courtesy of brother Arthur.' Reuben grinned.

'Aye, sheep that's been stolen from the lush pastures

of the Yorkshire coast. Don't you or your brother ever dirty your copybook by stealing from around here, else Dales folk will string you up as soon as look at you.' Francis glanced at his friend; he'd heard of the odd sheep or two going missing of late, and he'd a good idea who was responsible.

'Sad old Swaledales they are, worth nowt to nobody. I'm a little bit more choosy. Believe me, Francis, the Dutch wouldn't look twice at our local breed. Anyway, don't you bother your head; your cellar will soon be full, and Jane will love you for ever with the silk I'll be bringing you.' Reuben stood up and wiped his mouth. 'I'm going to have to leave you now. I've dallied too long, and I want to get back home by nightfall, if possible, to see what my brothers have been up to while I've been away. I hope our Arthur hasn't been shooting his mouth off; he never was any good at keeping a secret, and he likes to brag about his latest conquest.'

'You can do without that. Tell him to keep his gob shut tight. He doesn't know of our arrangement, does he? I don't want the customs people knocking on my door – I keep a respectable house.' Francis looked worried.

'You hypocrite, Francis Verity. A respectable house! Now that is a laugh. Ransacked drink and tobacco and, aye, I know the odd room rented out with an obliging lady in it, if requested. You are more crooked than I am.' Reuben grinned and slapped his friend on the back of his leather jerkin. 'Your secret is safe. Now kiss that wife of yours from me, and I'll return in just over a fortnight, on the ninth of March, God willing.'

40

'Take care, my friend, and look after that neck of yours,' Francis said as he watched the tall, dark man leave his dining room. Sometimes Reuben Blake pushed his luck a little too far. He hadn't said anything, but involving John Andrews in his latest smuggling escapade was not a good idea. John Andrews was trying to go respectable, to change from being King of the Smugglers to being seen as the pillar of respectability in Saltburn, and he'd think nothing of blaming his old friend when it came to smuggling contraband, if it gave him some recognition. Francis shook his head. Reuben Blake would do whatever he wanted to do, regardless of anything he said, so he would simply hope for the best and wait for the most precious delivery, as promised.

Reuben was thankful to see the lamplight in the kitchen window of his family home as he approached the ancient longhouse with its barn attached. The dark shape of home was welcoming. It was situated with a large syca-more tree by the side of it, protecting the house from the northern winds that often blew across the valley. With the sleet that had started to fall and hit his face, Reuben was glad to be back, as he unsaddled his horse and walked into the kitchen of his home at Banksgill on the stroke of midnight.

'So you are back, are you? I was going to give you another ten minutes and then I'd be away to my bed. It's only rogues and vagabonds out and about at this time of night.' Elspeth Blake glanced up from her darning and looked at her eldest son.

41

'Aye, I'm back, Mother. It's a bleak night out there. It's raining down in the valley, but up here it has turned to sleet, although you don't seem to have had as much snow as in Swaledale. I got caught in a blizzard, else I'd have been back yesterday.' Reuben sat down in the chair across from his mother and gazed into the embers of the dying fire. He then glanced across at his white-haired mother as she sighed and placed her darning mushroom, with one of her son's socks over it, on the table next to her. 'So that's where you've been, is it? Up to no good, no doubt, I know there's something afoot with you all. Every time I look up, Arthur and Lennox are whispering and hatching something, and neither of them is fit with a secret.'

'It's nowt to worry your head about, Mother. Nothing is going on; just a few horse-deals that we are putting together, but it will mean we will have to be away for a day or two shortly.' Reuben smiled and took her gnarled hand, holding it softly. 'What have you been up to? You shouldn't have waited up for me. I'm old enough to look after myself nowadays.'

'Don't you soft-soap me, I know when my lads are up to no good. You take care, my lad. I'll not be left here on my own, with you lot in Carlisle gaol or even worse. Think on what I say to you: your father would not be suited with your wild ways, God rest his soul. Now have you eaten? There is some cheese and bread in the pantry; and put the kettle on what's left of the fire – it's got water in it.' Elspeth rose from her chair and made her way to the pantry while Reuben placed the black iron kettle deep into the red embers. There was no deceiving his mother; she too knew every trick in the book, being descended from the Border reivers. He'd often thought he got all his traits from her; there was nothing she ever missed and she would lay her life down for one of her lads, if she was ever asked to.

'Now, get some of this cheese and bread into you.' Elspeth placed the plate in front of him. 'I suppose, if you've been in Swaledale, you'll have been visiting that Francis Verity. He's another wrong 'un. You keep bad company, my Reuben. I worry about you, and why you simply can't settle down, I don't know.' Elspeth gave a sigh.

'Don't lecture me – there's three of us unmarried. Perhaps we can't find anybody who would look after us as well as you. So you are to blame.' Reuben grinned as he bit into his bread and cheese.

'You talk tosh. No woman is daft enough to have any of you, that's what it is.' Elspeth poured him his tea and put the partly empty kettle to one side, to be refilled in the morning. 'All you think about is horses and sheep. By the way, Arthur's finished breaking in that young colt while you've been away. He says it'll make a bonny horse and will bring in good money this Appleby Fair.'

'Hmm . . . Talking of Appleby Fair, Mother, I've something to tell you.' Reuben hesitated.

'You've not found another gypsy lass to break your heart again, have you? I thought you'd learned your lesson a long time ago.' Elspeth looked at her son and knew there was something wrong.

43

'No, it's better than that.' Reuben caught his breath and watched his mother as he told her his news. 'I've found the baby – our baby that Vadoma was carrying. She's the bonniest creature I've ever seen, and she's wearing the bracelet that I bought for her mother and me. She's the spit of Vadoma, and you'd love her if you saw her.'

'Now, lad, she could be anybody. Happens she says she is your daughter because she knows you are worth a bob or two.' Elspeth gasped and looked at the joy in Reuben's eyes.

'She doesn't know she is mine – I never told her. And she was abandoned as a foundling on the inn's steps, with just the bracelet and wrapped in a shawl. She's my daughter, Mother, and she needs to know it. I'm going to bring her back here where she belongs. My lass, my Ruby, my reason for living.'

Chapter 3

Ruby pulled up her skirts as she stepped out across the moor in the direction of the coal pit, where she was to deliver some of the miners their dinner. The cold wind cut through her as she hastily picked her way through the snow. Although no more had fallen since the night Reuben Blake had called on them, it still lay deep in places, preserved by the cold mountain air. The long fell grass that grew in tufts made her walk hard, and she was glad when she reached the face of the open pit, which ran like a dirty deep scar along the moorside. Fell ponies pulling carts were lined up, awaiting their loads, and dirty-faced miners puffed on their clay pipes as they lifted their picks and shovels, digging out the poor-quality coal for use in nearby farms and villages.

'It's a raw day, Ruby, and the ground is as hard as my arse. It's tough work. I'll be glad when the better weather is here.' Edmund Lund walked over to her and leaned on his spade. 'It's more like peat we are cutting out – the seam's nearly at an end. It won't be long before there's nowt worth staying for. Nobody in their right mind would choose to live here if there's no work.' He reached into Ruby's basket and took a piece of freshly baked bread from it and a chunk of cheese, which both soon turned black with coal dust as he ate them, and then he took a swig of ale from the jug that accompanied the meal. He looked around him at the low grey clouds and shook his head, watching the clouds scurry across the sky and threaten rain.

'I don' think I could ever leave here – I love it. I don't mind it being so wild. Another month and it will have warmed up. You'll find another seam and then you'll be back, happy.' Ruby smiled at her next-door neighbour, who always looked on the dark side of life.

'Nay, I don't know, somehow I don't think so. I remember my grandfather telling me how these pits used to supply the castle at Richmond. Even your place used to be called the King's Pit Inn, back in those days. Now they cart it in from up in the North-East: Newcastle and the like. Carting coal all that way just because it burns better, when there's a pit on their own doorstep, there's no sense in it.' Edmund watched as his fellow workmates, seeing that Ruby had brought them their dinner, joined them and helped themselves out of her basket.

'What's up, Edmund? You are not moaning again, are you? A bonny lass like this delivering us our dinner, and all you can think to do is moan. You wouldn't have done it if you'd been thirty years younger.' Rob Jenkins patted his workmate on the back and winked at Ruby.

46

'If I'd any sense thirty years ago, I'd have moved away from this godforsaken place and found myself an easier living. Anyway, you can hold your noise, Rob Jenkins – you often complain,' Edmund said and finished eating his dinner.

'It's a grand place. Closest to God, that's what we are up here. You've only to look around you – at the views of High Seat, Rogan's Seat and Beldoo Hill – and there's no better view on a grand day.' Rob grinned.

'Aye, on a good day: the one day of the year when the wind isn't blowing and the rain lashing down. See, it's coming again; it's starting to rain, and I'll be going home sodden again,' Edmund replied and wandered off to the scanty shelter of the depth of the coal face before the weather came down harder.

'Lord, he knows how to moan, does that man. But he is right: you'd better be getting yourself home. The weather is changing and it looks as if it could bring snow again. I hope that Jake Hartley doesn't think of staying the night with us again if he visits Tan Hill tonight. He nearly took the roof off our cottage with his snoring the night he stopped with us, and he never shut up about Reuben Blake – he frightened my young 'uns to death with his stories about him. They were made up and all. Reuben's not that bad. Folk have just given him a bad name,' Rob said and looked at Ruby. 'I always feel sorry for him, as he got partly blamed for your father's death and it was nothing to do with him. It wasn't Reuben that lifted his fist. And then he returned home on the very same day to find his own father had died, after

47

falling off his horse. He'd a bad day then – I wouldn't have wished it on anybody.' Rob sighed. 'Get yourself home, Ruby. Everybody has had their fill, and it's a good walk back to the inn.'

'I'll get home, as I think everybody's been fed.' Ruby watched the miners, who were hurriedly eating their bread and cheese before returning to the coal face. 'How do you know Reuben Blake?' she enquired. 'I'd never really met him until the other night. My mother never mentions his name, because of my father.' She'd kept thinking about the dark stranger who had entered the inn, and she couldn't make her mind up whether she admired or hated him.

'My wife's family know them all – they live over at Stainmore, two farms away from theirs. The lads are all a bit wild, a law unto themselves. You don't ask questions if you see a wagon trundling up to the farm in the middle of the night; but at the same time, if one of their neighbours was going hungry, they'd be the first to make sure they were fed. There's worse in the world, believe me.' Rob smiled. 'He's a handsome bugger, isn't he, even though he's twice your age? Don't let Martha know that you've been talking to me about him, else I'll be banned from my pipe of tobacco and my noggin of an evening.'

'I'll not say anything, he's not that handsome. And to be honest, I never looked twice at him.' Ruby picked up her skirts and pulled her basket over her arm as the first drops of icy rain fell.

'That's what all the women say, but they really look at him on the sly. Reuben's vowed he'll never love another

48

woman, as his heart was broken by a gypsy lass – that's what I heard,' Rob shouted after Ruby as she quickly made her way back across the open moorland.

'That's alright then, because there will be no love given from me,' Ruby yelled back. She grinned as she picked up her pace and ran between the tufts of grass and snow deposits to the warmth of the inn.

'It's bloody well raining again. I don't know how we are supposed to make a living on days like these. Nobody comes our way, and there's only so much drink you can serve the miners,' Martha moaned as Ruby came, breathless and fresh-faced, into the kitchen.

'It will pick up in another month or two. There will be more folk following the drovers' trails, and travellers with their wares, as well as those who already pass over these moors as they wander on their way. You know you love it up here in the summer. I've heard you saying all too often that you'd never leave this place until you were dead in your box.' Ruby put down her basket and hung her shawl up and kissed Martha on the cheek. 'Besides, you would never live down the dale, you are too set in your ways.'

'I might be, but these old bones of mine ache in the winter months. Rheumatics have set in and I'm not getting any younger. I look at you and think: where have all those years gone? If I'd have known then what I know now, I'd have chosen a different life.' Martha wanted a better life for Ruby, a life away from Tan Hill. The coal mines were not as profitable as they used to be, and the takings in the inn had been down of late.

'Well, I love it up here – you couldn't drag me away. Spring must be just around the corner because I heard my first curlew cry as I made my way back here. Soon the moor will be alive with nesting grouse and skylarks overhead, and we'll have sheep penned up in the yard, with their drovers snoring their heads off in the spare rooms. You always look on the dark side of things at this time of year, Mother. I can set the clock by it, you are so predictable.' Ruby smiled at her mother.

'Aye, I know. It's been a long, lean winter, and the sun on my face will make me feel better shortly. Now can I leave you to wash these dishes? I could do with a bit of a nap. That soup we had has made me dozy and my head dull. Fifty winks on my bed will get me in a better mood.' Martha took off her apron and yawned. 'You can polish the brasses, if you've a mind to – not that any of this ignorant lot up here will bother if all's clean; they simply fetch more muck in with them every time they visit.'

'Go to bed and get up in a better mood. You seem to have been in a right way with yourself of late. Things are not that bad. We are not going hungry and we are our own masters, and that's a lot better than some of the poor devils who work in the lead mines around about.'

Ruby watched as Martha walked dejectedly through the bar to the stairs. Since the visit of Reuben Blake she seemed to have been worried about something. Everything seemed to be depressing her of late; perhaps he had brought back the memory of Fred's death, an event that had always prayed on Martha's mind. Whatever it was, it was to be hoped that, with spring, her spirits would lift, Ruby thought as she filled the sink with hot water from the kettle and began washing the earthenware that Martha had made her bread in that morning. Martha enjoyed baking, but invariably she left the washing up to Ruby; and likewise the thankless task of keeping the pub's brass fender around the bar clean. Martha was not one for cleaning, full stop, Ruby thought as she set about her task, and it had been a good day for Martha when she had been found on the inn's step.

At the Tan Hill Inn, Martha tossed and turned on top of her feather mattress. It was bitterly cold in the inn's bedroom, so she pulled over her the patchwork quilt that had seen better days. She moaned softly; she wasn't that tired, it was just that she needed to have some time to herself. She'd done nothing but worry since the appearance of Reuben Blake. Had he realized, when he looked at Ruby, that she was not her daughter, especially after that comment about Ruby's dark features? She couldn't lose the girl, not now – not after all this time of her treating her like her own. Besides, she needed her, without mentioning the love that she felt for Ruby.

Martha breathed in deeply and sat on the edge of the bed, looking out at the grey, wet moorland before going to the chest of drawers that she kept her most precious possessions in. Within lay a box that had not been opened by her for nineteen years. It had been pushed right to the back of the drawer, out of sight and out of mind –

better for all involved, she had thought when she had hidden the secret attached to the shawl that had been wrapped around Ruby that summer morning. She unlocked the small mahogany box, trembling as she turned the key, to reveal the hastily written note on its torn and ageing paper. She looked at it and read the words, thinking of the wrong that she had perhaps done to the young woman downstairs, and to the man she had always despised since her husband's death:

I cannot keep my child; her life will be worth nothing with my own family. Please, if you are a good Christian, see that she gets to her father, Reuben Blake, at Banksgill Farm, Stainmore. Tell him I will always love him, and that the child was born out of a sacred love, which I will always have for him. Her name is Ruby.

The Lord bless you.

Martha stared at the note that she had kept to herself over the years. Fred, her husband, had not even been told of the handwritten letter, so great was Martha's longing for the baby that had been left for them both to find, as if by a miracle. After all, the Blakes at Banksgill were a wild bunch, and the child must have been born out of wedlock. She had convinced herself that the bairn would fare better being brought up by them, loved and fed as their own. And that's how it had been until the day Reuben Blake walked back into her inn.

The likeness between father and daughter was instantly

recognizable, and Martha knew he would return, whether she wanted him to or not. She'd seen Reuben glancing at Ruby's bracelet, knowing that he must recognize it. The thing that was worrying her was: did she need to tell Ruby about her parentage, or did she take a chance that, hopefully, Reuben didn't want to claim her as his own? Whatever she did, Martha hoped that Ruby – the love of her life – would forgive her. Her deceit had been done out of love, and she hoped that Ruby would understand, if told.

Chapter 4

'Are you right, our Arthur? I've told Tom that we need him on this run – he can be our eyes and ears.' Reuben turned and looked at the young lad who helped them about the farm. He was starting to regret asking him to take part, and indeed was regretting plotting their own part in the smuggling exploits. He'd helped and benefited from assisting John Andrews only a few times in the past few months, but this run was more serious and he risked not only his own life, but that of his brother and most trusted friend.

'You don't trust John Andrews, do you? You've done business with him, but have little faith in him. If it doesn't feel right, then we shouldn't be going,' Arthur said as he looked at his brother and then at the young lad, who appeared frightened at the prospect of being put in charge of the wagon and horses as the two brothers' lookout.

'Never trust a smuggler. Andrews's heart is black – there's only one thing he values and that is his life, and a rich one at that. He'd sell his own mother if he could.' Reuben cocked his pistol and stared down its barrel before placing it into his waistband. 'I hope I don't have to use this, but I'm taking it, just in case. Are you armed, Arthur? I've given Tom the shotgun; he's a good aim with that, if we do run into trouble.'

'Aye, I've Father's pistol on me. But, like you, I prefer not to use it. Fighting, stealing a few sheep and making sharp deals is something I'm comfortable with. However, I've not got the stomach to kill a man,' Arthur said. He took a sip of his tea and went quiet as Lennox, the youngest brother of the three, came downstairs into the warmth of the family kitchen and looked at the meeting taking place. The fire flickered and showed the walls to be covered with cupboards, all well stocked and occasionally displaying highly decorated pieces of china, collected by Elspeth over the years.

Lennox stood in his nightshirt, with his ginger hair tussled after a restless night's sleep, and yawned.

'You want your heads seeing to, trailing all the way to Saltburn to do a deal with a fella that I wouldn't trust as far as I could throw him. The customs and Revenue men will be all over you. I'll be bringing our mother to watch you dance on the gibbet at Richmond or Carlisle, if you are not careful. And why take Tom? I could do with him to help here. Mother's bound to know there is something afoot, if all three of you disappear.' Lennox yawned again, sat down in the dim light of early dawn and looked at his two headstrong brothers, and at Tom the stable boy, who had been co-opted into their scheme.

55

'She'll not think anything of it, if you stick to my tale. I've told her that we are going to the horse fair at Carlisle and might be gone a night or two. Don't you be making her worry – we'll be back before you know it. This is our chance to make good money; even the parson has put in an order for rum. Folk think nothing of taking from the thieving government, which is exactly what we are doing.' Reuben glanced down at his brother and swore as he put his jerkin on.

'It'll all end badly, Reuben. I have a bad feeling about it. You are mixing with different folk when you are on the coast; it's not like our Dales, and they'll not like you entering their world. Leave the sea and smuggling to them, and content yourself with horse-dealing and the like.' Lennox looked up at all three as they stood at the doorway of the family kitchen. Arthur and Reuben cared not for their reputations, while Lennox wanted nothing but a quiet life as a farmer, and worried daily about being tarred by the same brush as his brothers, despite his best efforts at keeping his head down and out of bother.

'It will be right – we can look after ourselves. Stop worrying, look after Mother and we'll be back before you know it,' Reuben said, as Arthur patted his brother on the shoulder and winked at him.

'I wish you would change your mind. Why can't you be satisfied with your lot in life?' Lennox sighed.

'Because I want more from my life. I'm sick of seeing other folks with more money than I can dream of. I want us all to have a decent life, especially my mother – she deserves better.' Reuben watched as his brother and Tom left the kitchen and walked out to their horses.

'But she is happy as she is, and she wants for nothing. You'll break her heart if you get caught.' Lenox shook his head.

'Get back to bed, try to forget what we are about and stop bothering.' Reuben turned his back on his young brother and walked out to his waiting horse. He hadn't said anything to his siblings, but he was beginning to wonder if his plans were foolish and if perhaps Lennox was right. However, the thought of making fast, easy money was too much of a draw to him and he was not going to miss his chance of grabbing it.

The three men stopped in their tracks and looked down and out to sea, having arrived on the cliffs above the fishing village of Saltburn, after stopping the first night on the bank of the Tees just outside Darlington. They had staggered their journey, resting the horses and sleeping out underneath the cart, despite the coldness of the early March weather. They were thankful to see the small hamlet by the sea as they walked past travellers and traders from the towns of Middlesbrough and the surrounding areas, with the thought of a good night's sleep in a warm bed at the Ship Inn urging them on. John Andrews would make them welcome and then would be glad to see the back of them, once they had loaded the cargo that he was to share with them as part of their deal.

'I've never seen the sea before. You can smell it – just

breathe in that air and it's full of salt,' young Tom said and gazed around him in amazement. 'I can see for miles, and look at all the ships and boats on the sea; it's as busy as any road.'

'Aye, out there are France and Holland – that's where our ship, the *Morgan Rattler*, is coming in from tomorrow. Into that cove down there, in the darkness of the night. John Andrews's men will row out to it, load the contraband into their rowing boats and then we've to move fast. The rags in the back of the cart are to be put around the cart's wheels and horses' hooves; the less noise we make as we come through the cobbled street, the better.'

Reuben looked out to sea. His heart was beating fast as he was out of his league – Lennox was right – but he'd not turn back now. He couldn't lose face in front of his brother and young Tom. He stared around him at the screeching seagulls and at the waves crashing on the beach. He was a long way from home, he didn't know these cliffs and they would be ripe for the picking, if the local militia and customs men caught them. But John Andrews had given his word on their protection while they made good their escape, back over to the wilds of the moors and fells that Reuben knew so well.

'Can you see that large white house standing by the edge of the beck that runs down to the beach? That's John Andrews's family home – that's how much he's made out of smuggling, and that is why we are here, lads, to make ourselves a bit of that,' Reuben said and grinned, trying to quell his worries and sound positive at the promise of easy money. 'Come on away. Let's get our bellies filled, have a good night's sleep and see what the crusty Scotsman, Andrews, has to say for himself. He's a tough talker and is as slippery as an eel when it comes to the militia and customs, but we can trust him, so stop your worrying.'

'I'm not worrying, but you don't sound so bloody confident, our Reuben. Do you think we should turn back and go home?' Arthur looked at his brother as he sat astride his favourite horse. Reuben had insisted that they had come on the fastest horses in their stable, and had a spare horse tied to the wagon for Tom. He was obviously preparing for the worst, in his head.

'It'll be right. I'm just uneasy because we are out of our territory. Tom, when we get to the Ship Inn, you ask to stay in the stables with the horses – they'll have a place for you to put down your head. John Andrews knows my face all too well and he's expecting to be introduced to Arthur, but he doesn't know about you, so let's keep it that way.' Reuben noticed the worry on the nineteen-year-old's face. 'You'll be safer there anyway. The Ship is no place for a pup who is still wet behind the ears.'

'The more you say, the more uneasy I am, Reuben. It's not like you to be like this – you are usually cocksure of your actions,' Arthur said and looked at Tom, who would have turned round and gone home if he could have done, as the horses and wagon rattled their way down the stony track to the settlement of Saltburn. All eyes turned upon them as they made their way to the Ship Inn, which was the main building on the shoreline, surrounded by fishermen's cottages, lobster pots and boats with nets draped over their bows. The fishermen and old salts watched as they went round the back of the inn; all knew what the visitors were about, for nothing was a secret in the small smugglers' cove.

The *Morgan Rattler* was due on the following night's high tide, and it was a time for the hamlet to pull together. Women would hide barrels of rum under their skirts, children would carry what they could, and the men who were involved would hurry and scurry to offload the goods and quickly place them in covered wagons to take to the white house on the cliffs above, where they would usually be divided and distributed by John Andrews, King of the Smugglers. However, this time was to be different: the first wagonload or two was to be for the locals, but the last one was to be filled for the strangers who were making their way into their lives. There was a reason why they would be last in the pecking order – a reason that only John Andrews and his household knew. Nobody dared question him, as he was a hard man who would see you dead in your bed if you did him wrong. The offcomers were riding into a trap and it would no doubt lead to a skirmish of some sort, with lives probably lost, if John Andrews had his way.

'They are all looking at us like they could kill us,' Tom said as he drove the wagon past the dilapidated, weather-worn inn and turned into the stable yard at the back.

'They know we are not from these parts – and when somebody comes into your part of the world, they are bad until you get to know a bit about them. It's alright, lad, John Andrews will see us right,' Reuben said and dismounted from his horse as they stopped outside the stables and looked around them. He had been there on many occasions, drawn there by the barmaid in whose arms he sought solace when he was far from home. He was used to the small coastal hamlet, but he knew Tom and Arthur felt uneasy. The trouble was that so did he, this time of visiting; something was niggling him inside – his deal with John Andrews had been agreed to easily, but a quick profit had made the deal too good to turn down. He'd just have to keep his wits about him.

'Away, lad, it's good to see you. I've been expecting you.' The tall figure of John Andrews came out from the inn's back door. His mop of ginger hair was far brighter than that of Lennox, and his Scottish accent was still prominent, even after living on the Yorkshire coast for most of his life.

Reuben looked at Tom and nodded at him to take the horse and cart into the stable and not show his face to John, before he walked over to shake the hand of the notorious smuggler. 'Aye, it's good to see you, my old mate.' Reuben walked up to John and slapped him on the back, then turned to introduce Arthur. 'This big lump of a man is my brother. I'll warn you he is as big a rogue as me, and he's got an eye for the ladies.' Reuben grinned and urged Arthur to join them.

Arthur walked over to the Scotsman and shook his hand. 'Don't believe a word he says – I'm the sensible one. True, he is a rogue and a ladies' man, and I've learned from his mistakes.' He grinned, stood back and watched the man that his brother had struck a deal with. John Andrews was everything that Arthur had thought he'd be: big in stature, as well as being loud and outspoken. Arthur decided instantly not to trust him, and to watch like a hawk what went on within the inn for the next twenty-four hours.

'Aye, well, you are welcome under my roof tonight. And tomorrow, lads, will be a boon day. You'll be going back to your Dales rich men. Now come in and settle yourselves down for the night; the stable lad will see to your horses. Is your wagon man coming in with you or is he to find his own bed tonight?' John glanced at the lad who was busy tending to the team of horses that pulled the cart, but made no attempt to make himself known.

'He's his own man and he says he's happy to sleep with the horses tonight. Truth is, he's a surly bugger – you'd not want him under your roof. Although no doubt he'll be sharing a pint sometime with us all.' Reuben smiled and glanced quickly at the young Tom. He'd be better off staying in the stable; if there was any trouble, he was out of harm's way and, hopefully, safe.

The two brothers had both been given a room in the old inn and once they had eaten the meal they had been offered, they sat in the corner and watched their host as he served his regulars and whispered to those in his inner circle. The inn was full of crooks, robbers and locals, who all knew what the two strangers in their midst were there for, as they sat drinking, telling their tales and smoking their clay pipes while passing the night with a gill of rum or a pint of the Ship's own bitter.

'It's a den of thieves in here, Brother,' Arthur whispered to Reuben. 'They'd slit your throat as soon as look at you.' He sat back and glanced around him, resting his gaze on the bonny-looking woman who was serving behind the bar and kept glancing their way.

'Not all of them. There's the customs man over there, and that is Mary behind the bar – she's a good soul, albeit a relation of John's.' Reuben took a long draw on his clay pipe and winked at Mary as she smiled at him.

'Aye, that's about all, and the lass won't be there for much longer, if I have my way. She's never taken her eyes off me all night.' Arthur took a deep drink from his tankard and swallowed hard, while still looking at the blonde-haired lass who had taken his eye.

'That she will not be doing, my dear brother, as she is already spoken for tonight.' Reuben grinned.

'Is she wed – is her husband here? I haven't seen her with him all night!' Arthur growled and took another swig of his ale.

'Nay, she's not wed, but she'll be mine tonight. Mary and I have some catching up to do. Besides, she'll tell me how things are with the business that we will be about this time tomorrow night. So cool your ardour, young brother. Besides, she'd eat you alive – there's no satisfying that lass.' Reuben winked at Mary again and then patted his brother's knee as he saw the anger on his face.

'I should have bloody well known it was you she was looking at, not me! I swear, Reuben, I don't think there is a woman in Yorkshire under the age of forty that you have not bedded. I am fed up with having your cast-offs. Do you know what it is like to hear them exclaim, after I've bedded them, "You are not like your brother, are you? Not quite as, er . . . vigorous." It is so bloody maddening. I hope you get the clap.' Arthur drank back his pint and stood up.

'Where are you going?' Reuben grinned up at his younger, chubbier brother who, despite saying he was going to keep alert, had downed the drink like it was going out of fashion.

'I'm going to check on Tom – he's not shown his face all night. And then I'm going to bed, on my own! I'll see you in the morning, if you have the energy to walk after your night's activities,' Arthur said, with disdain on his face, as he slammed his tankard down on the table and walked drunkenly to the back door of the inn to check on Tom, leaving Reuben to look at his past love, Mary. She'd be tapping on his bedroom door as soon as she'd finished her work behind the bar; she always did, and he couldn't wait.

'Tom, where the hell are you?' Arthur yelled as he walked into the stables of the Ship Inn. It smelt of horses, hay and linseed oil, and the horses snorted as they took in the smell and noise of the visitor in their midst.

'I'm up here in the hayloft, and I was nicely going to sleep until you made your noise,' Tom yelled from above Arthur's head and looked down on the drunken brother as he pulled up his braces over his shirt.

'Why didn't you show your face to us tonight and have a drink? You might have stopped us falling out over a woman. As it is, Reuben's had her before, and I'm not having his cast-offs.' Arthur staggered and held onto some horse harness to steady himself as he looked up at the fresh-faced Tom.

'I did more good here. I found out all sorts while I had my supper with the stable lad. Things that I'll tell you and Reuben in the morning, when you've both got clear heads.' Tom smiled at the state of Arthur; it was no good telling him anything in the condition he was in.

'Aye, tell me in the morning. Just as long as you are alright. I thought I'd better check. I'm away to my bed now. This stable is starting to spin around – that bloody ale was strong stuff.' Arthur grunted and made his way back into the Ship Inn and stumbled up the stairs to his bed, collapsing in a heap on top of the covers. He was thinking of what Reuben was going to be getting up to with his glamorous barmaid and cursing him, before he eventually went to sleep.

'I've missed you. I thought you'd forgotten all about me, Reuben,' Mary whispered as she lay back in the arms of her lover, whom she had been waiting for since the minute John Andrews had mentioned his visit. She kissed his neck and ran her hand down his chest as she looked into his eyes. She knew that he would never stay with her or marry her – he wasn't that sort – but she did love him, and a night lying in his arms making passionate love would have to suffice, if she was to keep seeing him.

'Nay, I'd never forget you, Mary, you should know that. How many times have I made my way over here simply to spend the night with you? You are the bonniest lass along this coast, and you know how to satisfy a man.' Reuben bent his head and kissed her passionately. They'd spent an hour pleasuring one another and now, in the darkness, they were content to lie side-by-side and wrap their arms tightly about each other.

'You and your brother shouldn't have come. John will kill me if he finds out that I've told you what I'm about to say, but I don't want to see you dead on the beach tomorrow night, for the sake of him saving his own skin.' Mary looked at Reuben and balanced herself on her elbow on the pillows. 'I bet he's not told you that he himself is working for the customs officers – that he keeps them off his back by tracking down other smugglers. They've even made him a captain in the Cleveland Voluntary Infantry, as the community respects him so much. He's setting a trap for you, Reuben. After he's got the first boatload or two of contraband, he knows the militia and customs men will be waiting for you up on the cliffs. They are coming from Scarborough. I heard John talking to the Revenue man, and he's told them to wait for you at midnight, although he will have made sure the *Morgan Rattler* has been emptied of most of its cargo by then, and there will only be you left on the beach. The ship's coming in on the nine-thirty tide, not midnight, like he's told you. I'd leave first thing in the morning and escape with your life.' Mary sighed and lay back down. She risked her own life by telling tales on her cousin.

'Lord, I knew I couldn't trust the bastard! I'll not be leaving with nothing – one way or another, I'll play him at his own game, and he'll not get away with this,' Reuben threatened. 'Now, don't let him know you've been with me this night, as I don't want anything to happen to that bonny face of yours. I'm indebted to you, Mary, you've probably saved us all from the gallows.' Reuben held her tightly and kissed her. 'I'll not forget your loyalty. I love you, lass, but I'm not one for marriage. You do know that?'

'Aye, I know, and I'm a fool for loving you. You probably say that to every woman that you bed. But I can't help myself when it comes to you, Reuben Blake. Just keep that head and body in one piece and don't get caught, whatever you do.'

Chapter 5

'Well, I think we should bugger off home. I don't care if you've to go shame-faced to half the Dales folks back home, when you say you can't give them what they've ordered. I'd like to keep my bloody head.' Arthur spat out a mouthful of saliva as he walked along the pebbled seafront after having breakfast and hearing what Mary had told Reuben. 'Tom said he'd something to tell us – he was full of it last night, but I was too lost in my cups to listen to him. He must have heard something as well,' Arthur growled. His head was throbbing, and now he had the added worry of perhaps being thrown into gaol, if caught smuggling; or, even worse, shot and left for dead by the big-mouthed Scotsman.

'We are not going home with nothing. We'll think of a way to make something out of this mess.' Reuben sat on an upturned lobster pot and looked out to sea. 'How can Andrews be in the militia? Everyone for miles around knows he's the biggest smuggler – they must be bloody blind.' He lifted his head as he heard the voice of Tom, shouting at them both.

Tom came striding towards them and grinned at Arthur. 'How's the head this morning? I bet you slept well, if nothing else – better than I did anyway. I thought I'd be having my throat slit at any time, but it seems I'm still here this morning.'

'You have far too much cheek sometimes for a farm lad, Tom Adams; it's a good job we both know you well. Now, what did you want to tell us last night?' Arthur asked and breathed in deeply.

'Well, the stable lad hates John Andrews – so much so that he didn't hold back with information.' Tom gazed around him, making sure nobody could hear what he was about to say. 'The ship is coming in early tonight. The sign to John Andrews's smuggling mates is that someone will come into the Ship Inn and say to Andrews that his cow is calving – that means the *Morgan Rattler* is in the bay and ready to be plundered. Now the stable lad also said that Andrews is a two-faced sod and he's lining us up to take the rap for his smuggling. He's been told to get two teams of horses and carts ready for Andrews's haul, and to delay our leaving to get our share of the plunder,' Tom said excitedly, thinking he was first with the news.

'We know. Casanova here got told this by the woman he bedded last night. But Reuben still says we are not going home empty-handed, the stubborn bugger.' Arthur cursed and looked at his brother.

'Aye, as Arthur says, we know, lad. We were just

69

wondering what to do about it,' Reuben said and shook his head.

'Well, I'll save you your blushes from going home empty-handed. Jim Westbury, the stable lad, took a fancy to my horse – the piebald that you don't think much of. We came to an agreement, if you are willing to go along with the deal.'

Tom looked at the two brothers and hoped he'd done right by them all.

'I said he could keep it, if he made sure our horse and cart was the first in line to be loaded. He said that John Andrews's lot would be too busy filling the cart to recognize whose it was, and as long as I wrapped up and kept my identity unknown, they'd not think twice about me sitting on it and driving it away. He'd be driving the second of their carts, so he'd cover for me. All you've got to do is wait with what should have been our cart, and then slip away while they are busy ransacking the brig again. John Andrews will not be on the beach; he's keeping his nose clean by drinking with the customs man tonight, knowing that the Revenue men and local militia are to be upon the cliffs at midnight, waiting for us. By then we should be well away, and all that will be left will be just John Andrews's men on the beach.' Tom wondered if he'd convinced the brothers of his plan.

'The stable lad can't be much of a horseman – that horse is soft-mouthed and hates taking a bit in its mouth. He can have the horse, but is it worth risking all our lives for? What if the lad is lying? I trust nobody except Mary in this place,' Reuben said and looked at Tom.

'He's not lying, he hates John Andrews – he whipped him to within an inch of his life for forgetting to rub down his horse. There's no love lost between him and a lot of the folk in Saltburn,' Tom said. He hoped the brothers would listen to his plan; it was either that or return home empty-handed and out of pocket. They'd do the job even if it meant risking their lives, if caught.

Reuben sat in the Ship Inn at the same table as John Andrews and the customs officer. It was not quite nine-thirty in the evening, and John Andrews kept looking at his pocket watch while making conversation and plying the customs man with drink.

'It's a clear night out there, a full moon and a high tide.' Andrews winked at Reuben as he filled up his tankard again and gave a sickly smile.

'Aye, it's a grand night – you are lucky to live in such a grand spot,' Reuben replied.

'It's a night for blaggards to be about – my lads will be extra wary tonight,' the customs man said and growled as he looked around him. 'At least you run an honest business, John, not like some on this coast.'

John winked at Reuben again and urged the customs man to sup up, promising there was plenty more where that had come from. He stopped suddenly as a young lad came in and tapped him on the shoulder and said, 'I've to tell you the cow's calving, but it looks as if all is going well.' John smiled at Reuben and the customs man. 'That'll be my prized cow – she's been carrying me a bonny calf these last few weeks.' He grinned and took a long sip.

Reuben got up from his seat and looked down at the old rogue who was intent on giving him up, to save his own neck. 'I'll have to go for a pee; nature will not wait. I'll be back before long.' He made his apologies. 'I'll stir our Arthur as well. He's busy up in his room with a young strumpet, the dirty dog, and he could show better manners.'

'He's alright – let the lad alone, he's best enjoying himself.' John smiled, thinking that the two brothers had no idea of what was happening under their own noses.

'Aye, I'll join in, if he wants me to.' The customs man laughed and took another sip before talking to John.

Reuben looked at both of them and winked at Mary behind the bar as he left the inn. He'd not be returning for a good while, if he had the choice. He rushed across the inn's yard to the stable and grabbed his horse, which was already harnessed and saddled. Jumping into the saddle, he made his way silently to the bay, where in the moonlight he saw the masts and hull of the *Morgan Rattler* bobbing gently on the incoming tide. It was crawling with local smugglers, with casks and barrels being placed in rowing boats alongside, while on the beach men and women made themselves busy loading the two carts that stood there; the first one was nearly full, and Reuben prayed that young Tom was the driver, as he watched him from a distance flick the reins and urge the two horses forward with the heavy cargo. He looked next to the cliffs and listened to the sound of the waves crashing on the shore and the wind through the rough grass, and watched the smugglers still running around like rats on the beach, not suspecting that the first wagon was not going to be theirs to share. He turned quickly as he sensed his brother sneaking up behind him.

'I didn't think you were going to make it. Does John Andrews suspect anything? Young Tom has nerves of steel; he's seated on that wagon, grunting when he's spoken to, and now he's making good his tracks. I've loosened the wheel on the second cart, so as soon as they set off with that load, it'll come off. We need to be away, so I've slowed them down, with the help of the stable lad,' Arthur whispered as he held onto his horse's reins and kept to the shadows below the cliff alongside his brother.

'Nay, Andrews suspects nothing; he thinks you are shagging up in your room. Let's be away. Tom will have to drive that wagon hard if we are to get a few good miles between them and us. By the time they realize what has happened, the militia will have shown their faces and then they will be too busy saving their own skins to bother following us.'

Both brothers watched as Tom disappeared from view up the track that led from the cove and, instead of heading for the white house that belonged to John Andrews, he'd be driving the cart hard along a homeward path. Now they had to make good their escape and hope that, amid the smugglers' greed, they hadn't realized that the visiting Dales folk had outwitted their leader and caught them all in his own trap.

As Reuben and Arthur led their horses silently up the cliff face out of the bay, they stuck to the shadows, not daring to turn round and watch the scuttling smugglers below them. Once on the clifftop, they looked down upon the group and out to the shining silvery sea, with the ship bobbing on the waves. The second wagon was nearly full, and it would not be long before the men realized what had happened to the first wagonload, and then all hell would break loose.

'Away, our Reuben, let's get going while we still have our skins.' Arthur pulled on his brother's jacket before mounting his horse.

'You go and catch Tom up. I want to stop and watch what goes on once they realize they've been played for fools. I also want to see if Mary was right and the militia is about to arrive,' Reuben said and looked at his brother, who was anxious to put miles between himself and the beach full of crooks.

'They'll see you, as the moon's bright. If they catch up with you, they will flay you to within an inch of your life. Come away – just for once, value your own neck,' Arthur begged his brother. Then both siblings turned, to hear yells from the beach and the cliff road beneath them. The wheel had come off the wagon as it made its way across the sands, and chaos was erupting as John Andrews's men realized they were going to be caught in their own net of deceit, if they could not get the wagon's wheel on before the militia rode along the clifftop.

'Looks like you did a good job on that wheel. I hope the stable lad doesn't get the blame.' Reuben smiled at his brother and patted him on the back. 'Come on then, you are right: let's be away, else – as you say – we will

74

not live to tell the tale. Tom must be cracking on; let's hope he puts enough distance between them and us and that the militia does save our lives, if no one else's, this night. We'll hide for a while in Guisborough Forest until it breaks light; nobody will find us there.' Reuben mounted his horse and whipped it with his reins. Now they had to speed on their way home and not get caught with their load of contraband.

'What the hell is he doing here?' Reuben exclaimed as he and Arthur caught up with Tom and the covered wagon, with the stable lad from Saltburn trotting alongside on the piebald horse they all thought they had left behind.

'He couldn't have stopped – he'd have been bloody well killed – so he's coming with us. He's got a grand-mother that lives at Leyburn and he's going to make his way there.' Tom pulled on the horses' reins and stopped the team, which he had pushed to their limits across the heather moorland. 'I'm frightened that they'll follow us. I feared for my life while I sat on the wagon and they were loading it. They've muskets and knives, and they know how to use them.'

Reuben looked at Tom and then at the stable lad, who was saying nothing as he sat bareback on the piebald horse that was of little value to the brothers.

'Aye, well, he did save us all, and so did you, Tom; we have got a lot to thank you both for. What's your name, lad?' Reuben asked the stable boy; even in the moonlight, he could tell he required some decent clothing and a good meal in him.

'I'm Jim – Jim Westbury. I thank you for the horse and for letting me join you. I couldn't have stayed. John Andrews would soon have realized that I'd betrayed him. I hid under the cover of the wagon as soon as Tom started to make his way from the beach. I'd already seen that this horse was waiting for me at the top of the cliffs, although I've no saddle. Did the militia arrive? I bet they squirmed like toads in a barrel, and it serves them all right.' Jim grinned.

'We didn't wait to see – we were best getting out of the place. We'll travel slowly enough with this loaded wagon,' Arthur said and looked at the cart, which was packed high with barrels and wooden boxes under the oil-cloth tarpaulin.

'Right, let's make headway and get a bit further on our way home. Make for Guisborough Forest, we'll stay there for the rest of the night. Head for Highcliff Nab – you can just see it in the distance. It'll be a good vantage point to climb up in the morning, for me to see if anybody is following us.' Reuben pointed to the rocky tor that could barely be made out in the moonlight.

'The sooner we are back in scenery that I know, the better. I think nowt of this part of the world,' Arthur growled. 'And I'm ready for a good feed: my mother's meat-and-potato pie would be more than welcome at the moment. You don't even know what you've got in this wagon of yours. You'll look foolish if it's full of stuff we can't make use of.' Arthur nodded at the covered wagon, which was full of items that had been bound for John Andrews's house.

'I'll be able to sell it and find homes for it, don't you worry. It will be alright – if John Andrews was thieving it, it is worth brass. Now come on, let's reach the forest, get some sleep and then we'll have a quick look at our haul in the morning before setting off for home.' Reuben gazed at the three men, who seemed tired and worried. 'We will be alright, so stop worrying, although I don't think I'll be visiting Mary again in a hurry. I only hope she will be alright,' he sighed.

'She'll be right – stop worrying about your woman. It's our necks that we're worried about. Now come on to the forest, and a few winks of sleep before we get away from these moors and back home, as fast as these nags will take us. Get this wagon into action, Tom. I'm not moping about, thinking of a woman. Reuben, you need to stop bedding them and, for once, give your complete heart instead of staying with them for just one night,' Arthur lectured as he and the two others moved off, leaving Reuben looking at them.

'You needn't talk – you never have any women queuing up for you. Besides, you know why I can't ever truly love another, and I've even more reason not to, nowadays,' Reuben said as he joined the three of them and sat comfortably on his horse as they made their way down off the moor and into the forest.

'What do you mean? What's your reason?' Arthur said with interest as he watched his secretive brother.

'You'll see. Once we are back home, I aim to do something that I should have done a long time ago, if I had realized what was right under my nose,' Reuben said.

Then he whipped his horse into a canter and rode ahead of the party as the wagon rattled and jerked its way along the rocky road to the safety of the cover of the forest.

Morning came all too soon, and with daylight came the added worry of being spotted by John Andrews's men, who would be searching for them. Pulling back the cover on the wagon, they all looked at their cart of contraband, before carrying on their journey.

'Well, I hope you know a good home for gunpowder, because we seem to have a keg or two of it,' Arthur moaned.

'I'll sell it to one of the lead mines down Arkengarthdale – they'll take it off our hands. Jack Fothergill will not ask any questions, he'll buy it. We've brandy and gin and the odd box or two of tobbacie, so it's been worth it,' Reuben said as he pulled the canvas back over the haul, trying not to show his disappointment at the load. 'There's no silk, though. I promised Frank Verity at the Kings Arms some for his Jane, but she'll just have to do without.'

'Never mind the bloody silk! We were lucky to leave with our bloody lives. No more exploits like this from now on, Reuben. It isn't worth it. Even if you don't value your neck, I do. What if young Tom had been killed? His mother would never have forgiven you; she'd have been left a widow and without her son to bring her any income. It's time you stopped being so reckless! Silk for Jane is the least of your problems until we get clear of these moors.' Arthur eased himself into his saddle; he was disappointed with the haul and was afeared that if they did not get back into the dales they knew, they were in danger of losing their lives.

'Alright, I know I was out of my depth when it came to smuggling. I thought I could get away with a lot more than we have. But it was good to feel the blood surging through the veins and to outwit John Andrews. I wonder what chaos erupted last night if the militia arrived – they deserve what they got.' Reuben grinned as he mounted his horse's saddle. 'Let's be away and hope that we get home in one piece and not too wet – by the look of the storm clouds that are coming in from the north. At least the weather will keep any followers at bay.' He stared up at the grey clouds that were scurrying above his head; it was going to be a miserably wet ride home and nobody was in the mood for celebrating, with a haul mostly of gunpowder, which would be hard to sell without too many questions being asked.

The journey back was hazardous; the moorland drovers' tracks were rough and stony and, with the threat of the smugglers or the militia following them, they were all glad to finally get back to the dales and valleys they recognized. The sight of Richmond Castle and the glitter of the winding River Swale had never been more welcome, as they made their way steadily back to Stainmore. Just south of the small village of Marske, Jim made ready to leave the group. He was glad to break away from the three men he barely knew, but worried about how to explain to his grandmother his arrival on her doorstep.

'Take care, lad, we are thankful for your help.' Reuben looked at the stable boy who had been treated so badly by John Andrews. 'Here, take this – it'll pay for your keep for a week or two until you find a job in Leyburn.' He reached into his pocket and passed three guineas out of his purse. 'We have you to thank for our escape.'

'God speed, sir. I thank you for giving me a chance to escape from servitude with John Andrews. One day he will be hanging from the gallows, no matter how much wool he pulls over the eyes of the ones in power,' Jim said as he sat astride the piebald horse, which he had instantly known was not of much use to folk who needed to put a bit in its mouth to ride it. He was merely thankful for a way out of his former life.

'Aye, God be with you, and thank you again.' All three men watched as Jim squeezed his knees into the piebald's sides and galloped out of sight, leaving them feeling weary and ready for home themselves.

'Well, we've made it this far, through rain and hail, and we are not far from home now, lads. If you are owt like me, you are ready for your beds. Come on, the last few miles and then we will have to face the wrath of my mother when she realizes that it was not a simple trip to buy a horse at Carlisle. That'll be worse than anything John Andrews could do to us.' Reuben looked at his brother Arthur, and at Tom, who was complaining that his backside hurt from being on the seat of the wagon for so long over the rough terrain. 'Lord have mercy on our souls – that woman has an evil tongue on her when she wants.'

'I don't give a damn. I'm desperate for her pie and a good night's sleep in my bed,' Arthur growled.

'And I just want to get my backside off this wagon and get warm; even my stable bed looks good at the moment.' Tom shifted his body, trying to get comfortable, and gazed at the brothers. He had known that working for the Blakes would be interesting, but he didn't think he'd be risking his life for them.

'Aye, let's get ourselves home. We have had enough excitement to last a lifetime, and I'm thankful we have got away with our lives.' Reuben too was ready for home as he wrapped his coat around him, with the early spring wind cutting through him like a knife. He longed for his hearth, and to visit the Tan Hill Inn to claim his long-lost daughter while next doing business down Arkengarthdale.

Chapter 6

It was Monday and now that the weather had improved, Ruby had washed the bedding from her and Martha's bed. It didn't get changed with the frequency that it should, she thought, as she fed it through the clothes mangle, watching her fingers as the grey-coloured sheets were squeezed of any excess water between the two heavy rollers. The sheets then fell into the wicker washing basket, for her to carry across the road to the open space of moorland, to be hung on the washing line that she always thought had the best view in all of England.

She balanced the heavy basket on her hip and, with wooden pegs bought from a passing gypsy who called each year on the way to Appleby Fair, started hanging the sheets on the line, which caught the winds that blew from all directions. Her skirt around her stomach was wet from the fight of washing the sheets, and her long, dark hair blew wild and free as she picked them up and placed them on the line; the wind flicked the sheets, making showers of water splash her face as she pegged them securely, so that the wind could not blow them into neighbouring Weardale. With her task done, she looked down the road as she noticed a horse and cart coming along the road from Arkengarthdale. The driver appeared familiar and she caught her breath and quickly made for the safety of her home as she realized it was Reuben Blake who was driving his horse and cart to the Tan Hill Inn's door.

'Martha, he's back. Reuben Blake is tethering his horse and cart as we speak. I don't want to serve him. Why has he returned? We've never seen him since my father died, and now he has come back within weeks of his last visit.' Ruby felt her heart beating fast; she experienced something strange when she looked into his eyes. It wasn't that she found him attractive or was scared of him, it was more as if he knew her innermost thoughts as he stared into her soul with his steely-grey gaze.

'That doesn't surprise me – he's got unfinished business here, and I knew he'd be back.' Martha caught her breath and reached for the inn's bar for support, as she felt her head go dizzy and her heart beat fast, knowing full well what Reuben Blake had returned for, and that her own and Ruby's lives were going to be turned on their heads.

'What do you mean, Mother? What business has he here? We don't owe him anything, and he doesn't owe us. Why would he come back?' Ruby asked and looked at Martha's ashen face.

'Ruby, there's something I should have told you a long

time ago. It's just that I never felt the need to, until he stepped through the door on that wild night. It was the devil that brought him to my door that night, and I wish he would go back to the hell he appeared from.' Martha walked from behind the bar, slumped into a chair and pushed her grey hair through her fingers before gazing at Ruby, her words being silenced quickly as the tall form of Reuben entered the ancient inn.

'Now then, Martha. Afternoon, Ruby. Don't either of you swamp me with kind words and heartfelt greetings. By the look on your face, Martha Metcalfe, you know why I'm here.' Reuben placed his hat on the table next to Martha and Ruby, then sat down in the chair opposite them, splaying his long legs out in front of him and watching them both.

'Aye, I know why you are here, but the lass doesn't. Let me tell her gently, and explain why I didn't do as I was asked,' Martha pleaded as she felt her heart nearly bursting out of her bodice.

'Tell me what? You are both talking in riddles!' Ruby said loudly and glanced from Martha to the man she knew was feared by her. 'Perhaps you should leave – you are upsetting my mother,' Ruby went on. She looked down on Reuben and stood her ground, seeing how distraught Martha was.

'Whisht, lass, it is time the truth was told. You are old enough to take it now, and I've had you too many years anyway.' Martha sighed and gazed up at Ruby. 'Forgive me, I've known this day would come, from the minute we found you on the step that early summer's morning,

84

but I thought I could give you a better life, and I'd longed for a baby of my own so long.' She reached for Ruby's arm and gripped it tightly. 'I'm sorry, lass, but Reuben Blake is your father, and he'll be here to claim you as his own and to do with me as he must. Your mother left a note in the basket with you, giving your name and asking for you to be taken to your father, Reuben, but we never did. Forgive me,' Martha sobbed.

'No, no, you are wrong – he can't be my father! I'd rather rot in hell than find out he is my father,' Ruby cried and looked at the man, who was examining her as she rebuked his parentage. 'He can't be, he can't be.'

'So you've known all these years, Martha, and you've deprived me of my lass because of your own selfishness. How could you? Ruby, I am your father. That bracelet you were found with, I gave it to your mother when we promised to be faithful to one another. I have the same one. They entwine together when they are linked to one another; the silversmith in Richmond made them specially for me, so deep was my love for your mother.'

He reached into his pocket and took out a silver bracelet in the shape of a blackberry briar, which linked with the one that had been worn by Ruby all her life.

'I loved your mother, and she loved me, but our love could never be. She was a Romany, I was a gorger, so our love was fated from the start.' He looked at the bracelet in his hands, and then at Ruby as she fingered the bracelet on her arm. 'We loved one another, and we would both have loved you, if given the chance. Her name was Vadoma Faa and she came from proud Romany stock – too proud to have one of their daughters unmarried and with a child by me.' Reuben bowed his head. 'You look exactly like her. I knew as soon as I saw you, that wild night, that you were my blood; there's no hiding your parentage, lass. You even have our stubborn, headstrong ways and temper.' He smiled at Ruby, but could see only hatred and confusion in her eyes as she spat back at him.

'So I'm the daughter of a gypsy and a horse thief! And you, Mother, have kept the secret all my life. How could you! I hate you all!' Ruby pushed back a chair and glared at both Martha and Reuben. Her past was not one that she had wanted to hear, and she would have been more grateful not to have known her parentage and to make up a perfect family in her imagination.

She pulled her shawl around her and rushed out of the inn, with tears running down her cheeks. She was going to the one place she felt safe: the top of nearby Water Crag, where she could sit in peace and make sense of the news that had broken her secure world. Why had Reuben Blake ever entered her life? Of all the fathers she could have had, he was the one she did not want, and for her mother to be a gypsy was shameful. The gypsies passed the inn's doors every year, with their gaily coloured wagons and horses. They were always hawking their goods, lucky heather, pegs and fortunes told; country folk knew their ways, but a lot did not trust them. Her mother was one of them, a true gypsy called Vadoma Faa – a name that was not even English, but Romany; she herself was of Romany descent and there was nothing she could do about it.

She ran through the long fell grasses and started to climb up to Water Crag, from where she could look out over the wild moorland and gather her thoughts in the peace and quiet of the countryside. Her heart beat fast and she was out of breath by the time she reached the grit stones, which she had sat upon many a time to take in the surrounding sights. For miles around, the wild moorland stretched out in front of her: to the west, in the distance, were the heights of the Lake District fells, blue, hazy and as old as the world itself; to the east, the sprawling North Yorkshire Moors; while to the north, the North Pennines sprawled out; and the verdant Yorkshire Dales were to the south of her.

Had her mother travelled to all these places in front of her, and where was she now? Ruby looked straight in front of her and followed the course of the Ease Gill with her eye towards the fells of Stainmore, where she knew her father now lived. He'd been so near and yet so far. Why hadn't he realized she was there at Tan Hill, and why hadn't he married her mother, despite the differences between them? After all, Reuben Blake was known as a hard man, with a mind of his own, and they could have run away together if they had loved one another so much.

Ruby felt tears trickling down her cheeks and she sobbed, feeling that her heart would burst with the confusion of emotions. Martha had known all those years who her father was, and she did wrong in keeping Ruby as her own child. Martha should have done as her true mother had wished and taken her to her father, no matter what she thought of him. Although Ruby had always known that she had been left as a foundling, she was grateful to have been adopted by Martha and Fred and had never thought of them in any other way than as her parents, but now this had changed. She had always realized that her skin was darker than most people's, but now she knew that her eyes were like her father's, and that she had a closer affinity to the natural world than to that of her adoptive parents.

Her mother's roots lay within her. She fingered the bracelet and stared out over the moorland, the wind whipping her hair against her face as she stood up and looked above her to the higher ground of Rogan's Seat. If she climbed there, she would have an even better view of the moors and Dales, but the day was not one for sightseeing. She would return home to Tan Hill Inn and see what Martha and Reuben had discussed in her absence. Whatever they had planned and said, she would have her own say about her future; she was old enough now, at nineteen, to make her own decisions about life. She needed neither of them, if they did but know it. However, there was a gnawing curiosity about the life her father led, now that she realized she was Reuben's daughter. There was also a feeling that she could never forgive Martha for not telling her the truth all these years. What else might she be hiding from her, Ruby wondered, as she wiped her nose on her shawl, dried her eyes and walked briskly out across the heather-clad moor back to the inn. She'd hear what her father had to say, now that she had come to grips with the news, and see what was going to alter, with Reuben Blake in her life now.

'You did wrong by me, Martha Metcalfe – you knew she was my baby. You should have done what Vadoma asked of you.' Reuben looked at the old woman, who didn't dare even glance at him.

'I thought I was doing the best for her. You were only young and a bit of a wild one, you couldn't have cared for her properly. Besides, we gave Ruby everything she needed – brought her up like she was one of ours.' Martha lifted her head and gazed at Reuben, although in her hearts of hearts she knew she'd done wrong.

'She'd have been looked after – my mother would have made sure of that. She always wanted a lass, and I'd have loved and cared for Ruby. I'd have married Ruby's mother, if her family had been in agreement with it, but instead they gave me a good hiding and went on their way, and I've never seen Vadoma since. You've got me wrong, Martha. All I do is try and make a living in this world. I'm no different from you, except that I've not been living a lie for the last nineteen years.'

Reuben sat up and leaned forward to look at the old woman, who he'd not deny had done a good job of raising his daughter, but now he wanted her back.

'Now, what are we to do? Will the lass be staying with you or can I take her back home with me, to show her what she's been missing all these years? Her grandmother and uncles will make her more than welcome and, after all, she is my blood.'

'You'll no doubt do what you have to do. But Ruby will want her say – she's headstrong and stubborn, and she'll do what she wants to do. All I ask is that if she does go with you, you look after her well and let her return and visit me when she wants to. It'll break my heart to lose her, although it won't be long before some young lad comes along and sweeps her off her feet. She keeps them all at bay at the moment – there's nobody good enough for her up here, at the mines.' Martha wiped her eyes and blew her nose; she'd been dreading this day and now that it was here, she'd have to face the consequences.

'Then we will let her choose. I thank you for seeing to her every need. She's been raised well, I can tell that. She's got my temperament, so it can't have been all smooth sailing. She says what she thinks – I discovered that on my first visit. Now, while Ruby sorts her thoughts out, can you make me something to eat and pour me a drink. I've been down Arkengarthdale this morning. I set off before it was light, and my belly is complaining.'

Reuben stood up and looked out of the inn's small windows. His daughter could have been brought up by a lot worse souls than Martha and Fred Metcalfe. At least she had been able to wander the moors and dales while growing up, he thought, as he watched for his headstrong offspring to return.

Martha made her way to the kitchen and hesitated at the bar, turning to glance at Reuben. 'Will she return, do you think, and will she ever forgive me?'

'She'll return, and hopefully her temper has cooled

down. She'll be regretting her words, if she's anything like me. Now whether she has it in her heart to forgive you, I don't know. You've shown her your love over the years, and that is something she should be grateful for.' Reuben sat back down in his chair. He wanted Ruby to say that she would leave with him; nothing would please him more, but he didn't want to have to force her to his way of thinking.

Ruby caught her breath and stopped herself from trembling as she flung open the inn's door and stepped inside.

'You are back then? Have you calmed down?' Reuben looked at Ruby as he helped himself to another piece of cheese from his plate.

'Aye, I'm back, but I don't know why. It seems that all my life has been a lie, with the truth being withheld from me.' Ruby stomped into the room and stood between her father and Martha.

'I'm sorry, lass, I did wrong. I just wanted to give you a good home. Here, I've got your mother's note that was left with you. I've kept it all these years, waiting for the right time to show you it.' Martha's hand trembled as she passed the note to Ruby as she stood defiantly between both of her so-called parents.

'Why didn't you do as it says? I should have been with my real father, not here.' Ruby sobbed and looked at the badly written note, which was the only proof of her mother that she had.

'I thought I was doing right, and you were such a bonny li'l thing,' Martha cried.

91

'But it wasn't the right thing. Vadoma wanted her to be with me – she knew that I'd care for her,' Reuben said and stood up beside Ruby. 'I lost both the woman I loved and the baby she was carrying. I've never loved anyone since losing them. It was a cruel, selfish thing you did, Martha Metcalfe. Ruby's my daughter – the note tells you that, and you've only to look at her to know it. What we are going to do from this day onward, I don't know.'

'Well, I know I can't stop here. I'm sorry, but I can't trust you, Martha. There may be other things you haven't told me. I've always loved you and I knew I wasn't your child, but you knew from day one who my father was and never thought of telling me, so how can I ever trust you again?' Ruby sobbed.

'I did it for you – you were better off with me.' Martha tried to put her arm around Ruby to console her.

'No, you didn't; you did it because, like you said, you needed a baby to call your own and I fitted the bill.' Ruby inhaled sharply and controlled her breathing. 'I'll go and live with you, my father, where I should have been for the last nineteen years, if you'll have me.' She looked at the man whom she had at first been wary of, but now she realized that Martha had only been telling her negative things about Reuben, knowing all along that he was her father.

'Aye, you can come home with me. You have a grand-mother and two uncles who will be just as surprised as you were at the news. They'll make you more than welcome. But don't be so hard on Martha; she's raised you well, she's showered you with her own and Fred's love, and she deserves more than you walking out of her life completely. Once you've made peace with yourself, I want you to come back and visit Martha, as you owe her a lot.' Reuben watched Martha and saw the relief on her face.

'I'll see. I feel numb at the moment, and I no longer know what or who I am. Do you say I have two uncles and a grandmother? Where do they live?' Ruby asked with interest.

'Back home at Banksgill. It is a long farmhouse, with sixty acres of land and just one or two horses too many, and sheep that my brother Lennox keeps. My mother will welcome you with open arms, and she will appreciate having another woman in the house to keep us all in line.' Reuben smiled as Ruby's face lightened.

'Lass, I will miss you so much. Don't go with him – stay with me, I need you,' Martha cried as Ruby went to the bottom of the stairs to pack what few possessions she had for her new home.

'No, I'm going to my true home. I'll always love you, Martha, but you are not my kin and he is, and now I realize who I am. I'm doing as my mother bade me. I think it's time now, and whether it will be for better or worse, only time will tell.' Ruby disappeared up the stairs to grab her belongings.

'I knew it was an ill wind that blew you into the Tan Hill on that night of the blizzard. You take care of my Ruby, else the devil will definitely have your soul, Reuben Blake.' Martha turned and scowled at him.

'He's attempted it many a time, Martha, but he's not won yet; and when it comes to Ruby, both you and the devil will be waiting a long time for this soul. I aim to be the father I always should have been. But I'll make sure Ruby visits you – she'll not be forgetting you, so don't worry.' Reuben walked to the inn's door and opened it, revealing the sun moving over the western hills. 'We'll be away; it'll be nearly dark by the time we get home.' He looked up and smiled at Ruby as she joined him with a packed bag in her hands.

Martha stepped forward with tears in her eyes, kissed Ruby tenderly on the cheek and whispered, 'I'll always love you. You were, and still are, my daughter.'

'I love you too, but I need to go with my father.'

Ruby bowed her head and walked out of the Tan Hill Inn, the only home she had ever known. Her heart was heavy as her father helped her up beside him on the wagon. Would her life with the Blake family at Banksgill be as happy, and would Reuben prove to be a father she could be proud of, or was he as black-hearted as she had always been told he was? A tear fell as she climbed onto the wagon and her father flicked the horse's reins. It was too late to change her mind now; she was on her way to her new life, whatever that might be.

Chapter 7

The journey to Reuben's home of Banksgill was made in silence on the whole. Reuben tried to make conversation as Ruby sat quietly with her thoughts, trying to keep back the tears that fell down her face as the darkness of the coming evening hid the sight of them.

The horse trotted steadily along the country roads and up the winding fell road to Banksgill. Ruby had looked across at the fells of Stainmore many a time; like the moors around Tan Hill, they were always the first to be covered with snow in winter, with the lower fields and meadows growing green and lush. Now she was on her way to live there with a family she didn't know, and with a man she had disliked all her life, but now felt that she had to show faith in. She swept a tear away as she thought about Martha, who had always shown her love and kindness; perhaps she should not have been so judgemental about the woman who had brought her up so well.

'They are all still up. Look, you can see the oil lamps in the window. My mother won't half make a fuss of you when she realizes who you are. When I left I told her to make the spare room ready for a guest, but I didn't say who. I didn't want to disappoint her, in case you refused to come back with me,' Reuben said quietly as the horse trotted into the farmyard and stopped outside the stables and barn at the side of the farmhouse.

'Tom, are you waken?' Reuben yelled as he climbed down from the wagon, then watched as Ruby reached for her possessions and clambered down from her seat and stood, gazing around her.

'Aye, I've been waiting for you. Did you make a sale then?' Tom, with his hair tussled, opened the stable doors, throwing light into the yard as he walked across with a storm lantern in his hand. He stopped short in his conversation as he noticed Ruby standing next to Reuben.

'Aye, I did. Not as much as I wanted, but at least we got rid of it.' Reuben grinned as he saw Tom looking at his daughter. 'This is Ruby. You can meet her properly in the morning, but for now the horse needs looking after – make sure you give her a good rub-down and that she is fed and watered before you go to your bed.' Reuben passed Tom the reins and picked up Ruby's bags, then made for the green-painted door at the side of the house. 'By God, my brothers' faces will be a picture when I say who you are. None of us ever thought of ever seeing you, let alone having you in our family.'

'So was he one of your brothers?' Ruby asked as she followed in Reuben's footsteps.

'Lord, no, that's Tom, our stable lad. Although he might as well be one of us, as he's never out of the kitchen, and my mother treats him like one of the family. He's a good lad.'

Reuben grinned as he opened the door that led into the back kitchen, where the copper boiler and the airing rack covered with clothes were housed. On the walls were pegs with hats and coats hanging from them, and an arrangement of footwear stood on the floor. This was obviously the back way through the house, and Ruby followed the candlelit stone-floored passage behind her father as he yelled of their presence. They passed a kitchen dominated by an oak dresser, with a pot rail upon it filled with plates, and a large square pine table with six chairs around it. The walls were laden with cupboards and ornaments. The room looked homely as they walked towards the front of the house. This home was not short of money, and it was everything that the Tan Hill Inn wasn't, Ruby thought as she followed her father.

'Hey up, are you all still awake? We have a visitor. I hope there's a brew in the pot and some supper left for us both,' Reuben yelled as he opened an oak-boarded door into the family's main living room.

All eyes turned and stared at Reuben and Ruby as they walked into the room, and Ruby felt as if she was nearly naked as they all regarded her.

'You are home then. I thought you were going to be out philandering when it got past nine o'clock. But it seems you've brought a lass back with you, although she's only young, our Reuben.' Elspeth looked at Ruby and sighed. 'Tha shouldn't be with him, lass. You should be at home with your family, and you want nowt with my lad.'

Ruby dropped her head and blushed, not knowing what to say.

Reuben smiled at his brothers' faces as they stared at the young lass by his side. 'She is with her family. We are her family, and she's my daughter!'

'Oh Lord, she can't be. She should be long gone from anywhere around here,' Elspeth gasped and tried to catch her breath as she sat back down in her chair.

'She is mine. Ruby, show them your bracelet,' Reuben said to her, and she held her arm out for all to see. 'Vadoma left her at the Tan Hill Inn, and she's been living there since she was left on the doorstep as a baby, with instructions from her mother to return her to me to raise. But old Martha Metcalfe kept her and said nowt. And Ruby would still be there, if I hadn't seen her when I stayed at the inn.'

'Oh, lass, if only you knew how much your father has dreamed of you, and worried about your own and your mother's safety. He's waited so long for you and your mother to turn up on our doorstep. There isn't a day goes by that your father doesn't mention your mother's name. I'm so glad he's found you.' Elspeth got up from her seat and hugged Ruby tightly. 'You are our blood – I can see that, now that Reuben says who you are. No wonder he said I'd to put some effort into getting the spare room ready for a visitor. I thought he'd finally found a woman to replace your mother, but I should have known better, as there's always only been one true love in his life.'

Elspeth wiped back the tears that were flowing down her cheeks and kissed Ruby, before grabbing her hand and looking at her long and hard.

'Aye, you are our Reuben's – there's no doubting that.' She turned to Arthur and Lennox and grinned. 'Well, are you two big lumps not going to make your niece welcome in our home? It is grand to have her within the fold of her family where she belongs.'

Elspeth went back to her seat, feeling her stomach churning. She'd hoped that the child she knew her Reuben had fathered was long gone. His relationship with a gypsy had only made her feel shame, and now his lass was standing in front of them trying to worm herself into her family. She'd try her best to make Ruby welcome, but she was half gypsy, and that was no better than her mother being a beggar, in Elspeth's proud eyes.

Both brothers moved forward and hugged and kissed Ruby and welcomed her into their home, before patting Reuben on his back and congratulating him on finding his daughter. It was a night to remember and rejoice in at Banksgill; at least one of Reuben's loved ones was back within his arms. There would be plenty to talk about and celebrate in the warmth of Ruby's new-found family.

Ruby lay back in bed, yawned and stretched. She knew it was just after eight o'clock because she had heard the grandfather clock in the hallway at the bottom of the stairs chime on the hour, waking her from sleep. She'd not slept in so late for a long time; usually she was awake and helping Martha clean the Tan Hill Inn and bake bread by six, but this morning she had been told to remain in bed for as long as she wanted, after staying up in the early hours talking with her new family. She'd found her eyes drooping and herself yawning, as the family told her about the farm she was on. Rather grudgingly she had to say that she was exhausted from the day's outcome, and had been shown to her bedroom by Elspeth, who had kissed her and told her once again how glad she was to receive Ruby into the family.

All of them had shown her nothing but kindness. Arthur and Lennox, although rough in appearance, with their wild hair and hard looks, were caring sons and brothers. And Ruby knew that no matter what bad things other folk had said about the Blake brothers, it was because they didn't truly know them. She was going to enjoy getting to know them and her father, and helping her grandmother around the house, which was absolutely spotless, with every room filled with good-quality furniture and ornaments that had obviously been handed down from generation to generation.

She lay back and thought about Martha. How could she have not told Ruby about her true family and done as Vadoma had asked? Martha had been keeping her away from all that was around her now, and painting her father in a bad light, although he'd shown her nothing but kindness last night. This was her family now, and this was where she belonged. However, Ruby's heart hurt, thinking about the way she had left Martha; she had no right to sound and act as heartlessly as she did when her father told her the truth. Martha had loved her and done her best for Ruby, and if she got the chance she would go and say sorry for being so selfish and heartless towards the woman who had brought her up.

Ruby was brought out of her thoughts by a knock and the sound of her bedroom door being opened.

'Morning, my dear. I thought I'd treat you to some breakfast in bed and a lie-in. You looked so tired when you climbed the stairs to your bed. The news must have been a shock to you. How do you feel this morning? Do you think you can put up with me and my boys as a family?' Elspeth smiled as she placed a plain wooden tray holding a cup of tea and two boiled eggs, along with some bread and butter, all on the best china, upon the patchwork quilt that covered the bed Ruby lay in.

'You really shouldn't have. I'm not usually this lazy. The breakfast looks lovely.' Ruby smiled at her new grandmother, who was what she had always dreamed of, as she sat upright in her bed. 'Everyone has been wonderful to me. I never knew that you all existed, apart from my father, and even then I didn't really know him.'

'Aye, and you've probably only heard bad things about him. I know how folk talk around here. He's a good lad, is my Reuben; he cares for those who care for us and does his best for us all, even if it does mean being a bit underhand sometimes. You have a good father – you'll not go without anything, now that you are back in his life. His one fault is that he can be too soft with the folk

101

he loves. It's as if love blinds him. He was like that with your mother.' Elspeth smiled. 'Now, enjoy your breakfast and then come down and join me in the kitchen. Arthur and Lennox are checking their sheep; all are in lamb, so they have brought them down from the fell, ready for lambing time. And your father is with the blacksmith and Tom in the stable. He's always with his horses, is that one – not that they make him a lot of money.'

'I'll be down as soon as I've finished this and got dressed.' Ruby looked at Elspeth, still not quite believing that she had a grandmother.

'There's water to wash in over there in the jug, and some lavender soap that I make every year from the flowers in the garden. It smells really bonny and is good for the skin. Did you bring enough clothes with you or did you leave in a hurry?' Elspeth asked as she waited at the door for a reply and gazed around the bedroom, checking that all was still in place.

'No, I'd time to pack what I wanted. I don't have a lot anyway,' Ruby said quietly.

'Well, we'll have to do something about that. Our Reuben will be spending some of his brass on you, if I know him. He's a bit of a dandy on the quiet; he likes to dress well.' Elspeth smiled again. She'd noticed the previous night that although Ruby was clean and tidy, her clothes were worn and tired. No doubt Reuben would be wasting some of his hard-earned money on the lass, despite her warnings that morning not to do so.

'I had noticed he's not the usual farmer,' Ruby said quietly.

'Nay, lass, he's not a farmer. I don't know where I went wrong with Reuben. His brothers, Arthur and Lennox, farm the land we have, but when it comes to Reuben, it's hard to say what he does. He loves breeding his horses, which Lennox and he argue over frequently, but he makes his brass through wheeling and dealing. He buys and sells things, but I learned a long time ago not to ask him where he's going or who he has seen, because you'll not get a straight answer. But the money comes in, so I close my eyes and hope it's not been made at the cost of a life. I know I will never change him. Your mother and her family would be more in keeping with Reuben's life than the one he's got here, because he's forever wandering – perhaps he's searching for her. I know she broke his heart when she left,' Elspeth sighed, 'and that I lost my eldest's heart to her.'

'He must have loved my mother, to have not settled down by now. I wish I had known her, and I wish she had kept me with her.' Ruby bowed her head and thought about the mother she had never known.

'If it had been up to her, she would have taken you with her. She'd have married your father as well. Reuben brought her home just the once for us to meet. She was a beauty, like yourself, with long, dark hair and dark eyes. You could tell straight away that she loved my lad, but it was a love denied by her family. Leaving you on the steps of Tan Hill Inn would have broken her heart,' Elspeth said with tears in her eyes, while she thought about the times she had argued over the gypsy lass, who had split the family with her beguiling ways.

'Well, I'm here now. Perhaps my mother will return some day, and then my father will get some peace and be able to stop searching for her.' Ruby smiled and looked at the breakfast set out in front of her, hearing her stomach rumble in the anticipation of food.

'Aye, lass, happen he'll not be happy until she does return into his life, that's for sure. Now I'm downstairs in the kitchen when you need me. My lads are always hungry and they keep these old bones busy. I'll be glad of another pair of hands to help me around the house. I have Anne, the maid; she does the cleaning for me and is the oldest daughter of the Handleys who farm next door, but she's no cook. So I hope Martha Metcalfe at Tan Hill learned you some cookery skills, as my lads will need feeding after my day.'

'Yes, Martha taught me to cook, although I'll never be as good as her. She was fine with pastry, and used to laugh at me enjoying making cakes; she said they were a luxury and an extravagance, where pastry was to be used every day.' Ruby thought of her baking lessons with Martha, when she had been shown basic recipes to keep the visitors at the inn fed and satisfied.

'Aye, well, she is right, although my lads like a bit of sweetness, and your father likes a good fruitcake. Along with a piece of cheese, he thinks he's in heaven. Now, have your breakfast and get dressed, and then we will see what the day brings. It will all be new for you, and it will take you a while to find your feet with us. My lads are a law unto themselves and you'll have to get used to their ways. I'll warn you now, they say what they think and don't hold back with their views.' Elspeth smiled. If nothing else, Ruby was going to be a good help in a nearly all-male house, she thought as she made her way back down to the kitchen.

Ruby looked at herself in the full-length mirror in the corner of her bedroom and surveyed herself with a critical eye. Now she knew why she had tanned skin all year round. She wondered if folk had known the truth about her all along. She was half gypsy and half horse-dealer's daughter: was that a thing to be proud of, or would she have been better staying in blissful ignorance?

For some people, gypsies were romantic; while for others, they were the scum of the earth. Ruby had never had any quarrel with them as they passed the Tan Hill Inn on their way to who-knew-where. Perhaps she had seen her mother and not realized it, just as she had not realized that Black Blake was her father. Whatever her parentage, she was now here at Banksgill and her newly found grandmother had welcomed her into the family with loving arms. This was her home now and she would make herself useful and show that she belonged here.

She gave herself another glance in the mirror, picked up her empty breakfast tray and left the welcoming bedroom, where the spring sunshine was shining through the windows. She would do her best to make Banksgill, and the Blakes, her home; and if things did not work out, there was always the Tan Hill Inn to return to. Despite not telling Ruby the truth, Martha would always

105

welcome her back. But a new life awaited her now and she would make the most of it.

'So you've shown your face. I told my mother to wake you over an hour or two ago, but she's soft and said you needed your sleep.' Reuben grinned as he walked around the back of the horse that the farrier was shoeing, and patted it on its flanks as he looked at his daughter. 'She'd not be saying that if we were lolling in bed.'

'I'm never usually up this late, but the previous day's events got the better of me. It must have been the small hours when we all eventually went to bed, and then my head was full of things that I could not stop thinking about. It has been a lot to take in.' Ruby listened to the farrier as he hammered the horseshoe on the anvil while it was still red-hot from the furnace in the corner of the barn, then dipped the shoe into the bucket of cold water to cool it down, before picking up the horse's hoof to see if it fitted correctly. The steam from the heat filled the old barn as Ruby watched the horse, which was obviously used to being shod, stand patiently while the farrier made adjustments, before bending in his leather apron with the horse's hoof between his legs and hands, and with his mouth full of small nails, ready to hammer them in place. 'Does it not hurt the animal?' Ruby asked her father as she watched the shoes being hammered on. She looked quickly up at the lad she had seen the previous night, holding the horse, who smirked and stopped himself from laughing.

Reuben glared at Tom and then answered Ruby. 'Nay, it would hurt the horse more if its hooves cracked through carrying a too-heavy load or travelling over hard roads.

106

The farrier here only used small nails; he hammers them into the part of the hoof that has no nerves in it, so the horse feels no pain. See, my Rosie did not even flinch. Her mind was on that trough of hay, which she's content to be eating; she's not bothered that someone is seeing to her feet.'

'They don't bother shoeing the ponies up at the coal pit, but they should because they pull carts full of coal all down the Dales. They need to be told,' Ruby said and carried on watching, as she'd never seen a farrier at work before.

'Aye, there's plenty that doesn't shoe their horses, and then they wonder why they go lame. It costs a pretty penny to keep my horses properly seen too, but they are worth it. Unlike folk, they won't give you cheek or judge you. I'd rather be in a field of horses than a room of folk any day,' Reuben said as he walked to the head of his horse and stroked her down her muzzle as the farrier moved out of the way.

'Are you not going to introduce us then?' Tom stood next to Ruby and looked at her, then grinned across at Reuben, curious to know who his latest conquest was.

Ruby gazed at the lad, who seemed about her age, with his sandy brown hair showing below his tweed cap; his eyes were staring at her full of mischief, as he stood waiting for Reuben to say who the visitor was who had come to the farm late the previous evening. He was not bad-looking, she thought, as he stood in his striped twill shirt and tweed waistcoat, with plus-fours to his knees and stout tanned leather boots on his feet.

'This, my lad, is my daughter, Ruby. So you can wipe that look off your face. There will be no gallivanting off with her – she's way out of your reach!' Reuben scuffed the cap from the top of Tom's head, making it fall on the floor for him to pick up. As Tom did so, Reuben kicked him gently on the backside, making him sprawl in the dust and dirt of the stable.

'There was no need to do that. I was only asking.' Tom picked himself up and dusted himself down. He turned and looked at Reuben, feeling embarrassed as he smiled and held his dusty hand out for Ruby to shake. 'Nice to meet you, Ruby. Don't believe a word your father says about me. I may be only his stable boy, but he knows I love his horses as much as he does. Us horsemen are a breed of our own.'

Ruby smiled. 'Nice to meet you, Tom. I can assure you my father has only spoken well of you, as far as I'm aware.' She gripped Tom's hand; it was a firm shake and she couldn't help but blush slightly as his hand lingered in hers a little too long.

'Aye, well, what he says is up to him. He's kept quiet about you, that is a fact. I never knew he had a lass.' Tom looked Ruby up and down and liked the appearance of the girl who stood in front of him.

'It's like I say, Tom: she's too good for you. My Ruby has only just been found and I'm not going to lose her to some wastrel like you.' Reuben patted Tom on his back. 'But you can teach her to ride. I thought that piebald would be her ideal horse.' Reuben nodded to the horse at the back of the stable. 'She's of good temperament and exactly the right size. Can you ride, Ruby, have you ever been shown?'

'You don't have to learn me. I've been riding the pit ponies since I was little. Rob Jenkins used to put me on the back of his, and he used to say I should have been born a lad. I liked being with the fell ponies so much, and now I know why. I don't ride like a lady, though, no side-saddle – in fact no saddle at all.'

Reuben laughed and grinned. 'By God, you are my lass. In fact once my horse is shod, we will see how good a horsewoman you are. We will have a ride around our land together and come back in time for dinner. I'll have to go into the house and tell my mother not to expect us back before noon.'

The farrier turned and looked up at Reuben. 'Aye, well, you can take her now, she's done and dusted for another while. She's a credit to you, Reuben, she's as fit a horse as I've seen in a long time.' Dick Waites patted the horse on its neck, closed his metal case of tools and took off his leather apron. 'So, you are Reuben's lass. You have got a father and a half, if you don't already know it. I'll not hear a bad word against this man – he looks after his horses and his kith and kin. You'll not go far wrong with Reuben Blake as your father, no matter what some people say.' Dick patted him on his back as he gazed at Ruby. 'Aye, you look like your father, and if you are as good with horses as he is, he'll be proud of you.'

'I don't think I'll ever be that, but I can ride, so that's a start.' Ruby watched Tom as he led Reuben's horse out

109

of the stable, already saddled and bridled, ready for their ride together.

'Aye, well, I'll be on my way. No doubt I'll be seeing you again.' Dick tipped his cap as he walked to his horse and cart, which were waiting for him in the yard.

'He's a good man, is Dick Waites, a bloody good farrier and honourable. There's not many like him left,' Reuben said, then turned to Ruby. 'Now, do you want your horse saddled or do you wish to ride her bareback? I think a saddle this time – let's start as we mean to go on. Tom, saddle her up and show Ruby how to do it while I go and see Mother and tell her what we are about.' Reuben nodded at Tom as he untied the smaller piebald horse that had been tethered in the corner of the stable.

'Her name is Thistle; her mother gave birth to her in a clump of thistles, so she couldn't have any other name,' Tom said as he walked the little mare to the front of the stable. 'She'll be ideal for you. Your father broke her in himself. She's quiet and good-natured and needed someone like yourself to love her.' Tom patted the small horse and then looked up at Ruby. 'Have you not known your father before? Are you and your mother the ones he's been searching for the main of his life?'

'It would seem so, and yet I've been living under his nose all along. He just didn't know it.' Ruby watched as Tom went to the wall of the stable, where all the harnesses and saddlery were hung, and then put a harness on the horse that was going to be hers. 'I know how to put a bridle on and I've seen a horse saddled before – you don't have to show me. I just don't like riding with one,' she said as Tom turned to show her how to place the saddle and tighten it up properly.

'Aye, well, your father sometimes rides without one too. He must be thinking of taking you a decent way, else he'd have not bothered himself.' He pulled hard on the saddle's belt and then lifted down the stirrups and patted the patient little horse. 'He'll be over the moon that he's found you. Now he needs to find your mother and then he'll be content. He's a good man, is your father; he's made me part of this family and makes sure my mother wants for nothing. I'm glad he's found you and I hope that we can be friends.' Tom smiled as he walked the horse, followed by Ruby, out of the stable into the spring sunshine.

'I have a feeling that we will be the best of friends, Tom. You can tell me about my new home, and I'll need a friend to talk to. I'm used to people coming and going as I serve at Tan Hill Inn. I'm going to find life a little quiet here.' She smiled at Tom; if he found her as attractive as she did him, then friendship – and more – would not be a problem.

'It'll be a bit of a change for you, but there are plenty of comings and goings at Banksgill. There's always something going on – you'll be surprised.' Tom grinned and then turned as Reuben, followed by his mother, came out of the farmhouse towards them.

'You'll be back for your dinner, Reuben, you promise me? No trailing until late in the day, as Ruby will still be tired,' Elspeth shouted from just outside the back door.

'Aye, aye, I hear you. We will be back when we are

111

back – stop your fretting. Plate us up some of the cooked ham and pickles, and then we can be back when we feel like it.' Reuben eased himself up into his saddle and watched as Tom held Thistle for Ruby to climb up into her saddle, next to him. She pulled herself up easily and took the reins with confidence, once she had arranged her skirts back around her legs, carefully not showing them to Tom. 'We'll have to get you something more suitable for riding,' Reuben said and stared at Tom, who was looking up at his daughter and smiling.

'Are you listening: back by one,' Elspeth shouted as Reuben pulled on his horse's reins and started down the road, with Ruby following him.

'Yes, Mother – one will be perfect.' Reuben turned and winked at Ruby, who was riding by his side, and whispered, 'Now is that one this afternoon or one this morning? She didn't make herself clear.' He dug his heels into the side of his horse and laughed. 'Now let's see if you can keep up with me and how well you can ride,' he said to Ruby as he speeded his horse into a gallop. 'Take care, you don't have to keep up with me if you don't want to,' he yelled as he pulled away from her, the dust flying up from the farm track as he galloped off.

Ruby watched her father and eased herself around the saddle, unfamiliar with the feel of it. She'd often gone at such a pace on the pit ponies, but Thistle was a hand or two taller and she was not used to the saddle. However, Ruby was not going to be left behind, and she too urged her horse on and galloped down the road to catch up with Reuben.

'Oh my Lord, she's as mad as her father,' Elspeth sighed as she watched both her son and her granddaughter racing one another and soon disappearing out of sight.

'Aye, she's her father's daughter alright – any fool can see that,' Tom said and straightened his cap on his head. Life was going to be more interesting at Banksgill from now on. Ruby was going to bring a new vigour with her, and Reuben already seemed like a different man with his daughter by his side.

Ruby sat tightly in her saddle, her heart beating fast and a grin on her face. She could feel every muscle being strained on the horse as she raced alongside her father, who kept looking at her and urging her to keep up with him as he reached the road that led to Reeth. She loved the feel of the wind against her face, and the speed as the horse ate up the ground beneath its hooves. She felt alive and, more than that, she had her father by her side, and at long last she knew why she felt as she did when she was on a horse and alone on a distant fell top. It all made sense now, as she quietly slowed her horse to a canter, once her father slowed down as they followed the road that ran alongside Arkle Beck and came to the small hamlet of Whaw.

The ancient hamlet, sitting squat with its Yorkshire stone-built cottages at either side of the road and its gardens, was beginning to come to life in the spring sunshine. Spring was always late in this part of the world, the northern wind being slow to loosen its icy grip along the fellsides. Her father brought his horse to a halt as the road crossed, giving them the option to turn back on themselves up through Swaledale or to follow the road further to Reeth.

'Well, you are a horsewoman, that's for sure. Your mother would be proud of you.' Reuben turned in his saddle and looked at Ruby, whose face was flushed, and she was gasping for breath.

'It's a good job old Rob Jenkins never knew how hard I used to push his pit ponies, else he'd never have let me ride them.' Ruby grinned to her father as she pulled Thistle to a halt.

'The poor bloody things. They'd been breaking their backs carrying that stuff they call coal, and then they get you riding them like the devil. I've found you just in time for the sake of their lives, if not mine.' Reuben patted his horse's neck and gazed at his daughter, with her long, dark hair hanging over her shoulders. She looked so much like her mother, and he felt his heart skip a jump as he stared at her.

'I only took the young ones; most were too long in the tooth to ride hard,' Ruby said and looked ashamed. 'Are we turning back now? Your mother will be expecting us for dinner.' She was worrying that Elspeth would be waiting for them.

'You mean your grandmother. She'll be right; she knows that we will turn up when I bethink myself. I thought I might take you to Reeth, introduce you to my oldest friend, Francis Verity, at the Kings Arms and his wife, Jane. I've some unsettled business to do with him and he'll not be best pleased with what I have to tell him. Introducing you will soften the blow. I thought we could perhaps stay the night, rest the horses and then return via the Tan Hill Inn. Then you can reassure Martha that I've not sold you to a travelling circus or turned you into a wild gypsy already. Although by the way you rode that horse, I don't think I need to try on the latter.' Reuben grinned.

'I don't know. What about Grandmother? I don't know if I should see Martha again for a while. I'm still angry with her, although I do feel bad about speaking to her the way I did.' Ruby felt guilty, but she would like to stay as a guest at the Kings Arms. She'd often looked up at the tall building at the crossroads in Reeth when she had visited the weekly market there, but never thought she might be a guest in one of its bedrooms.

'My mother knows me – she'll expect me when she sees me. As for Martha, you are better off making your peace with her. You said some words in anger and you should make up with her. She's brought you up well, and I'm thankful to her for that. Besides, Jane will want to smother you, when she finds out that you are my lass. We'll go and stay the night.'

Reuben sat in his seat and looked down Arkengarthdale, which he had ridden down a few weeks previously, with his heart and his head heavy with worry. Now he had his daughter by his side and he wanted to show her off to the world.

'If you say so, Father. But I haven't any nightclothes,' Ruby said with concern.

'Jane will see to your needs – she has more clothes than the Queen herself, and that's partly why I've to apologize. She wanted some silk from my latest exploits, but I left without it, so she'll not be happy.' Reuben winked at Ruby. 'She's a fair temper, but it soon blows over. Spirited, I think you call it.' He clicked his teeth and set his horse at a slow pace down the road to Reeth, with Ruby wondering what her stay with the Veritys would tell her about her father.

Chapter 8

'I expected you a few weeks ago, you devil. Where's my gin and whisky that I was promised, not to mention the silk that my Jane never shuts her mouth about?' Francis Verity leaned on an empty oak cask that he had rolled out into the yard of the Kings Arms, and caught his breath when he looked up at Reuben as he dismounted his horse with a woman behind him.

'Don't – just don't! Keep your words to yourself. I nearly lost my life that night for the sake of some whisky and gin, and I wasted nearly four whole days bringing back barrels of what turned out to be mainly salt, bloody coffee and some gunpowder. I do have a barrel or two of liquor that I'll see you get shortly, so hold your tongue,' Reuben said and shook his head. 'It all went wrong and I'm not going back again. That bastard Andrews had laid a trap for us and I had to take what I could get, which turned out to be not worth nearly losing my life for, and that of the lads that helped me. I only hope John

Andrews swings from a gibbet, if he got caught by the troopers. We did our best to set him up when we all found out his plan, the bloody bastard.'

'I've heard that John Andrews is in with the militia, so no wonder you nearly got caught – he'd want you off his patch. But his wrath is nowt compared to that of my Jane. She will have something to say to you, as she was looking forward to making herself a new dress for spring with some bonny French silk, and you know what she's like.' Francis gave a sigh, then watched Ruby as she quietly slipped down from her horse. 'But you are still with us, and that's all that matters. As it happens, I got some gin from Ted Bumfitt; he's distilled it himself. It's a bit coarse but drinkable. It strips your throat, but you learn to live with it after the first gill. Get what barrels you have to me as soon as you can – I've money waiting for you.' He looked over at Ruby. 'Who's this then? It's not like you to bring a woman here!' he sniggered as Ruby handed her reins to the lad, who took both horses away to the stables.

'Mind your manners and what you say, my friend.' Reuben turned and put his arm around Ruby. 'This is the apple of my eye, my long-lost daughter, Ruby. Her mother even named her after me, when she abandoned her at the Tan Hill Inn with a note asking her to be sent to me.' Reuben smiled as Ruby stood by his side, watching the burly publican who obviously knew her father well.

'Never! She's been at the Tan Hill all this time and you didn't know? By, now that is a turn-up for the books.' Francis looked Ruby up and down and then held out his

118

hand for her to shake. 'You are the image of your father and mother. By, I bet Reuben's a happy man with you by his side. Now he just needs to find your mother and then he'd stop his wild ways.'

Ruby shook Francis's hand and smiled. 'I'm glad I've found him. It has all been a bit of a whirlwind of late.'

'I bet, lass. It always is a bit chaotic when you've owt to do with your father. He's like a bad smell: always lingering about, and you wonder where it's coming from and where it's been.' Francis laughed and patted Reuben's back. 'I'm so glad, my old friend. You've pined for Vadoma and her baby for so long, and now you've found one of them. Come on in, I'll shout of Jane. She'll forgive you for not bringing any silk. Besides, you've brought us something far more precious – a true ruby, by God.'

Francis opened the back door into the inn and followed Ruby and Reuben into the main room, bellowing Jane's name as he kept shaking his head in disbelief. 'Ruby – she couldn't have called you anything better. And to leave you at the Tan Hill, right on the doorstep!'

'What is all the fuss about, Francis? Is the inn on fire?' Jane came out of the kitchen, wiping her hands on her apron and with a scowl on her face. 'I'm busy, man, making pies. Whatever it is, I hope it's worth dragging me away and leaving Maisy in charge.' She quickly changed her manner as she saw Reuben, discarding her flour-covered apron and replacing her scowl with a smile. 'My silk, has it come, and what colour have you brought me? I didn't think you were ever going to show.' She looked at Reuben and then at Ruby, noticing the lack of material in his hands.

'Sorry, Jane, I've no silk for you. My plans went a little awry, and I was lucky to get away with my life.' Reuben stepped forward and kissed Jane on her cheek. 'You do not need any fresh silks – you are bonny enough.' He winked at Francis.

'You can stop it with your flattery. It won't get you anywhere with me, Reuben Blake, and you know it won't.' Jane blushed and kissed him back.

'He might not have brought you any silk, but he's brought with him something more precious,' Francis had to tell her. 'This is Ruby, his long-lost daughter. Isn't she bonny? The image of her mother, Vadoma. And there's no doubting who her father is, just look at them standing together!'

'Well, I never. I wondered who you were. Step out in front of your father, lass, and let's have a proper look at you.' Jane grasped Ruby's hand and stood back and gazed at her. 'My lord, Vadoma would be proud of you. And yes, you have your father's features and you wear his bracelet – the one he showed me when he was planning to give it to your mother at Bartlett Fair all those years ago. I can't believe he's found you.' Jane wiped back a tear and then hugged Ruby close to her. 'You don't know how long he has been searching for you and your mother. Is your mother with you?' Jane looked behind the group, peering along the corridor for Vadoma.

'No, I don't know where my mother is. I wish I did,' Ruby said quietly.

'We'll find her, my lass, one day we will find her.' Reuben put his hand on Ruby's shoulder and smiled at Jane. 'She's been at the Tan Hill all these years and I never knew. Martha Metcalfe's brought her up as her own and has done a good job.'

'Well, I never. Now let's leave these fellas to it, and me and you will get to know one another. Knowing them, they'll have plenty to talk about, especially your father, by the sounds of his latest exploits.' Jane linked her arm into Ruby's. 'We will go up to our quarters and leave them to it. I take it you are staying the night?' Jane looked at Reuben as he followed Francis into the bar.

'Aye, you know me, Jane. I can never resist a night here, with your cooking and Francis's company,' Reuben said as he watched Jane take over Ruby.

'Oh, so it's just my cooking you come for, you old rogue. There was me, thinking we were good friends,' Jane answered back.

'You know what I mean, Jane Verity, and you know I love you as much as your tasty lamb hotpot. Aye, we will be staying.' Reuben grinned as he watched Ruby give him a backward glance as she was ushered up to the very top rooms of the Kings Arms by a chattering Jane.

'Now, tell me all about yourself. How did your father find you? I bet he was over the moon when he did. And what about you? How do you feel about it all?' Jane flopped down on the edge of a day-bed in the small living quarters in the eaves of the attic, bidding Ruby to do the same as she patted the edge of the bed. The room

121

was sparse but clean, and had a good fire blazing in the small, open fireplace. On one side of the room was an oak dresser with pots and pieces on it, and on the other was a window overlooking the village of Reeth, with views right across the valley of Swaledale. Down below her, the green and the surrounding shops were busy with shoppers and lead miners, and farmers with their families. Reeth was an important meeting place in the dale, and the inns and shops were always flush with trade. Ruby turned and looked at Jane. She could smell her kitchen upon her – the aroma of pastry and sweetness, from what she had obviously been placing in the oven on their arrival.

'I'm still in a daze. I can't believe I've found my true father.' Ruby smiled at Jane, seeing the warmth in her eyes.

'I bet you are, my girl. You couldn't have a better father. Some folk say he's a bit wild, which he was when he realized that he'd lost everything he had ever loved. But he's a good man, and your mother was a true beauty and so kind and soft-spoken – they made a lovely couple. We were good friends,' Jane sighed.

'You knew my mother?' Ruby asked with interest.

'Aye, I knew her. They used to stay here some nights, out of sight of her brother and parents. I wished they hadn't sometimes, as it was a love affair that was doomed from the start: gypsy folk and Dales folk shouldn't mix. One or the other gets torn from their family, with one only happy to be travelling and the other wanting to stay rooted. Your grandfather warned your father more times than I've cooked Reuben his favourite hotpot, but he'd not listen. He loved her and she loved him.'

'He must have loved her, and she him, if they risked their parents' wrath.' Ruby looked down at her bracelet.

'Aye, they did – they were made for one another. I remember when he gave your mother that bracelet; it was on that very green outside. It was the Bartlett Fair day, and the village was thronged with drinkers and fair-goers. He'd had a pair of bracelets made to show his love for her. It was then that Vadoma told Reuben she was carrying you. She was frightened of what they had done and she knew it would only end in tears. She was right, because when your father went to the gypsies' camp, her brothers nearly killed him and he was left for near-dead in a ditch just outside Appleby. And Vadoma and the Faa family had disappeared like the early-autumn mists. He's been searching for you and your mother ever since. He's courted women, but not like he courted your mother – she will always have his heart. She must have left you at the Tan Hill the following spring. I'm surprised, if she was planning to abandon you, that she didn't leave you with Reuben, as she'd know that he'd love you, no matter what.' Jane squeezed Ruby's hand.

'She left a note asking Martha to take me to him, but Martha decided to mother me instead, I don't think she thought highly of him, and she wanted a child of her own.' Ruby swept a tear away from her eye.

'Aye, she shouldn't have done that. No child should be taken away from their parents. Who was Martha to judge? Your father would have worshipped you; and

Elspeth, even though she can be a funny old stick, would have loved a lass in the family, with her only having three boys. You've got a good home with Reuben, you'll want for nowt.' Jane smiled and hugged her.

'I know, I've been shown nothing but love since I arrived at Banksgill. I've my own room and my own horse, and my father keeps saying that he will take me shopping. I think he's a bit ashamed of the clothes I'm in, but they are the best I could afford.' Ruby indicated her washed-out clothes and blushed.

'Aye, he's a bit of a dandy – Reuben's always to look right and have everything around him right. That's why your mother caught his eye: he likes things that glitter, like a magpie he is.' Jane laughed. 'We can soon sort the clothes out, don't you worry. Follow me, I'm going to make your day, and make your father smile and save him some money.' Jane pulled on Ruby's hand and led her down the stairs to a bedroom that was locked, smiling as she turned the key. 'You can sleep in here tonight. It needs to be used; it's been empty long enough, and my lass will not be needing it any more.' Jane opened the door and stepped back to let Ruby follow her into the bedroom.

'What a lovely room. You say your lass? Do you have a daughter?' Ruby asked as she gazed around the room, which was pristine, with a cherry-wood dressing table and matching drawers and wardrobe, and a single bed covered by a hand-crafted patchwork quilt that had obviously been made with love. The whole room had ornaments and trinkets in it suitable for a young woman.

124

'It was my daughter Hannah's. We lost her to consumption four years ago, and she would have been twenty-one this year. She'd just accepted the hand of a wool dealer from Halifax and they were to be married the following year, but it was not to be.' Jane smiled wanly and looked at Ruby. 'I, like your own mother, know what it's like to lose a daughter, but mine will never come back. Not in this world anyway.'

'I'm sorry, you must miss her,' Ruby said quietly.

'Aye, it's not anyone's fault. The good Lord does what he does, whether it makes sense to us mere mortals or not. Hannah will always be in here – nobody can take that away from me.' Jane put her hands on her heart and smiled. 'I do miss her, and your mother and old Martha Metcalfe will miss you, whether what they did was right or not. Both obviously loved you, and it will have hurt Martha when your father took you away from her; she'd think of you as hers, after such a length of time.'

Jane looked at Ruby and then lightly touched her arm.

'Anyway, the bed is always kept aired and I'll bring you some water up for the ewer. You can sleep in here tonight, but more importantly, the wardrobe is full of Hannah's clothes and shoes. You are about her size and, if they don't fit, I'm sure you can alter them. You take whatever catches your eye – it's no good the moths enjoying them. They need to be worn again. Hannah would have wanted it that way, and Reuben always used to make a fuss of her, so it's only right they go to you.'

125

'I don't know what to say. Thank you. Do you not want to keep them? They must be precious to you.' Ruby caught her breath as Jane opened the wardrobe door to reveal the most beautiful hand-made dresses she had ever seen.

'We both have her memories, and they will never go. You take whatever you want. There are shawls and undergarments in the drawers. I'm glad they are going to a good home.' Jane smiled. 'I'll go and see what your father and my old man are up to. The red dress will suit you – it is right for your colouring. Come down to dinner in it. I'd like that, and so would Francis.'

Jane stood in the doorway for a while and watched Ruby looking at the clothes in the wardrobe. They couldn't be going to a more suitable person, she thought as she closed the door and went back to her kitchen to quell the tears that were in her eyes, before joining the two men in their conversation. At least Reuben had regained his daughter; she knew that she and Francis never would.

Ruby looked at the wardrobe of dresses and sat on the bed. It was strange, knowing that she was to sleep in a bed and wear clothes that she now knew had been kept as a dear memory by Hannah's parents. What had she been like? Had she suffered long and hard in the bed she was about to sleep in? It worried her to think she was to sleep in the dead girl's bed, even though she was sure she must have slept in a dying person's bed before and not known it.

The clothes, on the other hand, were too much of a

temptation, and Ruby got up from the bed and fingered through the dresses that were hanging there, waiting to have new life brought into them. She'd bought dresses from Mrs Foggery, who dealt with people's second-hand cast-offs on the market at Reeth, so wearing someone else's cast-offs was not new to her; and probably some of those dresses in the past were from someone who had died. However, this was different. She now knew who they had belonged to, but the temptation was too great and she knew that Jane had given her blessing for her to have them with love.

She couldn't stop smiling as she held each dress up to her and admired herself in the mirror. Her father would really appreciate the gift of new clothes, she thought, as she hastily unbuttoned her bodice top, casting her threadbare old dress aside, and stepped into the red-and-black plaid dress that Jane had recommended she wear. She was right: the dress fitted her perfectly and the colours highlighted her appearance. She looked like the daughter of Reuben Blake now, not the lost foundling from Tan Hill. She'd have a new dress for every day of the week, Ruby thought as she laid them all out upon the bed and gazed at them. Jane must have spent hours sewing, putting love into every stitch for her precious daughter – unlike Martha, she had spent time and money on her daughter.

Then Ruby thought of the times Martha had made new underwear for her out of the flour sacks, which had been better-quality cloth than the drawers she herself had been wearing; and of the shoes that Martha wore, with holes in them, and mended more times than was fit. It wasn't the clothes and finery she should have been judging Martha by, it was the hours of love given to her, and there had been plenty of them. Money was hard to come by at the Tan Hill Inn, unlike the busy Kings Arms in the thriving village of Reeth, and Ruby realized as she sat on the bed with all the finery around her just how much Martha had sacrificed to raise her as her own. Her harsh words must have hurt, Ruby thought, as she hung her head and regarded her reflection once more. She would do as her father had suggested and call at Tan Hill on their way back and make amends. She should not have been so quick to judge. Martha had loved her, and had only had Ruby's welfare in mind when raising her. But for now, Ruby would enjoy the clothes she had been given and make her father proud as she joined him later at supper.

'You looked a picture last night, Ruby,' Reuben said as he and Ruby started out on the journey home to Stainmore. 'It meant a lot to Jane to be able to give you Hannah's clothes – they were precious to her.'

'I know. Hannah's death must have broken her heart. She was due to be wed – how can life be so cruel?' Ruby said as they gently made their way, side-by-side on their horses, up the drovers' road through the wilds of Arkengarthdale. She looked across at her father and tried to choose her words so as not to hurt his feelings as she thought about Martha. 'You offered me a chance to revisit Martha at the Tan Hill when we rode down.

I think that I should, as I spoke in anger when I left her and I should have known better. She's shown nothing but love and care for me while I was growing up, and she was only doing what she thought was right.'

'Aye, she'd every right to think the worst of me back then. I was young and reckless, and broken-hearted, I may add. I was perhaps not fit to be your father then, but you'd have had a good home with my family. You should make your peace – Martha only meant well.' Reuben smiled at his daughter; she'd a kind heart. A quick temper was her failing, but he'd only himself to blame, and he'd been just the same at her age.

'Then let's go back past the Tan Hill. I can't bear to think of Martha being upset. I never had the fine clothes that Hannah had, but I had hugs and sympathy, when needed. I only wish I could meet my own mother one day, and then I could tell her that I've been looked after and set her heart at ease. It must have taken some strength to leave me on the step of the inn and walk away.' Ruby sighed.

'Vadoma wouldn't have had much choice, my lass. Her brothers and fathers would have made sure of that. The last thing they would have needed would have been another mouth to feed, and she'd brought shame to her family by getting pregnant by me. Her life, and her heart, will have been in turmoil all these years. I should have listened to my father and left her alone. It would have saved us all heartache.' Reuben looked ahead of him. If he could undo all that selfishness of youth he would do, as his and Vadoma's lust for one another had brought nothing but pain, not only to them, but to both of their families and those around them.

Ruby and Reuben tied their horses up outside the inn and gazed around them. Ruby felt a lump rise in her throat. She had spent all her life wandering around the wild moors, watched over by the coal miners and their wives, when trade had been busy in the inn. This was her home and always would be, she thought, as she walked to the roughly painted door and lifted the latch, opening it wide and letting the morning's light shine across the well-worn flagged floor.

'We are not open – bugger off! It's only ten and I've just got rid of my night's lodgers,' Martha shouted from the kitchen, not even showing her face to her visitors.

'Well, we will if you want,' Ruby said gently, walking into the warm kitchen where Martha was starting to bake her bread for the day. 'But I hope you won't throw me out until I've made my peace, and told you that I love you and that now I understand how much I must have hurt you with my vicious words. I was wrong – you did what you thought was right. My father has explained, and has even said that he can understand why you did what you did.' Ruby walked towards Martha, who looked bedraggled and tired.

'Aye, lass, you don't know how glad my heart is to see you and hear those words. I thought I'd never see you again and that you'd never forgive me.' Martha, with flour still on her hands, rushed forward and held

Ruby close as she sobbed and rocked her back and forth. She whispered in Ruby's ear, 'You are alright – he's treating you well, and his family has made you welcome?'

'Yes, I'm spoilt rotten. I have my own room and Father has given me my own horse, and we've just spent the night in Reeth. I want for nothing,' Ruby said and hugged Martha close. 'I love you. I'm sorry for my hard words. I was thoughtless, and you know me to be hot-headed and too free with my speech sometimes.'

Martha stood back and looked at Ruby. 'My, look at you in your fine clothes. I could never have dressed you like that – and there's me putting flour all over them.' She smiled over at Reuben standing in the doorway, watching them both together. 'You've done her proud, Reuben, but you take care of her and love her, as well as giving her gifts.' Martha wiped her eyes.

'The clothes are not my doing. Jane Verity, down in Reeth, gave Ruby them, and more besides. They belonged to her daughter that she lost, and she thought they would have a good home with Ruby. She does look quite the young lady, apart from when she has her legs astride her horse like a man.' Reuben laughed as Ruby blushed.

'That's Ruby. She'd often be missing when she'd gone riding on the pit ponies. Rob Jenkins used to curse her something rotten for wearing his ponies out. He'd never say anything to her, but he'd complain rotten to me.' Martha smiled at Ruby.

'He should have said. I'd have stopped, if he'd told me off,' Ruby commented ruefully.

'What, and spoil his enjoyment of watching you trotting up the side of Bastifell with the wind in your hair, and the pony and you becoming one? There never was any getting away from your real parentage, lass.' Martha wiped her hands on her apron. 'Will you have a cup of tea? I can soon put the kettle on.'

'No, not this time,' Reuben replied. 'My mother will be having me hanged, drawn and quartered, as I said we'd be back for our dinner, but that was for yesterday's dinner. We've both been out overnight and she'll be worrying. Ruby wanted to right her wrong in being so sharp-tongued, and she's done it with my blessing. I'll not come between your love for one another. She can visit whenever she wants,' Reuben said, looking at both Ruby and Martha before leaving them to go to his horse.

'He's a good man, Mother. He's not like everyone paints him to be. He's deep with his emotions. I dread to think what he gets up to, with some of his dealings, but he's been good to me so far,' Ruby said, as Martha watched her for any telltale sign that she was not happy with her new family.

'Well, if it turns out that he and his family are not all that they seem, you've always got a home here. I miss you, my Ruby.' Martha leaned forward and gave her another tight hug. 'You keep yourself safe and if you ever need me, you know where I am. You come and see me on that new horse of yours.'

'I will, I promise. Now I must go, but I'll be back, so don't worry.' Ruby looked back at Martha as she closed the inn's door; she felt more content now. She had righted

132

her wrong and now she could visit Martha without worry. She should never have been so hard with her words.

'Are you right now, lass?' Reuben said and smiled as Ruby pulled her many skirts up around her knees, just like her mother had done years before, as she mounted her horse. 'Let's away home to the wrath of my mother. Yours is nowt compared to hers – it's the Scots in us, you know. Fiery and forthright, that's what we are, and you'll not be stopping it.'

Ruby looked around her. It sounded funny, her father saying, 'Let's away home.' The Tan Hill Inn had always been her home, but no more, now that she knew where her roots lay.

Chapter 9

'So now I've got two that trail around and don't let me know when they are coming home. I thought you'd perhaps behave yourself, Reuben, with Ruby in tow. I should have known better,' Elspeth said, with her hands on her hips as she looked at father and daughter standing in her kitchen, helping themselves to cheese and bread after their ride out together.

'You know what it's like, Mother. The day called me, and I decided I wanted to show Ruby off to Francis and Jane. You should have seen Jane's face when she realized who she was!' Reuben grinned at his mother.

'Jane gave me all her daughter's clothes – they are really lovely. She insisted that I took them, although I felt so sad for her. It was the last bond she had with her daughter,' Ruby said quietly. 'What do you think of this dress, Grandmother? I really like it, it is so warm, made with wool plaid and sewn so beautifully. I've never owned anything like it before.' She pulled the skirts out around her and smiled.

'Aye, tha looks bonny, lass. It was kind of Jane; they would have been made with love for her daughter. She's mourned Hannah these past few years, and perhaps she's ready to move on, and she'd be glad that your father has found you. Now, no more trailing. Arthur could have done with you, Reuben, as the sheep have started lambing, and he and Lennox are busy making sure that we are to make money this year. They haven't time to go galli-vanting whenever the mood takes them,' Elspeth chastised Reuben, who sat back in his chair at the table and gazed at his mother.

'I'll make us some money for the year at Appleby Horse Fair this coming summer, and at Brough Hill later in the year. I've some nice colts and fillies, readily broken in. They'll make just as much money as brainless sheep and are more pleasurable than looking at sheep every minute of the day.'

'I give up with you, Reuben Blake, I don't know what I've done to deserve you. I only hope Ruby has part of her mother in her, else Lord help us – I've two headstrong Blakes under my roof. Ruby, can you help me clean the bedrooms this afternoon or would you rather make supper for us all this evening? My maid, Anne, hasn't appeared this morning; the Handleys have probably kept her at home to help with their lambing, although they could have told me.' Elspeth sighed as she waited for Ruby to reply.

'Yes, of course. I need to pull my weight, now that I live here. Why don't I make a start with the bedrooms and then I'll also make something for supper? What would you like me to make? Is there anything in your pantry that needs eating first? It won't take me long to do, either. I'm used to hard work, from working at the Tan Hill.' Ruby quickly finished her cheese and bread and stood up. 'Where do you keep your cleaning stuff? I'll make a start straight away.'

'Here, I'll show you. Now, I'm a stickler for keeping all clean, so don't just dust upstairs. I expect everything to be polished, and the floors need mopping. That Anne sometimes doesn't do them and she thinks I don't notice, but I do. Dust soon builds up on wooden floors, so you've got to keep on top of it. The fires will need their ashes taken from out of them. I've not bothered lighting them this morning – it's spring, after all. Upstairs can do without heat until next winter; it's only more work for these old bones, and more expense.' Elspeth went to a cupboard set into the kitchen wall. 'Here, polish, duster, dry floor-duster, shovel and bucket. And make sure that all my lads' ewers and basins up in their rooms have enough water to wash themselves in, tonight and tomorrow morning, else they'll not bother and I'll have to give them a talking-to.'

Elspeth held everything out for Ruby to take, and then turned on Reuben. 'And you, stir your shanks – there's plenty outside for you to be doing. I'm going to have ten minutes in my rocking chair. I never slept a wink last night for worrying about you both. I should have known where you both were. You always trail off to see Francis when something is afoot.'

Elspeth took off her apron and looked at Ruby as she made her way through the kitchen and up the stairs to do the chores she had been given. 'Anything will do for supper, as long as I don't have to make it. Help yourself to the pantry,' she shouted after her, when she heard the metal bucket clanking on its hinges as Ruby climbed the stairs, weighed down with the cleaning materials. 'I could always get rid of Anne, if she proves to be a good hand,' Elspeth said quietly to Reuben. 'What's the point of paying someone, if you have got a granddaughter who does it for you?'

'Mother, a word of advice: don't put on her too much. Ruby's a lot like her mother, and she's got spirit,' Reuben said as he got up from the table and finished his cup of tea, before going out to muck out one of his stables.

'You mean she's a gypsy. You should never have met her mother. I'll make Ruby welcome, as I have her under my roof, but I'll not forget who her mother was. Your father warned you and went to his grave worrying about your dalliance. I don't know if she will bring us luck, living here or not, but we'll see, and you seem happier.' Elspeth shook her head. 'But she'll pay her way, like the rest of us.'

Ruby mopped and polished and cleaned all the fire grates, and did everything that had been expected of her. It wasn't as hard work as at her old home. Things had been kept tidy and clean by Anne, despite what her grandmother had said about her. The oak floors were soon mopped clear of any dust, and the mops were shaken out of the open windows, which Ruby had opened to let the sweet spring air into all the bedrooms. The fire grates were soon cleaned, and the furniture shone with Elspeth's home-made polish, which took no doing at all as all the furniture had been loved over the years and soon came to a healthy shine.

Arthur and Lennox's bedroom was just that: a bedroom with a wardrobe and a chest of drawers in it, no fineries or knick-knacks – unlike Ruby's grandmother's room, which had a chest of drawers with various trinkets and pieces of jewellery upon it, all of a certain age and beauty. She'd felt strange as she entered her father's room; bedrooms were private, and she stood looking around at what lay within it.

Unlike Arthur and Lennox, Reuben had all sorts of mementoes, none of any worth: on the chest of drawers next to his bed was a bunch of dried heather in a small glass vase, tied with a red ribbon; a leaden good-luck charm of a grinning, cross-legged pixie; and various pebbles that had obviously been picked up when out walking down by the river. They must have held memories for him, because anyone else would have thrown them out a long time ago, especially the heather, which had turned brown and shed its dead buds as Ruby polished around it. Had it belonged or been picked by her mother? It almost seemed as if her father was stuck in time since Vadoma had left his life. He must have loved her with all his heart, and she wished for him and for her that Vadoma would return one day. Then he could settle down and regain his happiness with her.

She sat on the edge of his bed, which was covered by a lovingly hand-made patchwork quilt, created from pieces of material that had been somebody's dress and blouse, and from other cast-off material that had been reused. The Blakes looked well off, but they were obviously thrifty, especially Elspeth. She was definitely the matriarch, although when it came to Reuben, he seemed not to be beholden to anyone but himself. However the family worked, she was part of it now and Ruby felt that she too would be expected to work for a living, whether she had been lost to them all her life or not.

'I hope you've all washed your hands?' Elspeth said as her boys returned from a hard day's work when darkness came on the fellside, making any further work on the land impossible before the following morning. 'Ruby has made supper for us tonight, and there's been a right good smell whiffing through the house while I've been doing your darning. It's grand to have another pair of hands. I should have had a lass instead of three lads.' Elspeth looked at her beloved sons, whom she always kept close to her, as they pulled their chairs away from the large kitchen table and examined the supper laid out before them.

'Aye, perhaps you should, if this is what we'd get every night.' Lennox grinned as he reached out for the dish of plain boiled potatoes and watched as Ruby sliced him a piece of bacon-and-egg pie, which she had cooked earlier and had allowed to go cool, for it to be eaten that way. 'That looks bloody good.'

'Lennox, language! Not at the dinner table,' Elspeth said sharply.

'Sorry, Mother. But it does look bloody good.' Lennox gazed up at Ruby and smiled.

'It's nothing special. I simply made what was to hand in the pantry. I used to make it often at Tan Hill, and there is a jam roly-poly for pudding, to make sure you are full for the evening. I hope I haven't made too much?' Ruby watched her grandmother and her father for confirmation that she'd done right.

'It's grand, lass, although we don't usually have a pudding in the evening. We have one at dinner time, and that way we can work it off. You weren't to know, and Lennox will love you all the more for double doses – he's the one with the sweet tooth.' Reuben smiled at his daughter as she passed him his plate of pie.

'No, it's right: you'll get used to our ways. The pie will be grand, but we will rewarm the pudding and custard for dinner tomorrow. I'm a believer in following the proverb "After dinner, rest awhile; after supper, walk a mile", as our Lennox puts weight on too easily anyway.' Elspeth tutted as she watched Lennox clear his plate just as fast as he'd filled it.

'You've not walked for miles, like me and Arthur. We've been up looking after those sheep three times today, and we'll be doing the same for the next month until the lambs are all born. A suety pudding would have filled that corner of my belly,' Lennox moaned.

140

'Have an apple out of the store, like the rest of us,' Arthur said. 'That was grand, Ruby, and I look forward to the jam roly-poly tomorrow. It is a bit heavy for this time of the evening – Mother's right.' Arthur smiled across at Elspeth.

'I'm sorry, I should have thought,' Ruby said and started to clear the empty plates from the table.

'It's right, lass, you weren't to know. You'll get used to our ways – don't worry.' Reuben reached for her empty hand and smiled. 'The main thing is that we have you sitting having supper with us now. I've wished for that for so long.'

'I'm glad that I'm here, but I should have asked before I made it. It will keep for tomorrow, as Grandmother says.' Ruby tried to not feel foolish as the brothers watched her. Why hadn't her grandmother told her earlier, as she'd seen the pudding steaming in a pan on the fire? Anyway, everyone had seemed to enjoy her supper and that was the main thing, and the family had accepted her, so she should stop worrying. This was now her home.

The early dawn's light shone through Ruby's bedroom window, the rays playing on her face, awakening her from her slumber. She yawned and stretched and looked around her. She couldn't lie in bed with the sun shining and beckoning outside, she thought, as she threw back her bedclothes and dressed quickly. The early morning was the best time of the day, she believed, as she stared through her bedroom window.

The fields spread out in front of her with a shimmering

white carpet of dew on them, and the sun was just starting to rise above the fells, giving the promise of a good day's weather ahead. Ruby quickly laced her boots up and quietly opened the oak bedroom door, walking softly along the landing and swearing to herself as the bottom rung of the staircase squeaked with her weight as she made her way to the kitchen. She stopped quickly in her tracks as she saw Lennox next to the fire, which he was bringing back to life with the aid of kindling and coal. He turned quickly and looked at her.

'What are you doing up at this time of the morning? I wouldn't be up this early if I didn't have sheep lambing,' he said, turning to blow gently on the smouldering sticks, hoping to entice the small flames to grow and catch hold properly.

'I can't sleep when the sun's beckoning me. It's too good a morning to be lying in my bed. I thought I'd go a walk before the rest of the house awakes.' Ruby stood back and watched the flames leap in the fire that Lennox had started.

'Aye, it is promising to be a grand day. Just you watch – the sheep always seem to make life hard for themselves and will not lamb today; they'll wait until it's the wettest day they could choose. They always do.' Lennox pulled on his leather kittle and looked at Ruby. 'You've made my brother happy, coming to live here with us. I still can't believe that I'm your uncle. '

'No, it is strange to me, but I'll get used to it, I suppose. And I'm not that far away from the Tan Hill. I can go and see Martha whenever I want, my father says, now that I've got my own horse, so I've got two homes.' Ruby watched as Lennox pulled his boots on. 'Are you going to look at your sheep now? Do you think there will be any newly born lambs this morning?'

'Aye, no matter what I said earlier, there will be one or two. I called one ready to drop her load last night. She looked as if she was having twins, so she'll be my first to check on this morning. Do you want to come with me? We'll be back before the rest of them are up.' Lennox glanced across at Ruby; her company would be welcome and he'd like to get to know his niece, away from the rest of the family.

'Yes, I'd like that. I used to walk the fells around Tan Hill and see the sheep lambing. It is a lovely thing to watch, and it makes you realize how life is precious, seeing the mother automatically take to her baby as soon as it is born. I wonder if my mother thought like that of me? And if she did, why didn't she fight to keep me?' Ruby said a little sadly.

'I'm sure she wanted to keep you, but she'd have had no say in it. And her family wouldn't let her, I presume. A mother's love can never be replaced. Our mother cossets us all too much; in fact she smothers me and Arthur, and there's only your father who dares to stand up to her. She means well, but I swear she still thinks I'm ten sometimes. I fair wanted a bit of your pudding last night, but it wasn't worth the argument. Still, I can look forward to it this dinner time.' Lennox grinned as he opened the kitchen door. 'Put your shawl on, as it still feels nippy out there. Spring has only just raised its head in these parts.'

'Do you not need a drink before you go?' Ruby indicated the kettle on the side of the hearth.

'No, we'll be away. The sooner I've seen to the sheep, the better, and then Arthur can give them another look before dinner. It's no good asking our Reuben. He's no interest and, besides, he'll be busy pampering his horses with Tom. They are both as bad as one another. I think he's adopted young Tom as well as yourself – Reuben makes that much of him. Let's away, there's plenty to do this day.'

Ruby sat under the shelter of a drystone wall in the morning's warming sunshine. The sun was climbing in the sky, and the air was fresh and clear; in the distance were the Lakeland hills and in front of her, even further away, were the border hills of Scotland. It was glorious, listening to the skylark singing above her own and Lennox's heads, and watching the newly lambed sheep nudge her two lambs to drink from her, encouraging them with bleats and soft nudges as they found their feet and instinctively made for her teats. Lennox had been right: the sheep had just given birth to a set of twins and was now licking them clear of the afterbirth.

'I must have seen this a thousand times, and I still think of it as one of the best sights ever,' Lennox said as he leaned back against the wall next to Ruby.

'Yes, it's grand. I could nearly cry. I like sheep, especially Swaledales; they are tough and hardy, like the Dales around them. They have to be, to survive up here, I suppose.' Ruby looked at Lennox, who with his wiry ginger hair was a bit like the sheep he loved.

144

'Aye, it is no good having them soft breeds, like Leicesters, up here on these fells. You need something tough to survive our winters, and the rain that never stops some days. Tough sheep and tough folk: that's what we are because we have to be, lass. It's a tough life that we have in this part of the world.' Lennox got up to his feet and offered Ruby his hand. 'Away, lass, let's be making our way home. This new family looks fine. Besides, we will both get a talking-to if we are not back in time for breakfast, and your father will be wondering where you are.'

'My father is a good man, isn't he?' Ruby asked Lennox as she held onto his hand to be pulled up.

'Aye, he is. A soft lump that lost his heart to someone he shouldn't have done, and that made him a bit wild for a while. But you have got a good father; he doesn't always stick to the rules of life, but he never hurts anybody if he can help it. You'll be alright with him and us, so don't you be fretting. We've already claimed you as ours, so don't you worry your head. You'll have to come with me in the morning, if you wish. There's nothing better than seeing new life come into the world. But for now let's get home to my mother, else we will never hear the end of it all day. Lord, my mother can witter, and if she gets something in her head, she never lets it drop!' Lennox laughed as they both walked across the rush-filled green field and looked down upon the farmhouse, with a good smoke rising from the chimney, and Tom saddling the horses up in the yard for the day.

'Tom is up and going in good time this morning,' Ruby

commented as they strode out down the pasture towards home.

'Aye, he's a good lad – his mother's brought him up right. He can be a cheeky beggar if he wants to be, but we put up with him. He was a godsend when your father and Arthur went over to Saltburn. I doubt they would have returned at all if it hadn't have been for Tom and the other stable lad's quick-thinking.'

'Why, what went on there?' Ruby asked innocently. 'I heard my father mention it when he was talking to Francis Verity.'

'Let's say he had a bit of trouble, of his own making. I'll add: with John Andrews, a well-known smuggler of those parts. Your father should keep to things that he knows, and not go out of his area. Anyway, he lives to tell the tale, until the next time he gets the urge to do something stupid.' Lennox opened the pasture's gate and waited until Ruby had passed through it, before closing it and joining her to cross the farmyard.

'You are up earlier than the other morning. What's up: have you wet the bed?' Tom said cheekily to Ruby as she passed by him while he groomed Reuben's horse in the morning's sunshine.

'No, I just enjoy spring mornings, and I've been with Lennox, looking at his newly lambed sheep. It's been grand – I've enjoyed every minute. Are you always that cheeky?' Ruby stared at Tom and saw a grin come across his face, as Lennox made his way in through the back door of the farmhouse.

'Only when I know I can get away with it. I watched

you going off with your father on your horse: you ride well. Do you fancy joining me one evening when I've finished my work? I'll give you a run for your money.' Tom grinned at her with a twinkle in his eye.

'Maybe, I'll see,' Ruby replied. She'd keep cheeky Tom waiting, she thought as she walked in Lennox's footsteps and turned to smile at him. Nothing would suit her better, she thought, as she heard her name being called out and was told to hurry to the table because she was already late for breakfast.

Chapter 10

The dark-haired, brown-eyed girl stood with her head bowed and her hands folded as Elspeth chastised her for not appearing to do her work the previous day. At the age of fourteen, Anne was already doing an adult's work each day in order to help put food on the table at her family home.

'I know your family is busy at this time of year, but we all are. If you'd only have sent word with your young brother, George, I'd have understood, but not to turn up at all is just not good enough, Anne,' Elspeth said and looked at her neighbour's daughter and her part-time maid with disdain.

'I'm sorry, Mrs Blake, but me ma was busy with my brothers and sisters, and my pa and our Bob were making sure the lambing was going alright. I was needed more at home than here, so my ma said,' Anne replied quietly, and then gave a slight glance at Ruby as she sat at the kitchen table, listening in to her dressing-down.

'Aye, but she'll still expect me to pay you. Never mind, you are here now. Ruby, here, cleaned the bedrooms for me yesterday, so they are done. You can scrub the kitchen floor before my lads come back in for their dinners. It could do with a good scrub – mucky boots have been coming back and forth over it. Why they have to bring half the land into my kitchen on their feet, I don't know.' Elspeth shook her head, taking in the look of disgust on Anne's face, before she went into the main living room to sit down and write a letter to her sister, telling her the news of Ruby's appearance and asking how things were over in Dentdale.

Anne glanced across at Ruby as she filled the salt cellars – a job given to her by Elspeth before she realized that her young serving lass was going to appear that day. She pulled a face. 'Have you been taken on by the old bag? Lord, does she moan and complain. I'd not come, but we need the money at home.' Anne slumped down in the chair next to Ruby and looked across at her, as she played with a spoon that had been left on the pine kitchen table.

Ruby sniggered and glanced at the stroppy young lass, who was large and clumsy for her age. 'No, she's my grandmother. But you weren't to know that, and don't worry – I'll not tell her what you think about her,' she added quickly, as she noticed the horror on Anne's face and the speed with which she suddenly decided to get on with her job as she jumped up from her chair.

'I'm sorry, I didn't know. You'll not tell her what I said, will you? She'd throw me out without pay if she knew what I thought of her.' Anne looked at Ruby, with worry on her face.

Ruby whispered, 'You are right, she does moan, and I've only known her a few days.'

Anne stared at Ruby as she put on a sacking apron from behind the kitchen door. She was curious: how was Ruby the granddaughter of Elspeth Blake? None of her sons were married. She hesitated for a moment and then decided to ask. 'So whose daughter are you? You can't be Lennox's, as he never hardly talks to anyone but his sheep, and Arthur's not far behind him,' Anne said with curiosity, as she reached for a metal bucket and soda crystals from under the pot sink in the kitchen. 'So you must be Reuben's; you aren't the gyp—' she said, breaking off her sentence as she realized that perhaps she was going to offend and should have been more careful about what she said.

'I suppose I am. And you can say it: "the gypsy's daughter". Although I've not been brought up as a gypsy. My father found me, and I'm just getting used to who I am because I've never known my true mother.' Ruby gazed at Anne as she screwed up her nose.

'My mother is always talking about your father. She feels sorry for him. I'll have to tell her that he's found you, if nobody else. She'll be glad for him. You look like him, and part gypsy. I should have guessed, with that long black hair of yours. It must be funny living here. Are you thinking of staying, because your grandmother might not need me if you do, by the looks of it.' Anne nodded to the salt cellars being filled. She'd worried

150

straight away when she'd heard that the bedrooms had already been cleaned; that was her job for a Tuesday, and she usually took all day doing them.

'As far as I'm aware, I'll be staying here. However, you needn't worry, Anne. I'll not be after your job, although I will make myself useful around the place,' Ruby replied and watched as Anne stood with the bucket in one hand and a scrubbing brush in the other. The girl definitely said what she thought, and Ruby couldn't help but ponder as she watched Anne go out into the yard and get some fresh water from the pump for the job in hand. As she did so, she watched Tom talking to her, a smile on his face, and Anne was obviously encouraging his attention as she giggled and chatted to him. So Anne had her eye on Tom, but did he feel the same about her? Ruby wondered. Tom soon got bored of the young girl's flirting and returned to the safety of his stable, leaving Anne with the kitchen floor to scrub, much to her dislike.

'That Tom Adams, he thinks a lot of himself and he's only a stable lad. His family is exactly the same as mine, trying to make a living in this godforsaken place. He'll wish he had spent more time of day with me, when I've moved to Carlisle and have made a name for myself by marrying a well-to-do gent. He'll realize then that he should have spent more effort on me,' Anne said as she carried her heavy pail, full of cold water, then got down on her knees and started to scrub the stone flags.

'I'll get out of your way. I'll put these salt cellars away, and then I'll go and give my horse a groom. My father gave me the horse called Thistle the other day, and it's

151

only right that I look after her.' Ruby got up from her chair and placed the wooden salt box upon the fireplace to keep the contents dry, then put the salt cellars on the highly polished oak dresser and smiled down at Anne as she scrubbed the floor. The smell of carbolic soap filled the kitchen as the girl sat back on her haunches and stared up at Ruby.

'You've landed on your feet, haven't you? There's nowt you'll ever want for again in your life,' Anne said as she looked hard at Ruby and then set to the task in hand.

Ruby said nothing in return. Anne was wrong. There was one thing she would like in her life, and that was to find and know her true mother, and then her life would be complete.

'So you've met the straight-talking Anne?' Tom said as Ruby entered the stable. 'You should get out of her way – most folks do, as she doesn't hold back with what she says.'

'I gathered that. I take it you are not a fan? Although I think she is of you.' Ruby smiled as she watched Tom, polishing and oiling a saddle as he sat on a bale of hay and looked up at her.

'She's forever flirting with me. She's far too young for me, and too forward. I try and make myself scarce when I see her coming, but I don't always manage it.' Tom grinned. 'Are you settling in? I suppose it will take you a while.'

'Yes, it feels strange. I don't quite know what I should do and what I shouldn't. And my grandmother is in charge of running the house, along with Anne, so I don't want to step on anybody's toes. I thought I'd come and groom Thistle. I'll give her a good brush.'

'She's been done. I did her with your father's horse before he went out up the fell this morning. He's gone to make sure his horses up there, that graze the fell, are all in good health. He'll be selling some of them when it comes around to Appleby Fair this summer and Brough Horse Fair in the back end. It's when he makes his money; despite what his brothers think, he's well respected for his breeding of horses. You can see for yourself that he's got a good eye and takes care of them. You can give Thistle another brush if you want, it'll not harm her. I was about to turn her out into the paddock – she might as well get the benefit of the spring day as be in the stable.' Tom put down the saddle that he was polishing and stood up and looked at Ruby. 'You take her; she's on her halter, and I'll walk over and open the gate for you.'

'Alright, we'll do that.' Ruby walked over to the stall where Thistle was and patted her horse, whose coat was immaculate after Tom's care of her. 'Now then, lass, let's give you some fresh air in your lungs and let you kick up your heels. I'll not be riding you today.' Ruby unfastened the halter from the iron ring that was attached to the whitewashed stable walls and held firmly to it as she walked the small horse out of the stalls.

'You've got a good lass there – she's one of my favourites. Aren't you, lass?' Tom stroked the horse's head and looked at Ruby as she held Thistle. 'Breathe gently up her nose; it's an old trick my father once learned me. She knows your smell then and knows that you are a friend,' Tom said as he stroked Thistle's soft pink muzzle.

Ruby looked at Tom and then gently blew on Thistle's muzzle and up her nostrils. The horse shook her head for a minute and then seemed unperturbed by the action.

'There, you are friends for life now. She'll always remember you.' Tom smiled as Ruby held tightly to the halter and stepped Thistle out into the light of the farm-yard, leading her horse with pride across to the pasture in front of the house.

They both leaned over the pasture gate as they watched Thistle kick up her heels and run the full length of the paddock, with the wind blowing through her mane and Thistle snorting as she enjoyed her freedom.

'It's a lovely sight. I love to see a horse running free,' Ruby said as she rested on the gate with Tom next to her.

'Aye, they know how to show their pleasure – it's a grand sight to see. Now you've made friends with your horse, is there any chance that we could be friends?' Tom looked at the lass who had caught his eye as soon as her father had brought her into the farmyard. He knew Reuben would wish somebody wealthier and better for his newly found daughter, but he'd put up with the consequences of his wrath.

Ruby turned and glanced at Tom. He was a good-looking lad and soft-hearted, it would seem. 'Of course, I'd like that. Nothing would suit me better.' She smiled and watched Thistle kicking up her heels, not wanting Tom to see the colour in her cheeks.

'Your father will perhaps have something to say about it, but can I ask you again: would you fancy a walk or a ride out on our horses together one evening when I've finished my work for the day?' Tom held his breath: had he acted too soon? Would Ruby think the worst of him for rushing her with his invitation to become friends?

'Nothing would suit me more, Tom, I'd enjoy that. You can show me around my family's land. I still can't believe I am part of this family,' Ruby said and watched Tom, who was blushing just as much as she had been.

'No, I can't, but I'm glad you are here,' Tom replied, then looked out over the pasture with a huge smile on his face. Ruby Blake was more his sort of woman than young Anne Handley, who couldn't hold a candle to Ruby's beauty. And despite what Reuben had said about Tom not being good enough for his daughter, he was perhaps going to court the girl, if given the chance. Reuben had surely only said it in jest anyway. He knew that Tom was as good a catch as any man in the county – perhaps not a rich one, but loyal to the core.

Anne stared out of the kitchen door as she swilled the dirty water, from washing the kitchen floor, down the outside drain. She noticed Ruby smiling and laughing with Tom and swore under her breath. Not only had Ruby robbed her of her cushiest job, but now she was robbing her of any chance of stepping out with Tom. The cheek of the gypsy bitch; she'd only been here a few days and already she'd stolen things from her. It was

155

typical of her sort, Anne thought, as she wiped her hands and replied to Elspeth when she yelled out Anne's name to give her the next chores for the day. She'd have to put a stop to that, if she had her way.

Later that afternoon, Anne, now envious and annoyed by the attention given to Ruby, sulked as she entered the kitchen of the Blakes' home. It was as if she was not there, except to scrub the floors and do jobs that were below the gypsy brat. And to make things worse, Tom hardly ever spoke to her, being besotted by Ruby. Late as ever, Anne breezed in and donned her apron as she stood and asked for her day's instructions from Elspeth, then glanced round and noticed that Ruby was just disappearing up the stairs and ignored her.

'Do you want me to dust and clean the bedrooms today? It is Tuesday and that is what I usually do?' Anne asked as she made for the broom cupboard to get her cleaning materials.

'No, there's no need for you to clean them. Ruby is already busy at work up there. She's already cleaned Lennox and Arthur's bedroom, and she doesn't take half the time you do. I thought you could clean the brasses this morning. They have lost their shine and it is such a dirty job, and I don't want to get my own clothes soiled. And then this afternoon all the chamberpots could do with a good scrub out. I told Ruby to leave them for you to do. So they are all at the top of the stairs, waiting for you to empty and clean. It's not a job for my granddaughter,' Elspeth said flippantly. She paid young Anne well enough, and she should be prepared to do the menial jobs, for what she earned.

'Will *she* always be cleaning the bedrooms from now on? Perhaps you don't need me at all, now you've got *her* staying with you,' Anne said with disdain.

'Perhaps I won't need you. I definitely won't if you don't get a move on and wipe that look off your face. Ruby is precious to my son and is now part of our family. So for once, Anne, I suggest you keep your thoughts to yourself, else I will not be needing your services for much longer,' Elspeth replied sharply and pushed a duster into her hands. 'Now, brasses – and make sure they are cleaned properly.'

Ruby turned and saw Anne coming out of Elspeth's bedroom as she rolled up the final runner along the landing, to be shaken free of dust out of one of the bedroom windows. Thinking that she must be looking for the chamberpot to clean, Ruby announced that her chamberpot was at the top of the stairs, like everyone else's.

'Oh, sorry, I thought Mrs Blake's was missing,' Anne said and then disappeared down the stairs with two pots, one of which was the one she had been searching for. Ruby shook her head. Anne's mind was obviously elsewhere, she thought as she shook the runner violently out of the bedroom window and then put it back in place. Anne had not spoken to her when she had seen her briefly in the kitchen, so perhaps there was worry at home. Reuben had said the Handleys only had a small stretch of land and there were six of them in the family, so money would be tight, she thought as she stood back with her hands on her hips and admired how clean she had left the upstairs rooms. Whatever was worrying Anne, she was definitely not as chatty as she had been on the first day they had met.

Chapter 11

'Has anybody seen my emerald necklace and matching earrings? They were in the top drawer of my chest of drawers. They are always kept there. The box is there, but it is empty. I know I put them back there the last time I wore them, after the Christmas dance down in Kirkby Stephen.' Elspeth looked worried. 'Reuben, you know the ones: your father gave them to me when we were courting, and they were his mother's. I can't have lost them. I distinctly remember placing them back in their case just before I went to bed, and now they have gone.'

Elspeth seemed perplexed. She was about to go and have dinner with her closest friend and her husband at Border House, one of the finest houses in the area, and she had wanted to look her best in her finery.

'It's no good looking at me, Mother, I'm not likely to have use of them,' Reuben replied, as his mother tried to fasten a necklace of lower quality around her neck while he waited to take her in his carriage, which was waiting outside.

'Ruby, have you seen them while you were cleaning the bedrooms? I must have put them down somewhere. I wouldn't mind, but I always think they bring me luck. As I'll be playing a game of bridge after my dinner with Richard and Dora, I could do with their presence around my neck. I know it is stupid, but that's how I feel,' Elspeth sighed.

'I'm sorry, I've never seen them. And I never open your drawers, as they are private. I'm sure you will win your hand of bridge, with or without them. However, would you like me to have a quick search of your bedroom?' Ruby rose from her chair and placed down the mending that she had been doing to pass the evening.

'No, no, sit down. I'm already late and Dora is a stickler for keeping to time. They will turn up. I must be getting a little forgetful in my old age,' Elspeth said as she reached for her gloves and followed Reuben out of the house to dinner with her friends.

'It's not like our mother to lose something, especially something so precious to her,' Lennox commented to Arthur as he read the newspaper and smoked his pipe in the quiet of the evening.

'It doesn't surprise me. I heard her muttering to herself the other day – she is getting on, you know, and we might have to face the inevitable eventually,' Arthur said.

'Then who will do our washing and mending?' Lennox asked and glanced from behind his paper at Ruby.

160

'Perhaps it is a good job that our Reuben found you. You might be needed shortly.'

'Perhaps it is. I'll go and have a look for her necklace and earrings. I'm sure they will be somewhere in the house.'

Ruby left the mending that she had been given by Elspeth and climbed the stairs to go and search in Elspeth's room for the elusive jewellery. She opened the bedroom door and stared at the large, square bedroom. The trinkets must be in her drawers; there was nowhere else she could have put them, she thought, as she opened the drawers and looked nervously into them. They were full of things precious to Elspeth – hair slides, gloves and scarves, and a pair or two of earrings – but there was no sight of the emerald necklace and earrings; only an empty velvet jewellery case in the shape of a seashell, where they obviously belonged. Where Elspeth had put them was a mystery, but Ruby hoped that she would find them soon. Not only did they sound of monetary value, but also of sentimental value. She herself would be heartbroken if she ever lost her mother's bangle, so she could relate to the feeling of loss if they did not reappear.

As for looking after the three brothers, if Elspeth's mind was failing, she'd not bargained for that, and she did not relish the prospect as she closed the bedroom door behind her to sit in the kitchen, which smelled of Kendal Twist, the baccy both brothers were smoking in their clay pipes as they rested from their day's work.

Life at Banksgill was a lot steadier than life at the busy Tan Hill Inn, and Ruby was beginning to miss the comings and goings of the locals and the cheek of visitors whose eye she caught. She planned to go for a ride on Thistle the following day. Anne could do all her regular chores while she was away; it would stop her looking so surly and thinking that Ruby was a threat to her position as maid to the Blakes. She'd not been as friendly of late, giving Ruby dark glances as if she was a little jealous, so it was best to leave her alone. Besides, a breath or two of the clear moorland air would do her good.

Much as she loved her new home and family, Ruby sometimes found Elspeth a little too bossy and overbearing. She wanted a dogsbody – a granddaughter who could turn her hand to most things around the house. Ever since she had arrived, Elspeth had treated her more like a servant than the granddaughter she was, Ruby thought, as she gazed out of the large arched window on the stairs and up at the moonlit sky. If she didn't know better, she'd think there was resentment growing towards her. Had it always been there? Elspeth sounded as if she would not have blessed the union between Reuben and her mother, even if they had been able to wed. Elspeth was starting to show herself for the real grandmother that she was.

Ruby looked up at the stars, which were shining brightly; the shadow of the dark fells and moorlands stood out like sleeping giants. Yes, she would go and wander tomorrow. She needed some time to herself, if only to get away from the glare of the brooding Anne and from her grandmother's orders.

Ruby sat beside the banks of Deepdale Beck; the wind was filled with the smell of the peaty fellside, and the freshness of spring bursting forth filled her lungs. It was good to have time to herself. Sometimes she felt that her every move and every word were being scrutinized by Elspeth. And her father, Reuben, was always busy with his horses or doing business one way or another and hadn't time to spend with her. Although she was with her true family, she didn't feel as if she fitted in; there was not the love shown to her that Martha had shown her – in fact, she could almost detect a slight resentment towards her from Elspeth.

She looked down at her fine skirts and natty boots. They were fine, but they didn't make up for the love that she was missing from Martha, and she sometimes wished she was back at the Tan Hill Inn and still dressed in her old clothes and cheeking the drinkers in the old inn. But pride was stopping her from admitting that she had been happier with Martha – pride and loyalty to her father, who had shown nothing but love to her since her arrival at Banksgill.

Tom, the stable lad, was the person she felt most at ease with, and she smiled as she remembered the teasing he had given her as she mounted her horse to set off on her ride. He was a good lad, a little older than her, but had a nice sense of humour, and he also knew that Elspeth was not the most understanding of women. Elspeth had a problem with those she thought beneath her class, even though she was only a farmer's wife – albeit a wealthy one – with some airs and graces that did not belong in a farmhouse set in the wilds of the Yorkshire moors on the border of Westmorland. She looked down upon Anne and Tom, and they both knew it. Ruby felt as if she would have been given the same treatment, had it not been for the fact that she was Elspeth's granddaughter.

Ruby breathed in deeply and lay back on the grassy bank and stared up at the sun through the unfurling green leaves of the sycamore tree above her head, and listened to the gentle trickle of water and the song of the courting birds. It was good to be her own mistress for a little while, and it would suit the moaning Anne to be able to clean the bedrooms and not feel she was being pushed out of her work.

A few hours on her own would clear her head; after all, the last few weeks had been new to everyone, and it would take time for them all to really get to know each other. She closed her eyes and smiled as she heard Thistle munching contentedly on the moorland grass while she rested. She loved her horse, and her father had been good to her, giving her Thistle. Things were fine really; just new, she thought as she lay in the sunshine.

'You should have stayed away a bit longer. I don't know what's going on in the house, but all the brothers have been made by your grandmother to come in, and I can hear raised voices,' Tom said as he watched Ruby dismount from her horse. 'Whatever's wrong, God help the person she's mad with, because Mrs Blake has one hell of a temper.'

'All was well when I left. Anne had come and even she was happy, as she realized she could have the

164

bedrooms to clean today.' Ruby slid from her horse and handed Tom the reins.

'Aye, well, if you want a sanctuary, I'm in the stable. When the Blakes fall out, they really do fall out – such tempers they have!' Tom took Thistle by the reins and led her into the stable, leaving Ruby gathering the courage to enter the raging household, where raised voices could be heard as she entered the back passage and went through to the kitchen.

'You are sure, Anne? You didn't find them elsewhere?' Elspeth sighed and screwed up her face in anger as she turned to look at Reuben. 'I should have known for her not to enter our family – gypsy stock, that's what she is,' she spat.

'I'm sorry, Mrs Blake. All I know is that I found them under Miss Ruby's mattress. I don't know how they got there.' Anne hung her head and started to sob as she came forth with her news.

'Are you sure, Anne, you are telling the truth now? The devil take you if you aren't.' Reuben grabbed hold of Anne's arm and shook her.

'I'm telling you the truth, honest, sir. I'm as afeared of the devil as you are, and I'd not be telling you and your mother lies.' Anne wiped her eyes and stood in front of the family, all of whom were looking at her, not even hearing the back door open and close as Ruby entered the farmhouse.

Ruby entered the kitchen quietly and heard Elspeth shouting, 'She's a thief, I tell you, nothing but a thief!'

165

All three brothers, her grandmother and Anne stood with angry faces and turned to stare at her as she arrived in their midst.

'So you've dared to return and show your face, madam? Have you been meeting with your own kind and arranging for my jewels to be sold on?' Elspeth snapped at her, and glared as Ruby stood dumbfounded in front of her family.

'Mother, hold your noise – give my Ruby time to explain. It might be all a misunderstanding,' Reuben said and walked over to where his daughter stood. 'Are you alright? What were you thinking of, when you stole and hid my mother's emeralds? I'd have bought you some, if you had but asked.'

'What? What are you talking about? I haven't stolen my grandmother's emeralds – I've never even seen them.' Ruby's stomach churned and she felt a flush coming to her cheeks. How could they think such a thing of her?

'So when Anne found them under your mattress, when she turned it this morning, they had got there by themselves? I don't think so, Miss! You stole them out of my drawer. I should have known better than to let Reuben bring you home and treat you like our own blood. You are from gypsy stock; your mother bewitched my son, and now you are taking what you think is yours away from me. Even Arthur and Lennox dote on you. Thank heavens Anne here has been able to show us your true colours,' Elspeth screamed and shook her head. 'It was a bad day when you were found. I thought you, Reuben, were starting to get on with your life instead of moping and dreaming about that gypsy whore who ruined your life. And then you turned up!'

'Mother, watch your tongue. Ruby knows nothing about your emeralds. Just look at her face!' Reuben snapped at his mother.

'My father's right. I know nothing about them, and I didn't put them there. I do not need to steal anything. I've everything I have ever needed, you have made me so welcome. But by the sound of your words, you have tarred me with the brush of being a gypsy and you think the worst of both them and me. Well, you are wrong. I never touched your jewellery and neither, I am sure, would any relation of mine,' Ruby said and lifted her head high. She wasn't going to be accused of theft. She stared over at Anne, who stood at the back of the kitchen with her head down, next to the emeralds, which had been placed on the kitchen table.

'Mother, you might be wrong,' Lennox said quietly. 'Ruby would not do anything like this – she's a good lass.'

'You know nowt about anything. She's guilty: look at her rise and defend her own. What have I done to deserve three sons so stupid? But it is you, Reuben Blake, who have brought your gypsy child under my roof. Well, she can go back to where she came from. The Tan Hill is about right for her. It's as wild and as lawless as it gets,' Elspeth screamed.

'Mother, she stays here. Ruby's my daughter! I'll not have you saying these things or throwing her out of her family home.' Reuben put his arm around Ruby and glared at his mother.

167

'Father, don't worry. I'm not staying where I'm not wanted. It is no good staying, if everyone thinks I'm guilty of stealing, which I am not. I've never stolen anything in my life. And your mother is ashamed of me – she's made that obvious since the day I came here, even though she welcomed me with open arms.' Ruby pulled away from her father; she had to get away before she said how she really felt. She looked around the room: all eyes were on her. How could anyone think the worst of her? And how had the emeralds been found under her mattress by Anne? They hadn't been there the previous week when she had turned her feather mattress over.

She stared at Anne, who was suspiciously quiet at the back of the kitchen. But it made no difference; her grand-mother had made her feelings towards her crystal clear: she was the daughter of a gypsy, the scum of the earth, in the old woman's eyes, and not fit to live under her roof. Ruby turned and ran out of the farmhouse, with tears running down her cheeks and a hurt in her heart so deep that she thought she would rather be dead than be thought of the way Elspeth Blake thought of her. She sobbed and ran to the safety of the stable. She would hide there for a while and hope that her father would make his mother see sense and be able to prove that she was no thief.

'Hey, hey, what's the matter?' Tom asked as he watched Ruby rush into the stable and sit down, hiding in the darkest corner and sitting down amongst the hay. 'What are you crying for? Has Elspeth upset you? She's a fair tongue on her when she lets rip.'

168

Ruby gulped and sobbed and tried to reply to Tom, who came and sat next to her. 'She's accused me of stealing her jewellery. Anne found it under my mattress, but I didn't put it there – I'd nothing to do with it. But Elspeth's called me all the names under the sun. She thinks I'm the worst person who could be under her roof, with me being the daughter of a gypsy.' She sobbed and gulped, but at the same time Ruby felt angry. She'd not been given a chance to prove that it wasn't her fault before she'd been branded as a thief, and her mother called a whore.

'Well, that can't be right. I know you'd never do that. Why spoil a good thing? You've everything you need and more besides, and if you wanted, you only had to ask for them. Your father adores you, and he'd do anything for you.' Tom dragged his fingers through his hair and looked at Ruby. 'She's got a sharp tongue on her, has Elspeth, and that Anne can be sneaky.'

'Well, Anne said nothing, she stayed quiet at the back of the kitchen. I don't want my father to think the worst of me, but I can't stay, if that's how his mother feels about me. How can I possibly live with them all after that's been said to me? I swear I did not steal those emeralds. And I can't help my parentage.' Ruby sobbed and felt Tom's arm come round her as he tried to comfort her.

'The old woman's a snob; she always has been. Reuben's father was the better person, and it's him that your father takes after, apart from his pride in his appearance. I believe you, and so will your father, but your grandmother's bias is another thing.'

169

'Well, I'm not staying here another minute. I will go home to my true home, and Martha. She's the nearest thing to real family, and she loves me, no matter what my parentage. I don't want to leave my father, though, not when I've only just found him. And I don't want to look as if I'm guilty, either.' Ruby sighed and gazed into the eyes of Tom, who was showing her only sympathy.

'I don't want you to leave, either. I was beginning to get to know you, and I like what I see. It will be that bloody Anne's doing, I bet. She's as sneaky as a snake and she was moaning to me that you'd taken over her best day of working for Elspeth. And she's seen us two talking together.' Tom looked at Ruby; she was so beautiful and he wanted to protect her.

'Even if it is Anne's doing, Elspeth said exactly how she felt about me, and I can't bear to look at her, let alone be civil to her. It's no good, Tom. I'm going home to the Tan Hill, where I know I'm accepted for what I am.' Ruby dropped her head and fought back her tears.

Tom gently put his hand under her chin and raised her head, peering into her eyes. 'Then if you must go, can I visit you, Ruby Blake? Because as well as being special to your father, I think you'll be special to me. And I don't give a damn whether you've stolen the Crown Jewels or are Queen of the Gypsies – I like you for who you are.'

Ruby controlled her breathing and wiped her eyes. 'I'd like that, as we do get on and I will miss you if I leave,' she said quietly.

'Then that's that. You've got me as a friend, or perhaps more, if you let me?' Tom said quietly.

170

'We'll see, Tom, but perhaps more.' Ruby smiled at the young man, who she knew had feelings for her; he was a good friend, and only time would tell what would follow.

Chapter 12

'I wish you'd change your mind and stay,' Reuben said as he loaded his own and Ruby's horses with her belongings. 'My mother's already regretting the words that were said. They were spoken in anger and they weren't meant.' He pulled the rope tight and looked at his daughter as she mounted her horse.

'I'm sorry, Father, but she did mean them. Perhaps she's regretting them now, but that is how she feels about me. Besides, I'd never feel comfortable again in the house, after being accused of being a thief.' Ruby sat up straight on the back of her horse and looked down at her father.

Reuben shook his head. 'Damn my mother, she always did have an air of arrogance about her, and she's always been too quick to judge. Those bloody emeralds must have appeared under your mattress by magic, or Anne has something to do with it. I lectured her and tried to get to the truth of it all, but my mother caught me talking to Anne and said I was bullying the girl. She needs bullying, and more besides, if it was her who planted them there.'

'It doesn't matter. Leave her be; what comes around goes around. She'll get her comeuppance eventually. It doesn't make any difference to my feelings for you. You've shown nothing but kindness towards me, and I know that you will always be there for me. Your mother can't help but feel that way about me, because – let's face it – most people think gypsies are different to them and don't give them the time of day. They don't understand their ways, that's the problem.'

Ruby looked across at her father. At one time even she had thought like her grandmother, but that had changed as she began to understand the love her father had felt for her mother, and as he explained Romany ways to her during their time together. She had listened with interest as he'd explained how they lived and ate from the land, foraging for what was in season and bartering with locals the crafts they made. How family and honour were everything to the Romany. They were connected to nature and their own traditions, and they were really no different from anyone else. Her father had smiled and looked at Ruby with love as he told her about her mother's ways as they rode together and urged her to be proud of her heritage.

'Aye, well, what's said is said, and I wish it was different. My brothers are annoyed with my mother and all. You do know you are always welcome back, despite what my mother says? Now I suppose, if you insist, we'll take you back where I found you, but I've got to say it is with a heavy heart.' Reuben urged his horse onwards with Ruby by his side.

Ruby couldn't help but feel her heart surge as she led her horse into the rundown stable at the back of the Tan Hill Inn. She'd been away just a few weeks but now, with hindsight, it felt like years, as she had never felt quite at home at Banksgill. Now, as she entered the inn, she knew where her heart lay, and that she would be loved and not treated like an unpaid skivvy, let alone be accused of being a thief.

'Aye, lass, you are back, but what is to do? I thought I'd hardly see you again, but here you are with your father and all your goods and chattels. Does this mean you are coming back to live with me?' Martha looked at Ruby as she placed a bag of belongings on the floor, then went to where Martha stood and wrapped her arms around her.

'If you'll have me? Things have not worked out at Banksgill – not because of my father, I must add,' Ruby replied. She stood back from Martha and turned to look at her father, as he entered with another bundle of her clothes and belongings from the back of his horse.

'Aye, it was my mother. She can't stop her mouth from saying what she is thinking sometimes. And most of the time what she is thinking is totally wrong. I've told Ruby to take no heed to her spoutings, but it's upset her, so I've brought her back to you for now.' Reuben sighed as he saw the happiness spreading over Martha's face.

'Well, I can't say I'm not glad that you are back, because I am, lass. Life here has not been the same since you left. And I've not been feeling myself of late, so I'll be thankful for your company.' Martha hugged Ruby yet again and then smiled at Reuben. 'You'll stop and have your dinner with us? I have a good meat-and-tattie pie in the oven – it'll soon be ready,' she said to Reuben. She was thankful that he had brought Ruby back, and no doubt Ruby would tell her what his mother had said, for her to leave her new home.

'Aye, that will be grand. I'll just put my horse in the stable for now.' Reuben looked at his daughter. 'You need to tether Thistle on the fell later. She'll take no harm if you keep moving her to a new patch every day, Ruby.'

'A horse – you've got your own horse! Now that is being spoilt. And look at all this stuff you've brought back with you,' Martha exclaimed as Reuben went out to see to the horses. 'I could never have given you all this.'

'You gave me much more: you showed me love, without any expectations or demands, and you took me in for who I was.' Ruby hugged Martha. 'I'm sorry I was harsh with my words. I had my head turned by what I thought might have been, but now I know where I was most loved.'

'So have they not made you welcome at Banksgill? I bet Reuben's mother can be a piece of stuck-up baggage when she wants to be. I've only seen her the once, but I wasn't impressed,' Martha sneered.

'She does think herself better than others – that were the problem. I think I was a disappointment. No matter

175

how she tried to dress me up and make me a lady, she couldn't forget who my mother was,' Ruby said quietly.

'Well, she needn't judge: she came from nowt. I've heard it said that her father was the biggest rogue who lived this side of the border. He'd swindle his best friend out of a penny, if he thought he could get away with it.' Martha folded her arms and bit her lip. Nobody judged her Ruby, if she had her way.

Ruby didn't say anything about being accused of stealing a necklace, else she knew Martha would make her thoughts known to Reuben, and the last thing she needed was her father leaving her under a black cloud. 'Aye, well, it was only her. Everyone else made me feel so at home. I'll go back every so often and visit them, and my father will always be calling in from now on. We find ourselves a lot alike – and not only in looks.' Ruby smiled.

'Aye, I think I judged him wrongly at first. I always had Reuben down as a bad lot, but I'll hold my hands up; unlike his mother, I'll admit I was wrong. He's welcome any time, and any of his family are; even his old bag of a mother, if she changes her attitude.' Martha grinned. 'Now let me set a table for us all and get your father fed. You go and take your things up to your room. I've not touched a thing since you left. I just hoped that you'd return to me, and here you are, back in the fold.'

Ruby looked at Martha as she picked up her clothes and belongings that her father had left on the inn's wooden floor. She noticed that Martha had lost weight while she had been away; she seemed frailer, and until now Ruby hadn't realized quite how old Martha was.

She was a good few years older than her grandmother at Banksgill, and she wondered why she had not noticed Martha's age before. Perhaps it was because she'd always known Martha to look the way she did, under the shabby dresses and with her long grey hair. There were no falsities about Martha, Ruby thought, as she carried her things upstairs into her room, which was, as Martha had said, still the same as she had left it, in her temper.

It was good to be back. Despite the lack of posh furniture and pretty ornaments, this felt more like home, Ruby thought, as she went over to the window and opened it, letting the fresh moorland air into her bedroom. She stood next to the window and stared out over the moor; she could smell the peat and the wild mountain thyme, and she heard a skylark singing above the distant noise of the coal mines. This was where she belonged, despite her new-found love for her father. She'd not be returning to Banksgill, not while Elspeth Blake felt as she did about her. She knew where she was truly loved, and that was at Tan Hill, in its rundown and wild setting.

She smiled as she watched her father hammering a tethering post into the moorland across from the inn. He'd always be there for her, and she knew it now as she watched Reuben striding back towards the inn with his usual swagger. She was proud that he was her father and only hoped that at some time he would find her mother, Vadoma Faa, whom he obviously still loved.

'That's a good pie, Martha. That'll fill me for the day and the night, if I decide to stay out. I don't feel like seeing my mother today. I'll make her think about what she's done with that evil tongue of hers.' Reuben sat back in his chair and looked across at Ruby, wondering if she had spoken truly about why she had decided to come home.

'Now then, Reuben. Sometimes folk say things they come to regret, so when you go home forgive Elspeth – that will hurt more than you ignoring her. She'll maybe start thinking about what she's said. Not that I know what it was, because neither of you have told me what this upset is all about,' Martha replied.

'It's nowt, Martha. A misunderstanding, and she just doesn't like my mother's heritage.' Ruby got up and cleared the three empty plates from the table and looked hard at her father.

'She'll not tell you, but I will. My darling mother accused Ruby of stealing her precious necklace, and then said exactly what she thought of the one true love of my life. I knew my mother had a temper, but I didn't expect her to go to those depths to make my daughter feel unwelcome under our roof.' Reuben sat back in his chair and picked at a bit of meat that had got stuck between his teeth.

'My Ruby would never steal. How dare she accuse my lass of anything like that, the old bag.' Martha's face turned red and her breath shortened as she got upset about the accusation. 'I'll come and sort her out. She needs telling she's got it wrong.' She felt her heart beating fast as she gazed at Ruby.

'I never touched them, Martha. I don't want her bloody necklace. I've got all I want in this very room. I don't

178

need precious things in my life, as some folk do.' Ruby put the dirty dishes quickly in the sink as she watched Martha fighting for her breath in anger and shock. 'You shouldn't have told her, Father, look what it's done to her.' Ruby rushed to Martha's side and grasped her hand. 'Here, have a drink,' she said gently and held her cup of tea to her lips, which Martha sipped gratefully.

'I didn't mean to upset you, Martha. I know Ruby had nowt to do with the necklace not being where it should be. If you ask me, it was the lass who cleans for us – she can be a cunning vixen, and I think she's jealous of my lass. Now calm yourself, catch your breath, there's nowt to worry about.' Reuben looked with concern at Ruby and Martha, as Martha continued to fight for breath.

'Are you alright? I've never known you like that before. Have you seen the doctor of late?' Ruby asked as she saw her adoptive mother regain control of herself and catch her breath.

'I want nowt with going to see a quack – he'd only rob me blind, and I know what's wrong with me. My heart is knackered. You can't work like I have all my life and expect to live until you are over seventy. I'm sixty-nine this back end: my threescore years and ten are nearly upon me.' Martha gasped and held Ruby's hand tightly. 'I know you didn't steal that necklace, and perhaps it is a good thing it happened as I'm in need of you, but I didn't want you to know. I had started to feel ill, even before you left me,' Martha said with a tear in her eye.

'I'll pay for a doctor for you. I'll ride down into Reeth

and bring him back with me,' Reuben said and pushed his chair back on the stone flags.

'You will not, Reuben Blake. You'll leave this old biddy to her own ways. I've had a good life and I'm not about to leave this world this minute. The good Lord, I hope, will give me time to settle my affairs. All I ask for is to see this summer out, especially now I've got Ruby back under my roof. The Tan Hill will be hers after my day – I've made that right already, so you can tell your mother that she's going to be a woman of substance. The Hill might look nowt to some folk, but it will always make her a living.' Martha dropped her head onto her chest.

'Stop talking that way, Martha, we will have years together yet. I should never have left you,' Ruby said as she knelt down by her side.

'Nay, lass, you'll see; once the cold winds of November start blowing, I'll have left your side, but I'll always be with you, watching out for you. As for you, Reuben Blake, you keep searching for the lass that you love, if you think she's still with us on this Earth. But be here for our lass, as she'll need you as a shoulder to cry on, although she's got her own mind – but we all know where she gets that from.' Martha smiled up at Reuben and saw the concern on his face.

'I'll always be here for her, now that I've found her, Ruby knows that. In fact I haven't said anything to her, but after I'm done here, I'm going to make my way down Arkengarthdale. There's a farm up for sale down there and, after the carry-on at home, I've decided to find a home for myself. My mother's ruled the roost for too

180

long, and my brothers will be glad to see the back of my horses from their land. They've moaned enough about them in the past.' Reuben looked across at Ruby. 'So hopefully I'll not be too far away from you in the coming months – that is, when I'm not attending the horse fairs. I have got a few horses to sell, and no doubt there will be a few good horses that will take my eye.'

'That'll be Punchard Farm that's taken your fancy? Folk was talking about it at the bar the other night. It's got a good few acres, and rights for Arkengarth Common – your horses would be alright up there through the summer,' Martha said and looked with interest at Reuben. There must have been some strong words said between him and his mother if he was leaving home.

'Aye, that's the one. It will do me fine, and I've enough brass to pay for it, just about. And I'll be my own man, and will not have my mother nagging at me,' Reuben replied.

'You've never mentioned it until now. Your mother will be lost without you.' Ruby stared at her father, knowing that he was leaving home because of her.

'Nay, she won't. She never knows where I am half the time, and she'll be glad to get shot of me. And, Lord, if I can't leave home at my age, when can I? I should have been wed years ago, and so should my brothers, instead of kowtowing to my mother after our father died.' Reuben shook his head and grinned.

'All these years I've had you down as a wrong 'un and now I'm starting to see that you are a good man, Reuben Blake. Aye, a bit wild when you were younger, and you still do dodgy dealings that I hear about over the top of this bar. But your heart is a good one, and I know Ruby will be looked after when I've done with this life.'

'Stop saying that. You are not going anywhere, not while I'm here. We'll run the inn like we used to, and my father can come and go, if he is to live down the road from us. It seems that I'll have the best of both worlds, with you both nearby.' Ruby grasped Martha's hand tightly.

'Aye, well, don't build your hopes up yet. The bloke that is selling Punchard has not accepted my price, but he will, as he's desperate to get out of farming and I've made him a decent offer.' Reuben stared out of the window. Now that he'd looked at Martha more closely, her health did seem to be failing; she did need a doctor and perhaps he should go and get her one, with or without her permission. 'I'll be away. I need to get home before dark, and I need to settle my business with George Frankland and convince him I'm the one for his farm. Now are you sure I can't send a doctor up from Reeth? I'll pay for him,' Reuben said, knowing the answer before it was given.

'You'll say nowt to nobody, and I don't want charity, Reuben Blake. But I do wish you luck in buying your farm – it'll be the making of you.' Martha got to her feet and smiled at Ruby. 'There, you see, I'm fine once I've got my breath and calmed down.'

Ruby glanced over at her father. 'We'll be fine. I also hope that you manage to buy Punchard; it's a nice farm, and I've been there a time or two. George Frankland has lost all heart in farming it, since he lost his wife to cholera, so be kind to him,' Ruby said, then watched as Martha stubbornly walked into the kitchen on her own.

'Yes, I will. And you take care of Martha and yourself. You know where I'm at, if you need me, although I hope to move into Punchard before the end of the month. It's Appleby Fair coming up and I can't miss attending that; along with Brough Hill Fair, it's my busiest time of the year, so I need my horses and myself settled before then.' Reuben watched his daughter. He was reluctant to leave her back at the Tan Hill Inn, as he wanted her to be under his roof, but now he knew that Martha needed her; and even if his mother apologized for her outburst, Ruby would not return to Banksgill.

'I will, Father. I hope that you are successful in buying Punchard. It will be good to have you close by.' Ruby looked at her father; she wanted to hug him, but knew that was not the way of Dales people. She felt as if part of her was walking out of the door when she went with him to the door and watched him go to the stable for his horse, before making his way down Arkengarthdale. She was glad that she was back at the Tan Hill Inn, but if Martha was right, she was going to be courting heart-ache and sadness. Martha might be wrong, Ruby thought, as she cleared the dinner plates and went to seek out her adoptive mother to see that she was alright.

Reuben stared around him. Punchard Farm was exactly what he was looking for. It had a good meadow or two, and pastures for his foaling mares. The fell land stretched out, nearly heading into the next valley, and was good for his horses to roam in summer. As for the dwelling, the longhouse was typical of the Dales; it needed a bit of work on it, but that would keep him busy over the winter months. The sticking point was the price: George Frankland would not budge from the top figure he was asking.

'Come on now, friend, I'll offer you another twenty guineas. You either accept that or I walk away. You can be paid in cash, and I do not need to go to a bank. It can be in your hand and you can be out and down in Reeth, leading a nice quiet life, by the end of the month.' Reuben looked across to the other side of the dale and watched the lead miners working along the far side of the valley, then gazed at George Frankland as he stood in the farmyard and reconsidered the offer. The wiry, ageing farmer with his ruddy face shook his head and put his hands in his pockets.

'I don't know. I should wait to see what other folk can offer me. If I wasn't so fed up with my lot, I'd have been staying here, but this place has been nothing but bad luck for me.' George sighed and looked at Reuben. He knew his offer of 1,500 guineas was a good one, but he found himself having second thoughts as he glanced around him.

'Well, either take it or leave it. I'm not wasting any more of my time or your time, and I need to be on my way home.' Reuben approached his horse, which was tethered across the yard, and decided that he was on a hiding to nothing in trying to buy the farm, which would be ideal for him.

'Wait, I just need to be sure. This place has many memories for me, but now that I've no Gladys by my side and I'm not getting any younger, I need to be out of here. My knees no longer like these brant fellsides, and my bones ache in winter. A cottage down in Reeth, with money in my hand, would make more sense, but it's a big decision.' George scratched his head and looked at Reuben. 'Go on then; your price is fair and there's a lot to be said for having cash in hand. I don't like dealing with banks – I like to know where my money is.'

'By God, I'm glad you've accepted. You'll not regret it, George. You'll have your money in your hand as soon as I can get it to you. It'll be good for you, and it will mean a lot to me. I've lived at home too long. I need my own place, especially when at long last I have found my own daughter.' Reuben held his hand out to be shaken by George Frankland, who spat on his palm and then shook it firmly to seal the deal.

'Aye, I heard that the lass at Tan Hill was your daughter and that she'd gone to live with you. Old Martha's never been the same since she left, but she's a good age, is the old lass.'

'I've just brought Ruby back to live with her. We had no idea that Martha was ill. It's perhaps a good thing that I'll be living here, as she may need me in the coming months, from what Martha was saying. But you never know; Martha might buck up, now that Ruby is back living with her,' Reuben said as he patted George on the back.

'Nay, I don't think she will – everybody says she's not as good as she was. Happen I've done right selling to you, if it helps Martha out. Although I don't relish the thought of horses being all over my land when it's been grazed by sheep for all these years.' George smiled; he knew well Reuben's reputation, and he knew all too well that horses would be roaming his fields and moorland as soon as he left.

'It'll not be yours to worry about, George, when you have your feet up next to that fire in your cottage and the rain is pouring down outside and you think to your- self: thank the Lord I've not to go out in that. You can be a gentleman of leisure, especially with the price you have got out of me.' Reuben slapped George on the back. 'I'm going now. I'll be back with the cash, and if you can have the deeds made over to me, I'll move in at the end of the month.'

'Aye, right, you'll take care of the old place. We'll come to an agreement with the stuff that I'm thinking of leaving: pitchforks and the like are no good to me when I have my feet up in my cottage,' George replied as Reuben lifted himself up into the saddle.

'Yes, you have my word on that,' Reuben said as he pulled on his horse's reins. 'Now, I'm away to tell my mother and brothers of my deal. My mother will not want me to be leaving, but the other two will be glad to see the back of me. As for me, I think it's the best thing I've done in a long time. I'm sure my luck will be good here.' Reuben smiled; he had his own land, his own house and his own life, and he was free of his mother and her sharp tongue.

'What do you mean: you've bought a farm and are moving out? Where did you get the money from and why, after all these years, have you decided to leave us?' Elspeth looked at her eldest son in disbelief. She might not know where he was some days, but he had always returned home.

'I've been putting money away for years now. I always did plan to branch out on my own. Banksgill is not big enough to keep a family of three grown men fed and happy, that's why I've been ducking and diving, making money where I can. And I know that you, Arthur and Lennox mock me with my horses, but they have made me a pretty penny over the years. Besides, I don't think any of us have enjoyed the atmosphere in this household since Ruby was accused the way she was and left.' Reuben stood his ground with his mother as he told her of his new purchase.

'Oh, I knew she'd have something to do with it. I suppose she is to live with you there? Forget your ageing mother and your brothers and just do what you want. Why change the habit of a lifetime? You have always been a selfish one.' Elspeth spat at her son and watched as he shook his head in disbelief.

'Ruby is staying at the Tan Hill. Martha Metcalfe is dying and she has already bequeathed the Tan Hill to her, so Ruby's no need of me, you or anyone else – she's her

187

own woman. True, my farm is only a stone's throw away from the Tan Hill, but that is just a coincidence. It suited my plans and has grazing rights on the moor, ideal for my horses. As for Arthur and Lennox needing me, I think they will be more likely glad to see the back of me. They'll no longer have to take part in my schemes, and both will be able to put more sheep on the land, once my horses have gone with me.'

'She may not be living with you, but it is Ruby who's to blame. She's exactly like her mother, driving a wedge between me and my lad and, like a fool, you are letting it happen once more,' Elspeth said and slammed her fist down on the kitchen table.

'Listen to yourself, Mother. Ruby is my daughter. I should be there for her and, unlike you, I will not judge her in any way. She is the image of her mother, and I should have been there for her from day one. If I want to make up for lost time and indulge myself in spoiling her occasionally, I will. And if I'm away from here, all the better, after what you said to her.' Reuben raised his voice and walked over to the kitchen door to escape his mother's tongue-lashing and head out into the sunny day that was dawning outside.

'She's a gypsy – she's bewitched you, just like her mother did. If you hadn't found her, you wouldn't be leaving me,' Elspeth shouted at her son.

'I'm not leaving you. I'm simply making my own way in life, like I should have done when I was courting Vadoma. You can visit me any time and if you need me for anything, then you only have to send word. Now

I've some horses to round up, and I need to tell Tom my news. I have a good mind to take him with me; after all, he works mainly for me and he'll not be wanted when I'm gone,' Reuben said and watched his mother's face cloud over with anger.

'Aye, you take him. After all, we won't need him, and Tom worships the ground you walk on and is as daft as you when it comes to horses. Take the whole bloody lot – what do I care? You've never listened to a word I've said ever since your father died.' Elspeth sat down in her chair and scowled at her favourite son, whom she had always tried to keep safe from hurt.

'Then I'm leaving home with your blessing. I thank you, Mother. You are right when it comes to me, but perhaps if you had believed the words of your grand-daughter and not a housemaid, then both Ruby and I would still be under your roof. Ruby and her mother might be of gypsy stock, but neither could ever be accused of being thieves, unlike you – you would steal any hope of happiness from your sons, if another woman came to live under this roof. It is you who are selfish, Mother, and perhaps it will teach you a lesson to have me leave this home.'

Reuben didn't stop for another second, but closed the door behind him and walked over to the stables. He would take Tom with him; his brothers had no need of the stable lad and he did; besides, he knew Tom would not enjoy working there without the horses to keep an eye on. He'd hated having words with his mother, as he'd always been brought up to respect his parents. But

189

he'd done that for too long and now, with his own daughter to be looked after, he was going to change his life for the better, he hoped.

Chapter 13

Ruby was back in her old clothes; her new finery was of no use to her when there was the inn's floor to be scrubbed and pots to be washed. She looked up at the whitewashed walls of the inn, then pushed a lock of her dark hair out of her eyes and sat back on her heels, with the scrubbing brush in her hand. The floor had been filthy. She doubted it had been cleaned since she'd left, just like the other parts of the inn, which were showing the neglect of the last few weeks.

Martha was not the woman that Ruby had left; she was right, her health was deteriorating, and Ruby was worried about her. Sometimes she found herself standing at Martha's bedroom doorway, looking at her while she lay sleeping and praying that Martha was wrong in her self-diagnosis, but Ruby knew she wasn't. Martha often fought for her breath, her lips were frequently blue and her ankles swollen with excess water; her heart was failing and there was nothing anybody could do for her.

Ruby still regretted the words she had said in haste when she first found out the real truth about her parentage, and she was only glad that those words had been forgotten now, and that the love between Martha and herself was still strong.

She got back again on all fours and scrubbed the last remaining flags of the ancient floor, before opening the inn's door and stepping out onto the moorland to throw out the filthy water. Once she'd done that, she dried her hands on her apron and was about to go back to work cleaning out the pantry when she heard a voice yelling her name, a voice she knew all too well.

'Ruby! Ruby, hold on, wait a minute,' Tom yelled as he came along the rough road with a horse and cart piled with various pieces of furniture and horse tack, with four horses tethered to the back of the cart patiently following on.

'Tom, what are you doing up here?' Ruby looked at the cart and then immediately realized that Tom was helping her father to move house, even though she had not seen hide nor hair of Reuben since he had left her with Martha. She was also embarrassed that Tom had caught her looking at her worst, with a dirty apron on and in her scruffy clothes.

'I'm moving into Punchard with your father. He's got me moving all his stuff and horses. Isn't that going to be grand, both of us living just down the road from you?' Tom grinned, jumped down from the wagon and walked towards her.

'I knew my father was going to try and buy the farm,

but I didn't know he'd been successful. Aye, it will be grand, and it's good to see you.' Ruby blushed. She wasn't lying; it *was* good to see Tom. She'd found herself thinking of him frequently since leaving Banksgill. She had not forgotten the kindness he had shown her when she had been upset over the words said to her by her grandmother, and she couldn't help thinking about the way Tom had comforted her.

'Your father's been busy sorting his horses and moving his things about, as well as making things right with his brothers. They are alright with him and me leaving, but it has caused a bit of a rift between him and his mother. That will be why he's not been near in a while.' Tom frowned and then looked at Ruby as she shook her head.

'She's a force in her own right, is that woman – her words still ring in my ears. She'll not be happy that my father is leaving her, especially if she knows he's moving nearer me.' Ruby appeared worried.

'It's her own doing, and she knows it now. She's heard from one of her so-called friends that Anne Handley has been bragging that she got rid of you from Banksgill, and that she was glad you had gone. Elspeth didn't say anything to Anne, though. She deserves Reuben leaving her, for taking the word of a maid over her own flesh and blood. How are you – glad to be back at the Tan Hill?' Tom looked at the roughly built inn with its weather-beaten sign and the miners' cottages huddled around it, and thought how remote the inn was.

'I am, and I've returned just in time. Martha is ill. I'm glad I'm here for her, as she deserves my love and attention more than my grandmother. It's good to be back serving our ales and food to the local miners. I didn't think I'd ever miss it, but I did.' Ruby smiled at Tom. She'd missed him too since she had left Banksgill, if he did but know it.

'Aye, your father said Martha was ill. I'm sorry, Ruby.' Tom reached for her hand and squeezed it. 'Well, I'll get on my way – your father's waiting for me. He's busy getting ready for Appleby Horse Fair as well as moving, so he needs me to make his horses look their best, which doesn't take a lot of doing because he's always got good horses. I'll come up and see you, perhaps one evening. I can have a drink and get to know the locals, now I'll be living here.' Tom looked at Ruby. She was so beautiful, and even dressed as shabbily as she was, her beauty shone through. He'd definitely be calling at the Tan Hill Inn a lot in the future.

'Who was that lad you were talking to?' Martha enquired as she poured the newly brewed beer into a jug, ready for her lunchtime clients.

'It was Tom. He's the stable lad at Banksgill, or should I say he *was*. He's helping move my father into his new home and he's going to be living there with him. That doesn't surprise me because they are two of a kind: all they think about is their horses.' Ruby smiled and looked wistful.

'So your father's moved. That will be better for him and he will happen settle down, now that he has some responsibility. Is this Tom a grand lad? He seemed to have plenty to say for himself. I watched you both from the window.' Martha quizzed her, seeing the colour rise into Ruby's cheeks.

'Aye, he was kind to me when I was at Banksgill. You'll be able to meet him some evening soon, as he says he's going to call in for a pint. I'm glad my father's got the farm he was after – he'll be better on his own.' Ruby put her head down and placed the bucket and scrubbing brush away, avoiding Martha's prying eyes. Her heart had pounded when Tom had taken her hand, and she knew she couldn't hide her growing fondness for him.

'Tom, as you call him, may not simply be after a pint. Happen he's coming to see you as well,' Martha pried.

'Happen!' Ruby said quietly and then went about cleaning the pantry. She hoped that was exactly why Tom would be calling at the Tan Hill Inn.

It was Friday night and Reuben was in his bedroom, washing himself in the bowl that he'd brought from his home at Banksgill. It was the last week of May and the nights were beginning to draw out, with the sun shining down the dale and making him realize what a beautiful place he had chosen to live in. He looked at himself in the full-length mirror of his wardrobe and scrutinized the lines on his face, which seemed to have become more prominent over the last few weeks. He stroked back his long black hair and straightened his waistcoat and jacket, before making his way downstairs.

'Are you ready, lad?' he said to Tom, who was standing in the porchway gazing out across the dale.

'Aye, the horses are saddled and waiting. I'm looking forward to having a leisurely pint – we've deserved it lately. It will be good to see Ruby as well. But just look at the horses and caravans that are making their way over to Appleby; they've never stopped this last week,' Tom replied, as the sound of the iron wheels of the brightly painted caravans made their way up the road to get to the Fair Hill on the outskirts of Appleby, which was fifteen miles away.

'You've moved the horses that were tethered in the bottom fields to the back of the house, haven't you? I don't want to sound like my mother, but if there's one thing that travellers and gypsies can't leave alone, it's a good horse. They wouldn't think twice about helping themselves, dyeing the horse a different colour and then selling it on, for us never to find again,' Reuben said, standing next to Tom and watching the parade of bow-topped caravans making their way up the dale, to rest up for the night in a place of their choosing.

'Aye, I've made sure of that; they are all secure. It's no good us two putting all that work into making the horses look good, just for them to disappear. You'll be taking them to Appleby yourself in the morning – do you not want me to come with you?' Tom asked. He'd never been to the fair and he rather fancied a wander around, taking in the sights.

'No, I need you here, as I'll be gone a day or two. I do a lot of business with the Romany – they are a good judge of horses – and I've other business to do as well,' Reuben said and closed the farmhouse door behind him, as both men walked across the yard to their saddled horses and the pull of a pint at the Tan Hill Inn. He noticed, as Tom pulled himself up in the saddle, that he was not the only one who had taken pride in his appearance, as Tom looked spick and span as well.

Reuben smiled, as he knew exactly why – if Tom had mentioned Ruby's name once, he'd mentioned it a dozen times. Not only was Tom going to quench his thirst, but he was going courting, and with his lass. He'd seen them together talking and walking and, at first, had thought Ruby could do better for herself. Then he remembered his mother's words, chastising him for loving Ruby's mother, judging her for what she was. It mattered not if Tom was only his stable lad; he was a kind and loving soul, and Ruby was a child of the moors. She'd never be happy with someone grander, and as long as Tom's love was true, that was all that mattered.

The smell of campfires, and of the stews bubbling in pots above them, filled the air as Tom and Reuben made their way up the road to the Tan Hill Inn. Horses and round-topped caravans, along with flat carts and women dressed in bright clothes tending the pots, littered the roadside. The men were seated on the caravans' wooden steps, pipes in their mouths, their faces tanned from many a day out in all weathers on the roads and lanes of the countryside. Occasionally one would greet Reuben with a nod of the head, as if he knew him, and then watch as he and Tom rode past on their horses.

'I don't know how they can live like that. I'd have to

have a home. I'm always glad to see my mother in our home, and even though you are good to me, I always enjoy going home to my mother's four walls,' Tom said and looked at Reuben.

'Have you ever been inside a gypsy caravan? You'd be surprised. Gypsies love the best china, and their vardoes – as they call their caravans – are spotless, and the women take great pride in keeping their homes clean and their men fed. They are a superstitious people: they won't do a deal on a Friday, and they like to camp next to a holly tree, as they believe it protects them from evil,' Reuben went on, as he dipped his head in recognition of one of the families he knew as he passed them.

'I just couldn't be on the move all the time,' Tom replied as they approached the Tan Hill Inn.

'Aye, and they couldn't stay in one place all the time. They have to wander – it is in their souls. It takes all sorts to make a world, lad, and life would be boring if we were all the same. Now you take the horses, and I'll get you a pint and see my lass. There looks to be a few in the old inn tonight; the warm weather must have made folk thirsty. Martha will be rubbing her hands, thinking of the money she's making.' Reuben laughed as he dismounted and gave Tom the reins of his horse.

'It'll not do her any good, if she's as ill as everybody says she is,' Tom commented quietly.

'No, it won't, lad. That's why you have to live the life of a lord every day, because you don't know what the next day will bring. Now hurry up and see to the horses. A beer is waiting for us both – and my lass.' Reuben grinned as he watched Tom walk away with the horses to the stable; he'd decided to feel happy if Tom was to court Ruby, as he was made for her.

The main room of the Tan Hill Inn was full of miners, farmers and travellers, all drinking beer or a tipple of whatever they fancied. The air was filled with the smell of a mixture of peat logs and local coal; even though it was late May, there was still a nip in the air at the altitude the inn stood at. Smoke from the many clay pipes being smoked hung in the air, and Reuben looked around him to see if there was anybody he knew and could talk to. There was a group of farmers discussing what sort of lambing time they had just been through, seated around the fire. A group of miners was playing dominoes and getting raucous, as one accused another of cheating.

Reuben decided not to bother with any of them and to sit by himself in the corner by the window. If folk came to talk to him, all well and good, but he'd be more than content to watch and listen into the various conversations and enjoy his beer. He smiled as he saw Ruby's face light up at the sight of him, when he went to the bar to be served, and then watched as her grin broadened when she saw Tom enter the inn and join him at the bar.

'It's good to see you, Father. I hear that you have got yourself settled in Punchard,' Ruby said and then glanced at Tom, who had not taken his eyes off her since entering the room.

'Aye, you heard right. And young Tom here has come to keep me company and see to my horses. And are you alright? How's Martha? I see she's not behind the bar

199

tonight.' Reuben looked over Ruby's shoulder, hoping to see Martha through the kitchen doorway.

'No, I made her go and lie down for a while, as she was struggling to get her breath after helping out this afternoon. Besides, we may be busy, but I can handle who's in tonight. A pint for you both, is it?' Ruby reached for the stoneware jug and poured two pints of Martha's home-made ale into two flagons and smiled at Tom and her father. Earlier in the day she had approached Martha about receiving deliveries of ale from Richmond in the future, rather than Martha teaching her the art of brewing their own beer. If she was to be left on her own – God forbid – she didn't want to be brewing beer as well as running the inn. Thankfully, Martha had agreed, so Ruby had written a letter to the brewery to send her a delivery the next time they were passing her way. That had been a weight off her mind, she thought, as she passed a pint of flat-headed beer across to Tom and looked at the mischief in his eyes. Martha's brewing skills were not what they used to be, and she had heard a few complaints about the quality of the usually well-loved brew.

'Are you alright. Ruby? I'm as happy as a pig in muck, living with your father. It's the best move I've ever made,' Tom said and leaned on the bar. He took a sip of the beer and was surprised by the taste. Perhaps it would improve with the next mouthful, he thought, as he gazed into his tankard, then decided not to say anything as he looked up at Ruby.

'You'll not be saying that when I make you go up Great Pinseat in the middle of winter to check my horses.'

Reuben laughed and slapped Tom on the back, before looking at Ruby. 'I'll go and sit in that corner over there. I'll talk to you when some of this rabble decides to go home and let this one entertain you, which I'm sure he aims to do.' He took a swig of his beer and then pulled a face as he tasted it. 'Lord, lass, that's a fair brew you've got there. Give us a tot of rum – my belly won't stand that.'

Ruby blushed and poured her father a glass of rum. 'I don't think Martha's mind was on her job when she made this batch of ale, and a few have complained tonight. We came to an agreement that the brewery at Richmond is to deliver to us as soon as it can – it will save us both work.' Ruby passed her father his rum and watched as Tom took another sup of his beer.

'It's alright, once you get used to the taste,' Tom said and took another swig.

'You'll regret it in the morning, if not sooner. It'll go through you like a dose of salts.' Reuben grinned and left Tom and Ruby gazing at one another over the bar, between customers yelling for their glasses to be refilled or their money back, as they complained about Martha's latest batch of beer. He watched as Ruby and Tom flirted with one another. They'd make a good pair: both were good-looking and they had a lot in common. Unlike his mother, he simply wanted his daughter to be happy in life. He wasn't bothered whether the lad who took Ruby's eye was wealthy or of good breeding. The couple had to be happy with one another and that was all that counted, in his eyes.

But he didn't want to share Ruby quite yet. After all, he had only just found her, and he still couldn't quite believe that the lass with the stunning looks and easy ways was his daughter, he thought, as he watched her laugh and chat with the local miners and then give her attention back to his stable lad. Ruby was the image of her mother – and how he missed her. Vadoma was still in control of his heart, and always would be until the day he died. At Appleby Fair he'd do his usual search for her, but he knew that she and her family had disappeared like the early-morning mists.

Reuben sat back in his chair and stared out of the window at the coming night, and saw the sparks from the various campfires on the moor lighting up the night sky. Somewhere Vadoma would be sitting around a campfire, if she was still alive, and he wished he could be with her, or she with him, watching their beautiful daughter together and witnessing that their love for one another had not been wrong.

'I'll be away for a few days soon,' Reuben said to Ruby as he buttoned up his jacket and watched as Tom stumbled from his seat. 'I'm off to Appleby Fair. If you want anything, send word to Tom here and he'll come and find me. That is, if he ever recovers from the ale you served him tonight.' Reuben smiled, because Tom seemed decidedly ill as he walked towards the door. The inn was empty and the fire was burning low as he looked across at her.

Ruby shook her head. 'I told him not to drink it. I felt

guilty serving it, as it was not right, but I'd nothing else to give anybody, unless they asked for a spirit. If I do need you, I'll send word, but I shouldn't have to. I hope you get good sales with your horses.'

'Aye, now is the time I make my money. I hope I do have a bit of luck, in more ways than one, although Brough Hill is my favoured fair – I've always bought well and sold well there.' Reuben walked over to the door, with Ruby following him. 'Make sure you lock up tonight. There's a lot of travellers on the move at the moment and I want you safe.' Reuben thought of his hypocrisy in saying this, but he wanted to keep his precious daughter safe.

'I'll sort them out if they come anywhere near you. I'll box their ears.' Tom swung his fists and nearly lost his balance as he swayed, next to the doorway.

'You couldn't hit a bloody thing in the state you are in. Come on, move your arse and get those horses. I'm taking you home,' Reuben said and smiled at Ruby. 'It's either you or your ale that's made him so drunk. He'll regret tonight in the morning.'

Ruby stood in the doorway of the Tan Hill Inn and watched as her father and Tom, the worse for wear, led their horses out of the stable and, once mounted, disappeared into the darkness of the night. Martha was truly ill in the bedroom above her head; the ale had not been worth serving; and she was left standing in charge of the remote inn. However, her heart was bursting: she had her father's love and, even more, she had Tom's attentions. He'd never left her side all night and had vowed that he would come on Sunday to visit her – that was, if he remembered. She smiled as she locked the door behind her. She'd more than she had ever dreamed of having in her life. If only Martha was well, Ruby thought, as she looked into the bedroom where Martha lay asleep, before she went to bed. Life was cruel; it gave with one hand and took away with the other.

Chapter 14

Reuben leaned over the bridge that spanned the River Eden. It was a sweltering hot day, with the sun at last showing its strength as gypsy clans, travellers and tradespeople gathered in the market town of Appleby to celebrate the fair, which was granted its royal charter by James II back in 1685.

Reuben had found lodgings at The Grapes, the inn that stood just behind him, and had also found safe grazing for his horses in the inn's paddock. This was an arrangement that he made with the landlord every year, rather than risk his horses disappearing overnight if they were left tethered by the roadside, as so many people had done in the past – only to be found painted a different colour and sold at the Gallows Hill Fair later in the day. He watched as young gypsy boys showed their skill and horsemanship, riding their horses in the deep waters of the part of the river called 'the sands', and eyed up the horses, which were being made to look their best as they were washed down in the river's water and groomed. They were hard with their horses, but they also loved them and had good skills; nobody could handle a horse like gypsies, he thought, as his eye was taken by an especially good-looking pinto stallion that was being driven through the river and was not liking the unsure footing of the river bed, so threw its rider from its back, to the hilarity of his friends. He watched as the burly young lad jumped up to his feet and grabbed the stallion's rope harness, then snatched at it, pulling the horse to the bank, where he grabbed a whip and started to thrash the animal. Reuben shook his head and made for the river bank and over to the lad, whose pride had been hurt, but who was now taking it out on his horse.

'Tha doesn't need to bray it again. It wasn't its fault that it threw you – you pushed it too much.' Reuben put his hand out and caught the whip, which the lad was using a bit too keenly on the frightened horse.

'Mind your own fecking business. I'll do what I want with it,' said the young Irish lad, who was in his late teens and glared at Reuben as he tried to pull the whip from his hand.

'You'll only break his spirit, and that would be a shame in such a proud-looking horse as this.' Reuben ran his hand down the flinching stallion's neck, examined its teeth and felt down the length of its hocks as the lad stood and stared at him.

'He deserves the whip – he's too headstrong, the bloody thing. My da says he's a good horse, but he won't do owt for me,' the lad said. 'Are you interested in him?

206

We've come to sell him.' The boy stood back and watched as Reuben led the horse out of the water and up the river bank, then decided to run with it for a short while, up and down the road, to see whether or not it was lame and how it moved.

'Aye, I'm interested, lad. What are you asking for him? And don't give me any blarney – I'm not paying a lot for him. He's got a wall-eye; he will always have a wild side to him.' Reuben looked at the pale-blue eye on the right side of the horse's head, compared to the dark-brown one on the other side. Horses marked like that were not popular, but this one was different; he had something about him.

'Twenty guineas, plus a shilling for luck.' The lad held his hand out to be shaken.

'More like ten, lad, and sixpence for luck.' Reuben patted the horse and it snorted at him, as if it knew that a better life lay in his hands.

'Fifteen and you've robbed me – me da will skin my arse,' the lad said and spat in his hand, then held it out once more to be shaken.

'Fourteen and that's my last offer. I'll walk away and you'll be making your way back home to the Emerald Isle after the fair, still with this horse.' Reuben spat in his own hand and held it out for shaking.

'Ah, you are a hard man.' The lad shook his head and stood looking at the horse and Reuben. 'Fourteen it is, and sixpence for luck.' He held his hand out and shook Reuben's. 'He's yours, and my father will skin my hide when I tell him I've sold for that miserable sum.' He grinned to himself; his father would more likely rub his hands and know that he'd done a good deal, as the horse wasn't worth what he'd got for him. It was fit, but it was stubborn and skittish – no good for life on the open road.

'You'll tell me owt, lad. He'll be celebrating tonight. Here now, take your money and be on your way: our deal is done.' Reuben held his new purchase by the halter and walked away from the lad and his mates, as he heard them laughing and joking about him buying the horse. He wasn't bothered; he had a good buy, and the horse would have a better home with him on the fells of Arkengarthdale. It was a grand horse, once he'd calmed its ways, and a good bargain.

'So, you've bought one before you've sold your own.' The landlord of The Grapes leaned on his paddock gate and looked at the fresh horse in his field.

'Aye, but my four will be gone by evening. I'm away up to Gallows Hill, where I'm to meet the head Romany – the Shera Rom. I deal with him, and only him; have done every year for the last fifteen years. I know his money is right and my horses will be treated with care – he's a good man.' Reuben looked at the four horses he was about to sell, hoping that he was right and they would not be treated badly.

'You wouldn't get me dealing with them if I didn't have to, but they like their drink, and as long as they don't cause bother, I'll be right with them. Some folk haven't the time of day for them, but if you respect them, they respect you, I'd like to think,' the landlord said to Reuben.

'Aye, well, I take as I find and they are just like anybody else. There are good 'uns and bad 'uns – you've simply to have trust in whoever you are dealing with.' Reuben hung the rope halter over his shoulder. He was happy with his purchase, and now he'd get a good price for his four horses as well.

'I suppose so. I know everybody's thankful when the fair is finished and our town returns to normal. Although the farmers hereabout are quick enough to sell their wares to the gypsies, and there is anything you could wish for on some of the stalls on the hill and in town. My old lass has spent a fortune this morning on ribbons, various kinds of cotton, pegs and lucky charms. She doesn't like going past some of the gypsy women in case they curse her for not buying anything from them.' The landlord sighed and started to walk back into The Grapes.

'Aye, that's where I'm going now. And I'll walk up Flashing Lane and watch the horses being put through their paces. Keep an eye on my horses, will you? I don't want them mistaken for somebody else's.' Reuben smiled; he wouldn't say 'stolen', not wanting to blame anybody if they went missing.

'They'll be safe where they are at – you go and have your usual wander.' The landlord watched as Reuben walked out into Appleby's busy streets once more. It wasn't so much the horses he was searching for; it was the one face that he had been looking for every year since he had first been staying with him. One year Reuben might just find her, or so he hoped.

The town was full of farmers herding flocks of sheep

while their wives were selling butter, cheese, milk and baking. The locals might not like the travellers, gypsies and tinkers who filled their streets for a few days every year, but they made the best of the fair days, taking money from them and trading with them. Likewise the gaily dressed women of the gypsy community were selling their good-luck charms and pegs, and offering to tell fortunes to whoever crossed their palms with silver.

Reuben pushed his way through the crowds up to Flashing Lane, where he watched the horses trot and race the length of the lane, with the young men showing off the strengths of their horses and their own horsemanship. It was an amazing sight, but was also dangerous, as the horses were ridden and driven at speed, and no heed was paid to the safety of the crowd. Reuben searched the faces in the crowd, looking for Vadoma. He was fearful that even if she was there, he would not recognize her any more. After nearly twenty years, life would have left its mark on both of their faces and they might well pass one another and not even know it.

Satisfied that she was not in the crowds watching the horses racing, he made his way to the Fair Hill. There rows of horse-drawn vardoes were parked up, painted in beautiful bright colours of gold, red and green; the horses that pulled them were tethered beside them, and the families who lived in them were sitting on the steps or around their campfires. Occasionally Reuben was approached to have his fortune told, or to be asked if he wanted to buy one of the many linnets that were for sale in hand-made cages. But he was interested in neither.

He was searching for the girl and caravan that still held his heart, but as usual Vadoma and her family were nowhere to be found as he trod the rutted green field, disheartened and alone.

Dusk was nearly upon the Fair Hill as Reuben sat at the Shera Rom's campfire after doing his yearly business with him.

'You are with us once again, Reuben. Are you still at odds with yourself or does your heart let you rest this year?' the Shera Rom asked his guest, after a deal had been struck for the four horses they had agreed upon.

'I'm still searching,' said Reuben. 'I'll not rest until I've found her. I have found my daughter this year and she is just like her mother, and I will always be there for her. But I still search for Vadoma, and will do until my dying day.' He looked across at the wise, weather-beaten man and watched as he pulled a ball of clay out of the camp-fire.

'Be content that you have your daughter. The Faas have long gone and they no longer join our gatherings. They lost face when Vadoma courted you. Stop your heart from pining and make the most of your life and what you have, Reuben Blake.'

Reuben watched as the Shera Rom cracked open the ball of clay to reveal a roasted hedgehog – a hoawici – with its spines held firmly in the clay it had been roasted in.

'Will you join us, and have a drink of chao with us?'

Reuben shook his head and got to his feet as the Shera Rom's wife passed tin plates to her husband for him to

211

divide up the animal. His stomach did not relish eating hedgehog, no matter how good he'd been told in the past it tasted.

The Shera rom smiled. 'Then you take care, gadjo, keep that heart still and yourself safe. Until next year.'

'Aye, God willing,' Reuben said and walked away. He'd made his money for the year but he'd still not found his Vadoma. His last chance would be at Brough Hill Fair in October, unless he happened upon her, as he knew the Shera Rom had no reason to lie to him about her family no longer taking part in the usual gatherings. They could even be out of the country, travelling around Europe, for all he knew. He'd never be able to find her if that was the case. But he would still keep searching and would continue to do so until he eventually found her.

Chapter 15

Ruby sat outside on the steps of the stable. She needed a few minutes to herself as she held her head in her hands. She was tired, worn down and worried. Martha was not getting any better, even though she had still insisted that she could serve behind the bar when Ruby had taken delivery of the barrels of beer from Richmond, which were now secured inside the doorway of the stable. She could have cried as she felt wrapped up in self-pity and looked at the darkest moments in her life.

Perhaps she should never have come back to the Tan Hill Inn; perhaps she should have stayed at Banksgill and tried to make peace with Elspeth, especially now that she had realized her maid had a hand in misplacing the emeralds. At least she wouldn't look like a beggar girl in ragged clothes, and with hands sore from scrubbing and washing the many pots and dishes the drinkers at the inn used every night. However, Ruby loved Martha and knew thinking that was stupid. Martha needed her to be here, and she shouldn't be so selfish; it was just that she was weary and, to make matters worse, Tom had not shown his face again, after he had told her so fervently that he would, come hell or high water. Perhaps he'd had second thoughts. After all, she was the daughter of a gypsy, so who would want to court her and walk out with her?

She snivelled and wiped her nose on her sleeve and breathed in deeply, wiping her eyes as Richard Baxter from the miners' cottages walked towards her. She wasn't about to let him see her in a state, Ruby thought, as she got to her feet and decided to pull herself together. Richard was in his mid-thirties, and he never entered the Tan Hill Inn, unlike the other miners along the row. Instead he chose to spend a little of his money in Richmond once a month – rumour had it on back-street prostitutes, giving him a bad reputation with the other miners. He had thought too much of his money, not giving his wife enough to run the house, so that she had left him, running away with a carter from Leyburn.

'Morning, Richard, it's not a bad day. Are you not at the mine today?' Ruby pushed her hair back over her shoulder and looked at the tight-lipped man.

'No, I've had enough for this week. I worked by myself all day Sunday, and I did more work than all of them put together, the idle lot. The rest of them do far too much yacking and drinking, and then they wonder why they don't have any money. I'd rather work on my own and sell what I dig out separately from the rest of them.' Richard looked Ruby up and down and wondered

214

whether to say that he'd seen her crying. 'Are you alright – Martha alright? It's just that I couldn't help but notice you sitting on the step when I went out to the privy, and you seemed upset.'

'I'm alright, merely worried about Martha – she's not that well. And then I'd expected a personal visitor and he's not shown his face,' Ruby said and appeared embarrassed.

'A sweetheart, was it? Someone who was going to come a-courting?' Richard stared at Ruby. 'You know I could do with a bit of company. If you ever get lonely, come and look for me – I'll walk out with you. I've always thought you were a bonny lass. Now I'm free of the trollop that has left me, perhaps I could interest you in me.' Richard walked close to Ruby and smiled a sickly grin.

'Thank you for your compliment, but I'm sure Tom will be returning – not that I can call him a sweetheart, as we are just friends. Now if you'll excuse me, I'll have to attend to Martha and the inn. I've quite a few things awaiting my attention.' Ruby picked up her skirts and made for the inn's open back door, but Richard stepped in front of her and held her arm.

'You could do a lot worse for yourself than court me. I've my own house. I know it's not much, but it's better than nowt. I've brass in the bank and I'm a hard worker. You want nowt with a young lad; you want a man to cool that gypsy blood of yours.' Richard's eyes gazed at her, looking her up and down, and Ruby felt vulnerable and scared as she pulled her arm out of his hand.

'I'll thank you for keeping your hands and thoughts to yourself. I'll be having nothing to do with you, Richard Baxter. I've heard all about you, and I know your sort. Now leave me be, and go and spend your money for your satisfaction on one of those poor wretches that haunt the back streets of Richmond and offer their services to men like you,' Ruby spat. She wasn't going to be intimidated by a man that nobody had a good word for.

'Gypsy whore! Who do you think you are? Your father might as well be part gypsy, from what I hear. Don't think yourself so special, because you are nowt – abandoned and unwanted, had it not been for Martha and her soft heart.' Richard turned and swore under his breath. He'd been watching Ruby growing up from a young lass to a fine, good-looking woman and he'd been waiting for his chance. Her words didn't hurt him. What she had heard over the bar from his work colleagues was right: he did go seeking satisfaction in Richmond, but he was hoping that he could find it a lot nearer home. He shook his head and wished he'd not been as tart with his words, as he watched Ruby slam the door and go about her duties. He would have her, he thought, whether she wanted him or not. She was too much of a temptation to leave, and his fervour for her had been growing with each day lately.

'Are you alright, Ruby?' Martha came and sat in her chair next to the fire and pulled a shawl over her knees, then looked up at Ruby as she slammed the door behind her and swore.

'Yes, Mother, I'm alright. It's just that bastard next door,' Ruby exclaimed.

'Ruby, don't you swear like a man – it's not nice to hear from your mouth. Who are you on about anyway?' Martha sighed and reached out her hand for Ruby to take.

'It's nothing. Nothing for you to worry about. It's only Richard Baxter, he's mooching about outside,' Ruby said and then tucked the shawl around Martha's knees and smiled at her.

'You take care with that one, my love. We both know what's been said about him by his workmates. He's a wrong 'un and he doesn't respect anybody or anything, except for the money he makes, and he wastes some of that on prostitutes, when he's not counting it. No wonder poor Megan left him with the first fella that gave her the eye.' Martha shook her head. She'd always taken care of what she said to Richard Baxter as he didn't act like a decent person; he was lecherous and deceitful, and most folk gave him a wide berth. Of late she'd heard that he'd got worse. She only hoped that he was not going to cause bother for Ruby; she had enough on her plate without him lurking and watching her every move.

'He's a creepy devil. I don't like him. You don't have to worry about him, and I'll go out of my way to avoid him. I'm just thankful that he doesn't drink here. I wouldn't want to serve him when he was the worse for drink. He's bad enough sober. Now, you stay where you are and I'll continue serving behind the bar, as you look worn out,' Ruby said quickly, then went through to the bar to avoid any further questions about Richard Baxter. She hated him and always had done. He'd always been there, watching her every move, but since her return and his wife's departure, he'd got worse. She'd try to keep out of his way whenever possible, as he was not to be trusted.

She leaned over the bar and looked at the few customers the inn had on that Wednesday afternoon: not many, only those long in the tooth and those who thought more of their drink than of earning good money at work. It would be different, come evening, when the inn would be bustling as usual, with folk wetting their whistle after a hard day's work. She gazed out of the window and wished that Tom would appear. She missed him, and she could do with someone to talk to other than miners and drinkers. She picked up some dirty tankards to be washed from one of the nearby tables, then went to chat to two old men who passed their days playing dominoes in one of the corners of the inn.

'It's good to see you back, lass. You are a bit more pleasing on the eye than Martha,' one of the men said and smiled a toothless grin at Ruby.

'Aye, I've missed being here, I must admit. And I've especially missed you, Nathan, and that winning smile of yours.' Ruby smiled and teased the old man. 'Don't you tell your wife, though, else she'll be after me.'

'She'll be after him – but what for, I don't know. He's well past his prime; he can't even mount his horse, let alone anything else, so she needn't worry.' The other fella grinned at Ruby. 'I'm your better bet, because at least I've still got my own teeth.'

218

'Aye, but that's all you've got. At least I've got a wife; you go home to an old dog, and even that doesn't do as it is told by you.' Nathan grinned and then glanced up as the main door to the inn opened, spilling a sliver of bright light across the scrubbed and clean floor. 'Well, that's us out of the running. The cherry-picker is here, and this one is nice and ripe and ready for plucking.' Nathan winked at his partner and watched as Ruby turned and ignored his comment, then looked at Tom as he walked in through the doorway to where she stood.

'Tom, you've made it! I thought there was something wrong when you didn't make it on Sunday.' Ruby went over to him, feeling her heart beat faster as she stood next to him.

'I'm sorry, Ruby. I didn't dare leave the farm, with your father being away at Appleby, but he's back now, so I've sneaked in a quick visit to you. There were so many travellers on the road, and I didn't want to leave the horses on their own. We didn't usually see that many, when we lived up Stainmore.' Tom smiled and took his cap off. 'Are you alright? You don't know how good it is to see you.'

'It's good to see you too. I really worried about you when you didn't come, as planned, on Sunday. I thought perhaps you had thought better of seeing me, or I might have made you so ill with Martha's brew that you'd washed your hands of us,' Ruby said. She blushed as Tom looked at her and reached for her hand to hold.

'Aye, well, the ale was a force to be reckoned with. I did feel the worse for wear the following day. Your father did nothing but laugh at me and just said I'd learn. I was glad when he packed up and headed for Appleby. I went back to bed for an hour, but don't tell him,' Tom said and glanced at Ruby, thinking how he'd missed her so much.

'My father is alright, is he? Has he done good trade at Appleby?' Ruby held Tom's hand tightly and peered coyly at him. She'd never felt this way about a lad before. She'd looked at some of the young men and flirted with them over the bar, but none had made her heart beat as Tom did at that moment.

'He has. He's sold his horses and bought a new stallion – he's a bit wild, but your father will make him do. There isn't a horse yet that's got the better of your father. Have you time to step outside with me for a minute?' Tom gazed around him at the drinkers who were watching the romance play out in front of them; he didn't want to be the new topic of talk.

'I don't know. Martha has just got comfortable in front of the kitchen fire, so I don't want to bother her and ask her to manage the bar,' Ruby said.

'Martha is fine. Now stop thinking of me and look after yourself. Go on – go and step outside with this young lad, who has obviously taken the time to see you. Then, when you come in, you can tell me all about him.' Martha, having overheard the conversation, held tightly to the bar as she moved in from the kitchen and smiled across at the young couple. She had realized that this must be the lad called Tom whom Ruby had talked about with such fondness.

'Aye, we will look after Martha and whoever else needs serving with ale.' Nathan winked at his fellow dominoes player. 'Don't keep the lad waiting.'

'If you are sure, I won't be long,' Ruby said and blushed.

'You be as long as you want, my lass. We'll be alright. Go and walk out on the moor a while – it looks grand out there. It's too nice to be inside here with a load of old cranks.' Martha smiled at Tom. 'Go on, lad, take her hand and lead her outside. Us old 'uns will manage, no matter what Ruby says.' Martha winked and forced a smile to her face, as she caught her breath and sat down on a chair at the side of the bar.

'Thank you, I won't keep her long. As long as you are alright, and you don't mind,' Tom said, glancing at Martha.

'Lad, just go. I remember when my old man came courting. The last thing you want is an audience watching your every move,' Martha said quietly and watched as Tom pulled on Ruby's hand, eager to take her outside and not share with the drinkers inside the Tan Hill Inn what he had to say to her.

'We'll not be long, Mother.' Ruby felt her heart flutter as Tom tugged on her hand, urging her to join him outside in the bright sunshine.

'You be as long as you want – we are right, lass, nowt is on fire.' Martha watched as the two young ones left. 'Lord, I wish I was that age again. I wouldn't think twice about a bit of courting on the moor, now that I know what I do.' She sighed.

221

'We can do a bit of courting, Martha, if you are up to it,' Nathan said and winked.

'Not your sort of courting, Nathan Trotter. This is a respectable house and you are far too old, and you know it. It is best you stick to your dominoes and sup up your pint.' Martha grinned and then sat back in her chair. Hopefully Tom would give Ruby the love she would need to get her through life, if he was a good man; she'd need somebody, after her day. Somebody besides Reuben Blake. Martha knew he would be there for Ruby, but he was used to living his own life, and no matter how much he loved his newly found daughter, he was accustomed to his own style of living. He was like the gypsies he dealt with: he liked the open road. And Ruby needed somebody more stable in her life.

Martha closed her eyes and listened to the buzz of the gossip from her customers. This was her world, but for how much longer she didn't know. She just hoped she could see summer out and make sure the lad who was intent on seeing Ruby was right for her. God willing.

Ruby walked next to Tom across the moorland and was conscious that for once they both felt awkward about being together; they both knew that their feelings for one another were changing from friendship to something deeper.

'It's a grand day, but there's still a sharp wind,' Tom said and reached for Ruby's hand as they walked to the edge of the moorland and looked down the valley of Arkengarthdale. Ruby listened to the lead miners on the top of the moorland, busy hammering and smelting the ore.

'It is, but can we stop here? I don't want to go too far. I shouldn't really have left Martha's side, but I wanted so much to walk out with you,' Ruby replied. She looked at Tom and felt the urge to kiss him as he gazed at her with his forget-me-not blue eyes, which held her heart.

'Of course we can, lass. Here, I'll take off my jacket and we'll sit here and watch the world go by while we have a natter.'

Tom took off his jacket and laid it on the coarse, tufty moorland grass, then smiled when Ruby blushed as she sat down and pulled her skirt around her ankles. Tom sat down next to her and put his arm attentively around her, noticing that she didn't protest at him doing so.

'Ruby, I've never stopped thinking about you of late. I couldn't wait for your father to get back. And I thought you might have forgotten about me.' Tom held her hand tightly and looked into her eyes.

'I'd never do that. I've never stopped thinking of you, either. I've never felt like this before. I thought my heart was going to burst when I saw you enter the inn. I've been counting the days, even the hours and minutes, since I last saw you and feeling selfish for being so happy when I think of you, when I know Martha is so ill,' Ruby said quietly. She gazed at Tom as he leaned forward and kissed her ever so gently, making her feel light-headed and dizzy with the love she knew was in his kiss.

'Aye, I'm the same about you. I can't stop thinking of you, and your father keeps shaking his head whenever I mention your name. I think he knows I'm sweet on you,' Tom whispered as he held Ruby's head close to him and ventured another kiss, which Ruby responded to with love.

'He'd have something to say to you if he didn't approve, of that I'm sure. So he must be happy that you are visiting today. I thought he'd have called on his way back from Appleby, but he didn't.' Ruby put her arms around Tom's neck and held him tightly as he pulled his fingers through her hair and kissed her neck.

'He's calling later today, when I've returned. But never mind that – let us make the most of the time we have together.' Tom pulled Ruby back to lie down beside him on the moor and turned to look at her. 'I think I love you, Ruby Blake. I've never felt like this before,' he whispered as he kissed her over and over again.

'Aye, I think that's what it is. I know I've never felt like this before.' Ruby ran her hand around Tom's face and stared into his eyes as she lay back in his arms. 'But I'm not to be taken advantage of, Tom. I've got my pride, so just because I'm lying in the heather and moorland with you doesn't mean I'll be giving myself to you.'

'No, I know, and I wouldn't expect you to. I'll be content with kisses and knowing that you feel the same way as me, for the time being. Besides, your father would kill me if I got up to anything more.' Tom leaned on his hand and looked at the beauty that he knew he loved.

'That's alright then. I don't want you to think I'll be raising my skirts yet. I've to be sure our love is true before I even think of that.' Ruby kissed him and then lay back down with Tom's arm around her waist and his head next to hers, as they both gazed up into the blue sky overhead and listened to a skylark that was singing above the noise of the lead miners. The peaty air smelt sweet and the warmth from the sun made both of them feel content, as they lay together and looked at one another. They knew they both felt the same way about one another, and that their love would grow even more with time.

'I don't want you to go just yet.' Ruby pulled on Tom's arm as they walked back along the road to the Tan Hill Inn.

'I'll have to – your father will be expecting me. I'll come again on Sunday, I promise. If I call on a Sunday, the inn will be closed and you can rest easy that Martha has nothing to do while we are courting. The days will soon go, and I'll be thinking of you all the time I'm away.' Tom kissed Ruby outside the miners' cottages and his eye was drawn to the curtains moving, as Richard Baxter watched the couple's kiss right outside his home.

'I never thought I'd feel this way about anybody. I'm going to pray that Sunday comes quickly.' Ruby looked into Tom's eyes and felt her heart racing.

'No, me neither. I've never given lasses time of day until I met you, and then something inside me changed. You've bewitched me, Ruby, and there's nothing I can or want to do about it.' Tom smiled and held her tightly. 'But for now I'll have to go, as your father will be expecting me home before he makes his way to you.'

Tom walked towards his horse, which he'd tethered outside the inn, and pulled himself up into the saddle, with Ruby gazing up at him.

'Take care and hurry back to me,' she said as he smiled down at her.

'I will. You look after yourself and Martha, and I'll see you on Sunday.' Tom kicked his horse's sides and left Ruby staring lovingly after him. She'd be counting the minutes till his return.

Chapter 16

'Hold your noise, Nathan. I know you need your tankard refilling, but I'm going to have to go outside and fill my bar jugs up.' Ruby looked across at the old man, who had been in the inn all day and was now slightly the worse for wear, rattling his tankard on the table, demanding a refill.

'Aye, get a move on – a man could die of thirst in this spot,' Nathan grumbled and slurred his words, as Ruby grabbed the large serving jugs from the top of the bar and disappeared out of the back door, leaving Martha shaking her head and feeling useless in her own inn.

It was nearly dusk and the bats were starting to fly out of their roosts and screech overhead as Ruby made her way to the stable to fill her beer jugs from the barrels. The stars were just beginning to show in the darkening sky, and the warmth of the day was being replaced by a cool wind blowing from the north as she walked across the yard to the stable. The stable was empty of horses, as Ruby's pride and joy was tethered on the moorland across from the inn, while those belonging to the drinkers were tethered at the side of the inn, waiting for their riders to return to them, either sober or drunk.

Ruby made her way to the beer barrels, passing the sacks of grain that Martha had been using for her brewing as she went. She turned the tap on the huge wooden barrel to fill her jugs with the new brew, which seemed to be going down a little too well with some of the regulars. She waited as her first earthenware jug filled and brimmed over with froth, smelling of the sweetness of hops, then turned the tap off before refilling the next one. She quickly put the jug to one side as she saw the shadow of somebody entering the stable. 'I'll be out of your way in a minute – just let me fill my next jug and then you can stable your horse,' she said, without turning to see who it was that had entered the stable. No one answered, but as Ruby bent down for the second jug, she felt a hand go over her mouth and she was man-handled onto the grain sacks, roughly and without care or thought.

'You thought you could turn me down and then flaunt yourself, right outside my window, with that young pup. I need some of what you'd been giving him on the moor. And if you won't give me it, then I'll take it, whether or not you are willing.' Richard Baxter kept his hand over Ruby's mouth as he pressed his body down on hers and fought to undo his breeches while he forced her legs open with his own.

Ruby hit him again and again with her fists and tried

to shake him free of her. She tried her best to scream and shout, but couldn't loosen his grip on her.

'The more you fight, bitch, the more I like it. You are not so high-and-mighty now, are you, gypsy girl, rolling around in the muck of a stable? I'm going to ride you the way you ride that horse of yours.' Richard pulled on his belt, and Ruby tried to scream as she heard his belt buckle hit the cobbled floor of the stable and felt his hands trying to take down her drawers. Then her eyes grew wide as the outline of a second man stood in the doorway. Were there two of them about to have their way with her? She fought and struggled, then screamed as Richard's hand was forcefully removed from her mouth, and his body was thrown across to the other side of the stable by the other man.

'Are you alright, my lass? Make yourself decent while I sort this bastard out.' Reuben looked down at his daughter and gave her his hand, to get her back onto her feet.

Ruby shook her head and quickly pulled her skirts down and buttoned her blouse, which had come loose. She caught her breath as her father walked across to the crumpled body of the other man. 'It's Richard Baxter, Father, he lives at number three. He's a dirty old bastard, and nobody likes him. He'd threatened me earlier today.'

Reuben dragged Richard onto his feet and punched him hard; again and again he hit him, and blood spurted from his nose and Richard cried out for sympathy, but Reuben gave him none as he lifted him nearly off his feet and threatened to hang him up from the hook that was used to suspend the pig carcasses. 'I should bloody well kill you for touching my lass, you dirty, disgusting wretch. Instead I'll spare your life, if you get yourself away from my lass and this inn, and you pack up all your belongings and bugger off to wherever wretches like you belong.'

'You can't make me do that. She led me on, with her dark looks and wicked ways,' Richard blurted.

Reuben hit him again. 'You will be leaving. I know my lass would not encourage you. I'll set your bloody house on fire, if you aren't out and gone by morning.'

He took hold of the back of Richard's coat neck and dragged him across the yard while the man kicked and swore and cried out in pain, as he got dragged through the inn's doors to be shown to all the drinkers in the inn by Reuben.

'This bastard has tried to rape my lass. He's been told to pack his belongings and be gone by morning. If anybody thinks I'm being unreasonable and wants to speak up on his behalf, then say so now.' Reuben stood with the battered Richard next to him and looked around at the faces of the men, whose mouths were aghast. Ruby came in and stood behind her father, then glanced at the drinkers, who she knew would not come to Richard Baxter's aid.

'You can hang the bastard, for all we care. He's a wrong 'un – always has been. There's no love for his sort in here,' a voice yelled from the back of the inn as Reuben let go his grip of the offender and looked around him.

'We'll help you drive him out of his home. He's never been one of us,' another voice yelled, as Ruby made her way behind the bar to Martha, who gazed at her with upset and fear in her eyes.

'Do you hear that? You are not wanted here, and if you ever touch or even look at my daughter again, you'll be found dead down one of those disused mineshafts. Now bugger off and get your stuff packed – you are not welcome here.'

Reuben pushed the bleeding, battered man out of the inn and watched as he limped across to his cottage. Then Reuben sat in the solitary seat that he had named as his own, which overlooked the moor. He listened to the murmurings of the drinkers and shook off the glances that came his way; he'd been used to the same looks when he was younger. He'd always been hot-headed and it had been too easy to use his fists and ask questions later, but this time he knew he was right. Besides, he had to protect his lass.

'Are you alright, Ruby? He didn't touch you, did he? You know what I mean,' Martha said, and felt her legs going weak as she looked at Ruby and reached for her chair.

'I'm alright, thank you. My father arrived just in time, else I wouldn't have been. I couldn't fight Richard off me – he's stronger than he looks. Here, sit down, it has upset you.' Ruby rushed to give Martha a hand and watched as she struggled to catch her breath. 'I feel foolish. I should have been able to hold my own and not let him get the better of me,' Ruby said, feeling a bit unsteady on her feet herself as she thought about what could have happened to her.

'Aye, well, your father soon sorted Richard out. He was always handy with his fists and his old self came out tonight. That's what I remember him being like, and hearing the stories of who he'd been fighting – and Reuben didn't get the nickname "Black Blake" for nothing. After your mother's brothers had beaten him near to death, he learned to box and he learned it well, but sometimes he went too far. Richard Baxter is lucky to get away with his life tonight, seeing as your father's dander was up.' Martha sighed.

'I've never seen him like that – he's a different man,' Ruby said and looked over at her father.

'He's only protecting what's his. He did right, and he'll have got rid of Richard Baxter, something the other miners will thank him for, once they hear what has occurred here tonight,' Martha said.

'Aye, and they will hear of the shame of having my skirts raised and nearly worse, to my horror,' Ruby said.

'You've nowt to be ashamed of – everyone knows Richard's ways. Now hold your head up high and forget about him; he'll be gone in the morning. Take your father a tot of rum, on the house, and make sure that he's alright. This to-do will have shaken him up. I've never seen him so angry.'

Martha patted Ruby's arm and looked across at Reuben, sitting by himself. He'd fought for his daughter's honour, there was no doubt about that, but it had reminded folk of what a wrong 'un Reuben had been for a short while in his youth. Just when he had settled down to a quiet life on his own farm in Arkengarthdale he could well have done without the gossip that would follow.

'Are you alright, Father? Thank you for saving me.' Ruby sat down next to her father and looked at Reuben, as he turned away from the window and gazed at her when she passed him his tot of rum.

'I'm sorry, you shouldn't have had to see that side of me, but I'd have killed the bastard, if it was left to me. Now I've found you, there's nobody like Richard going to put his hands on you and force his way with you.' Reuben took a swig of his rum and reached for Ruby's hand. 'You are more precious than life to me, and he's the scum of the earth. He'd no right to even touch you, and I need to see him clear of here. Chase him out, like the rat that he is,' Reuben growled and slammed his drink down.

'Nobody likes him, but you nearly did kill him, Father. He'll be lucky if he can walk tomorrow, let alone pack his belongings and move out,' Ruby said and hung her head.

'He'll be gone, because I'm stopping the night here and, as soon as dawn comes, I'll pack up his cart and horse and send him on his way. He's got his own cart and horse, I take it?' Reuben asked.

'Yes, he stalls it at the end of the row.'

'Right then, tomorrow I'll send him on his way. Right now, however, I'll go and fill up those beer jugs you've

233

left on the stable floor, and bed my horse for the night. There's folk with empty tankards awaiting you, but I'll not have you going out there by yourself while that man's still here.' Reuben stood up and winked at his daughter and then smiled. 'I rarely lose my temper these days; in my youth I was a bugger, but no more.'

He started to walk away from Ruby and then hesitated.

'Tha needn't worry that I'll do the same to Tom, although I hope he's more of a gentleman when he comes courting you. Tom has my blessing to visit you – he's a grand lad. I think a great deal of him, and I know he can't stop thinking or talking about you. In fact his head's been in the clouds of late, and I've had to remind him to keep his mind on his job. You have a lot to answer for, Ruby. Your looks turn a man's head all too easily.' Reuben smiled and then made his way to bed his horse for the night and to bring the much-wanted beer in from the stable.

Ruby stood and gazed around her. Since her father had come into her life there had been nothing but upset. But he did truly love her and he approved of Tom, whom she would never have found, if it had not been for Reuben.

'Are you alright, lass? Your father's done the Tan Hill a lot of good tonight, giving that Richard Baxter a good hiding. He's had it coming for a long time. It'll be grand to see him on his way – he's puddled in the head and not fit around anyone,' Nathan said and looked at Ruby, with an empty tankard in his hand. 'Any chance of a fill-up?' He grinned.

'Aye, it's coming, Nathan. My father's gone out for

some. He'll not be long.' Ruby shook her head and smiled at the old fella.

'I'd better hold my noise then and not complain about my empty cup. Else I might end up the worse for wear,' Nathan said quietly and grinned at Ruby, before returning to his cronies and their dominoes.

If nothing else, her father had made the locals show some respect, but she'd never forget the temper he had shown when defending her, because it had been frightening.

Reuben peered into the window of the candlelit cottage that Richard Baxter lived in and watched as the man placed his few possessions into a sheet and tied it tightly, before sitting down on his kitchen chair in pain. Richard, it seemed, had taken heed of his threats; but to be sure, he'd see him on his way in the morning.

Reuben gave a sigh. Nobody touched his daughter as Richard had done and thought they could get away with it. He only regretted losing his temper quite so much, as he returned into the warmth and noise of the Tan Hill Inn. With the jugs filled with the new beer from Richmond, he was soon made welcome, and as folk got more drink inside them, Reuben was thanked for sorting out the man that seemingly no one trusted or liked.

By the break of day, Reuben had slept uneasily in the chair next to the window and, with the inn now empty of customers, and Ruby and Martha asleep in their beds, he went and stood at the back door and looked across at the miners' cottages.

Outside number three, in the sharp light of the morning and with cloud hanging around the surrounding fells, he watched as Richard Baxter slowly led his horse and cart to the front of his house and started to load his worldly goods onto it. Progress was slow, but Reuben was not about to go and help the man, as he watched him struggle with the table and chairs he was intending to take with him. The rat was leaving his nest and that was all Reuben was worried about. His lass would be safe now, and the miners at Tan Hill pit would not have to put up with Richard Baxter's unsocial ways. Good riddance, but Lord help the women he eventually lived among; he'd always be a threat to them. Still, his lass was safe and that was all that mattered, along with her happiness. And she'd have that, if she stuck to courting young Tom.

Chapter 17

Tom couldn't get to see Ruby soon enough once Reuben had explained why he had not returned that evening.

'Is she alright? He didn't hurt her, did he? He didn't do – you know . . . ?' Tom asked and felt embarrassed to be talking about suchlike to Ruby's father.

'No, he didn't, else he would have been bloody dead. I'd have made sure of that,' Reuben replied and then saw the worried look on Tom's face. 'I told Ruby I know that you are sweet on her, and I presume she is on you, but the same goes for you, lad: respect my lass and we'll not come to blows.'

'Of course, sir, I wouldn't do any other. Besides, Ruby's said the same herself to me – not that I tried anything, or owt like that.' Tom blushed and wished he'd not said quite as much as he had about his and Ruby's conversation on the moor.

'Good. That's where I went wrong. I should have kept my best friend in my pocket and not let it get the better

237

of me. Not that I regret being a father to my Ruby, but if we had waited, things would have played out a lot better, and neither I nor Vadoma would have wasted our lives, as at least I have. Ruby saw the darker side of me last night. It is very rare, as you know, that my temper gets the better of me, but I could have killed that Richard Baxter, if Ruby hadn't been there. She was a little quiet when I left her this morning and wasn't as forthcoming with her love for me.' Reuben sighed.

'She will be shaken up. You always feel worse when you've had time to think about the consequences if things hadn't gone as they did. It'll not be you that Ruby's worried about, I'm sure, as you'd every right to do what you did. Would you mind if I took the time to see her this morning? All the horses are out grazing and the stables are cleaned. I've only some harness to mend, and then I was going to go down into the bottom pasture. I noticed we have a gap in one of the walls, which I was going to put right before we place any horses back into the meadow.'

'You think a bit of her, don't you, lad? I'm glad. Ruby deserves a lad like you, not somebody who's worth nowt. Aye, you go and see how she feels, now the dust has settled, and make sure Martha is alright. She wasn't out of her bed when I left this morning. She looks so ill; her cheeks and lips are blue and she can hardly get her breath. Last night's carry-on will have really shaken her up.'

Reuben watched as Tom picked up his cap and pulled on his jerkin. He couldn't leave the house fast enough, Reuben thought, as he watched the lad nearly run across the yard to his horse. Tom was in such a rush that he'd not even thanked him for letting him go. Reuben shook his head; young love was a wonderful thing. He could just remember it, he thought, as he watched Tom gallop off down the farm track to see Ruby. The trouble was it was over in the blink of an eye, and your heart yearned for it for the rest of your life.

Ruby was clearing up the mess left from the night before, and when Tom walked in through the door, she looked up at him with tears in her eyes.

'Thank God you are here. I needed to see you and feel some comfort from you.' She placed down the empty tankards and rushed into Tom's arms. 'Did my father tell you what happened? I was fearful for my life, and then I feared that my father was going to kill Richard Baxter. I've never seen him with his temper risen. I honestly thought that he was going to kill him. His eyes . . . they were frightening.' Ruby buried her head in Tom's shoulder, and he held her close and kissed the top of it and stroked her hair.

'Aye, he's got a temper and his eyes, they do go as black as night when he is riled. That's where he gets his nickname from – Black Blake – but he soon calms down. He only loses his temper when he knows something's wrong. He's usually a good man. It shows how much he thinks of you; how much we *both* think of you,' Tom said and held her tightly. 'I'd kill the bastard myself if he was still here this morning.'

'Well, he's gone, thank heavens. I never did like Richard

Baxter – nobody liked him. But I never thought he felt *that* way about me. He must have been watching me, and us, all day, by the way he was talking. I've known him all my life. How could he even think the way he did?' Ruby asked and looked up into Tom's eyes.

'He's a bad lot, Ruby, but he's gone now. Lord help whoever he takes a fancy to next. Now, how's Martha this morning, and is there anything I can do for you while I'm here?' Tom kissed her again.

'I'm worried about Martha. She's still in her bed, and she says she's not up to getting out of it. It was a shock for her too, but her health has been worsening this last week or two. I wish she would have a doctor, but she says there's nowt he could do for her, even if he came, and I fear she is right. I just don't want to be left here on my own, which sounds selfish when she is fighting for her life.' Ruby let go of Tom, as she picked up the dirty tankards and placed them on the bar.

'You'll never be on your own. I'll always be here for you, and your father is only down the road with me. However, if anything happens to Martha, perhaps you should think of leaving the Tan Hill, as it is no place for a young woman to be running on her own. All sorts wander on this godforsaken road, even though it is as bleak as it can get.'

'No, I'll never leave here. And I'm definitely not going back to Elspeth and Banksgill. When I did leave here I realized how much I love this place. It might be ramshackle, and the customers may be rough and ready, but I know them for who they are, and they know me.

I don't have to put on any airs and graces and pretend to be something I'm not,' Ruby said with conviction and then smiled at Tom. 'Besides, I like my customers: they keep me on my toes and keep me entertained, especially when some drink a bit too much and talk rubbish over the bar. There are not many like Richard Baxter.'

'You are as stubborn as your father. He always has to have his own way too. Pig-headed, but don't tell him that.' Tom breathed in deeply, watching Ruby taking the tankards into the kitchen to wash.

She shouted through to him, 'I will – I'll tell him you called him an ignorant pig, and then what will you do, Tom Adams? You'd be as lost as he is without his horses. You are both that much alike.' Ruby laughed as Tom came through into the kitchen and put his arms around her waist, while she giggled and teased him.

'And you are as headstrong as any horse that the pair of us have broken in. In fact you are more like one of the stubborn mules that the lead miners use.' He held her tightly, and Ruby laughed as he tried to kiss her again and again. Their frolicking only ended when they heard a noise from above: a loud thump and a cry from Martha, which made them both stop in their tracks and look towards the stairs.

'Martha! Martha, I'm coming.' Ruby threw down her drying cloth and pushed Tom aside as she picked up her skirts and ran up the creaking old stairs as fast as she could to Martha's bedroom.

Tom heard her scream as he followed Ruby, and watched as she stood in horror, staring down at Martha's body sprawled upon the floor. Her body was lifeless, her mouth ajar and her eyes closed. Ruby bent down beside the old woman and hugged and rocked her, with tears running down her cheeks.

'Martha! Martha, please wake up – please wake up!' Ruby cried. She looked up at Tom as he bent down beside her.

He took Martha's arm and felt for a pulse on her wrist, then held her bedside mirror to her mouth to see if there was the faintest of breaths coming from her open mouth. But there was neither, so he put his arm around Ruby and consoled her.

'She's gone, Ruby, she's left this world. I'll place Martha back in her bed and make her look more respectable. There's nowt more can be done for her now,' Tom said as he held Ruby next to him. 'Shh, she's at peace now.'

'It was the rumpus with Richard Baxter that killed her. She got so upset, she had to retire to her bed, and she said she felt unwell and tired. I should have sat with her this morning instead of making a start on clearing downstairs.' Ruby sobbed and reached out for Martha's hand as Tom gently picked the old woman off the bedroom floor and placed her back onto her bed.

'It wouldn't help. She knew she was dying; she told you that her heart was failing and she knew that her time on this Earth was nearly at an end.' Tom glanced at the grey-haired woman, who had been so feisty in her day, and realized how aged she looked, and how delicate Martha really was beneath all the bluster.

'What am I going to do without her? I'll be lost here

242

on my own. I don't even know for certain that I can still live here, even though Martha always told me that the inn is mine after her day. Oh, Martha, I wish I'd shown you more care and listened to you more.' Ruby sobbed and sat at the edge of the bed, gazing down at the woman who had been her mother all her life. She remembered the harsh words she had said to the person who had shown her only love, when she had found out the secret that had built a wedge between them for a short time. 'I loved you so much; you were my true mother, and all you did was show me kindness and love. I was selfish and conceited, and you still loved me.' Ruby hung her head and wiped tears away from her face, as Tom put his arm around her and comforted her.

'Whisht now, Martha knew that you loved her. You should have no regrets. You looked after each other, and she'll have made things right by you – I know she will have done. She'll need laying out, and the undertaker and vicar in Langthwaite need to be told of her death. I'll do both for you. It will be Langthwaite where she will want burying, won't it? After all, it's the nearest churchyard, and I can't see Martha being a Methodist?' Tom asked, going through the practical things that needed to be done as Ruby lost herself in grief.

'Yes, yes, it's where Fred is buried and she'll want to be buried next to him, that I do know.' Ruby stood as the memory of Fred's death came flooding back to her and the grief of that day, when both her own and Martha's worlds had fallen apart; it had been the first sighting of the man she now knew to be her father.

'Right, I'll stay a bit longer and then I'll be away. It's best things get sorted straight away. Will you be alright on your own for a while or do you want me to get one of the women from the cottages to come and sit with you? Do you want me to stop with you tonight? I'm sure your father will not mind, under the circumstances. I'll tell him on my way down the dale, as he will be worried for you,' Tom said and put his arms around Ruby.

'I suppose he will. Perhaps if he had not been so vicious towards Richard Baxter, Martha might still be alive this morning. I could have looked after myself, and there was no need for him to be so violent. It seems that wherever he goes there is trouble for me and mine.' Ruby sighed. If only her words were true, she thought, but she knew that without her father's intervention the worst would have happened.

'Nay, now you can't blame Reuben for Martha's death. She was ill – she said so herself; her heart was worn out. It's just a coincidence that she died today, after all the upset.' Tom glanced at Ruby with worry on his face.

'Perhaps, but Martha was frightened of Reuben, and he didn't help her health any with his temper, no matter what you say. I have grown to love him, but there is still a bit of my father that I don't know, and will never know,' Ruby said. She pulled away from Tom's arms to look down at Martha at peace in her bed.

'Well, it was Reuben who told me to make sure you were alright and to ensure Martha was well this morning. He was worried about her, so her death will be no surprise to him. He also gave me a lecture about my intentions towards you, and I assured him that I would be honourable. I don't think I'd dare be anything else, after hearing about the fate of Richard Baxter.' Tom smiled. 'Not that I needed the lecture, as I would never do anything to hurt or upset you.' He kissed Ruby's forehead as they both walked out of the room, leaving Martha on her death bed.

'He's no need ever to threaten you – I know that, and he should too.' Ruby gave a sigh.

'He wasn't threatening. He thought he was protecting you, and he only set into Baxter because he bloody well deserved it. Reuben does nothing without a reason – I've told you before. He loves you, Ruby, and wants to do right by you. Don't let his temper colour your view of him,' Tom said as they walked down the stairs. 'Now, I'd put a sign on each door telling folk of Martha's death. You don't want to be serving folk with beer while she lies stiff above their heads. Although, knowing the folk around here, they'll want a night to see her on her way to the next world, and to celebrate her life with a few jars.' Tom smiled.

'Yes, we will see her off in style, she'd have liked that. I'll make sure she has a good wake. That is one thing I can do.' Ruby smiled, but she felt empty inside, as Tom left her standing at the serving bar and went to tell the outside world of Martha's demise.

It was the night before Martha's funeral, and the Tan Hill Inn was filled to the rafters with local folk mourning her passing. 'She was a grand woman, was Martha

Metcalfe. Salt of the earth – she would do anything for any man.' Jake slurred his words while propping up the bar and looking around at the ancient inn, which was full of drinkers and locals who had come to celebrate the life of Martha, before she was placed into the dark earth of St Mary's churchyard down in the village of Langthwaite.

'Oh, aye, would she now?' Jake's drinking partner joked as he listened to the old soak rattle on.

'Aye, she would. But she could be a tartar and all. She soon put you in your place if you stepped out of line. Martha once clobbered me over the head with her ousting shovel. I can't remember what I said, but it must have been summat bad.' Jake lifted his tankard and swigged back another mouthful. 'I'm going to miss her – we all will. It's to be hoped that her lass, Ruby, stays; that is, if she's been left the Tan Hill. I've not heard owt about what Martha's left to who.' Jake finally sat down in a chair, seeing that Ruby was coming his way.

'Well, although it is nowt to do with you, I can put you out of your misery, Jake. Martha has left me the Tan Hill and, by the looks of you, I think my mother would have said you've had enough for tonight, especially if you are to be one of Martha's bearers tomorrow,' Ruby said as she overheard the conversation and attempted to clear Jake's half-filled tankard away from him.

'Nay, lass, let me have my last sup – your mother wouldn't deny me that,' Jake said and quickly sipped what was left in his tankard, before getting up from the chair and looking at the new landlady of the Tan Hill.

'I'll make sure Martha gets to her resting place safe and sound, no matter how much drink I have in me tonight. I owe her that much, the old lass.'

'Are you alright, Ruby?' Reuben asked as he watched his daughter walking away from Jake, who was holding what was left in his tankard to him like a precious baby.

'Aye, I am. I'll just be glad when tomorrow is over. Tonight doesn't seem right: us all drinking down here, while Martha lies in her coffin upstairs. I know it's what she would have wanted, but I'm still finding it hard.' Ruby looked at her father.

'It'll soon be over. Tom says he's staying the night; he's got himself ensconced next to the fire already, so I hope he stays there and doesn't go creeping up the stairs to you, once everyone has gone to their homes. He's assured me that he won't, but I know what love and lust do to a young man,' Reuben said and stared hard at Ruby.

'Tom'll behave himself. He's too wary of you to get on the wrong side of you, and he knows that I'm not that easy – I've told him so. So you don't have to worry,' Ruby said coldly to her father, while she thought he should practise what he was preaching, as Tom had told her that Reuben was one for the ladies, when he felt that way inclined.

'That I'm glad to hear. Now that you are the owner of the Tan Hill Inn, you are a woman of property and you'll have many a man showing an interest in you, no doubt. You'll not go far wrong with Tom, though, he's a good lad. You'd get my blessing, if any thing becomes of it.' Reuben noticed how tired his daughter appeared. 'Now have we to get these good folk to their beds – it's nearly midnight. I think it's time to call it the close of the day, as all decent folk should be in their beds. We don't want Martha being sent to her grave by a load of half-blathered bearers that can hardly stand up. The vicar at St Mary's would not look at us in such a favourable light now, would he?' Reuben grinned as he got to his feet.

'It would only prove to him what he already thinks: that the devil owns the souls of those who drink here. He made that obvious when he came to see about Martha's burial, from what he kept hinting,' Ruby said. Then she stood next to her father and shouted in her loudest voice, 'Time to go home, if you please. It's the witching hour and I'm needing my bed. Now get yourselves home, and thank you for paying your respects to Martha before her burial tomorrow.'

Ruby heard a low murmur go round the inn, and the sound of drinkers finishing their last dregs before making their way past her and patting her on the back and giving their condolences. There were hard-looking miners, red-faced farmers and many a Dalesman going past her, wishing Ruby all the best and glancing up the stairs to where Martha lay. The same faces would be at her graveside tomorrow, most of them going without a day's pay to show their respects to the landlady at the Tan Hill Inn. Ruby only hoped that in time she would be able to fill Martha's shoes, and would be as well liked.

'Right, I'm away home. I'll be back by ten in the

morning, with my cart and horses, and we will do Martha proud on her last trip down the dale. I'll groom two of my horses and plait their manes, so that she gets a good send-off. Let's hope the weather goes in our favour. I think it will – all the signs tell me that it will be fine in the morning.' Reuben stared at Tom, who had stirred from his chair. 'You behave yourself, look after my lass and I'll see you in the morning.'

'Aye, she'll be right with me here, and I hear what you say.' Tom looked at Ruby as she walked her father to the door.

'You behave yourself and I'll see you in the morning,' Reuben repeated as he made his way out of the inn towards the stable, to get his horse and return to his home. All the time he was regretting trusting Tom to be left alone with Ruby. It was asking too much for two young folk in love to behave themselves, whether they were in mourning or not. He'd never had the strength of character to turn down a bonny face, so why should Tom be any different, despite his threats?

Ruby sank down into a chair and looked across at Tom. 'Thank God they have all gone – I'm on my last legs,' she said and put her head in her hands.

'Shh, my love, leave all be tonight. We'll both tidy everything in the morning.' Tom glanced around at the tankards left on the tables, at the dying embers of the fire and at Ruby, who he could tell was close to tears.

'I don't know how they can all drink and laugh and smile while Martha is lying in her coffin upstairs. I want to cry all the time,' Ruby sobbed.

'They are remembering her in their own way; that's what a wake is for. To remember the life of the loved one that's been lost, and to wish them well in the next world. You heard all that was being said about Martha by those who were sober and those who were the worse for wear. She was loved and respected.' Tom put his arm around Ruby and kissed the top of her head.

'I'm going to be lost without her. I don't think I can run this place on my own and I'll never fill her shoes.'

'You are just tired and sad tonight. Get yourself to bed and have some rest. After the funeral tomorrow, things will get better,' Tom said gently.

'I can't. I can't climb those stairs and sleep in the next room to Martha, knowing that she's to be buried in the morning. What if her soul is wandering around this place? She'll know my every thought.' Ruby reached for Tom's hand.

'Don't talk silly – she's at peace, she'll not be haunting or wandering anywhere no more.' Tom held Ruby tightly.

'Tom, lie with me tonight – I can't be up there on my own. Please come and sleep by my side, no matter what my father says. I don't want to be alone in my room,' Ruby pleaded and kissed him.

'He'd kill me if he ever found out. I daren't, but I want to so much,' Tom said quietly and kissed her back.

'He'll never know. Please, I need you. I need to feel loved and to have someone by my side. We needn't do anything, and you can simply lie by my side and love me,' Ruby begged.

'By, Ruby, we are tempting fate. You don't know how much I long to lie by your side.'

'Then come. I can't be on my own tonight.'

Ruby pulled on Tom's hand and found little resistance as they made their way up the stairs, with Martha's ghost smiling and looking at the young couple, knowing that they were to find comfort in one another's arms on the night before her funeral. Their fate had been sealed just as much as her own life had come to an end, and she hoped all would turn out well.

Chapter 18

'The day is too beautiful to be burying somebody. God can be cruel,' Ruby said as she looked up into the clear blue sky and watched the summer's new batch of swallows duck and dive over her head.

'Aye, but it makes you realize that you have to make the most of each day,' Reuben said as he watched Tom hold the horses steady, as the coffin containing Martha was loaded onto the back of his cart. 'Are you alright my lass? It's going to be a hard day for you. It is a good job I turned up in your life when I did, because at least you are not on your own.'

'Yes, Father, I'm alright, but I'll be glad when this day is over. I've locked the door of the inn. I'm closing it for today, out of respect. Surely the locals will realize that I'm not up to serving them today – after all, they had their fill last night,' Ruby replied and looked around at the folk who had gathered outside their homes, and on either side of the moorland road, to show their respects, as well as pulling the curtains within their homes.

'They'll understand. You can come back to mine this afternoon. It's not exactly a palace, with just two fellas living in it, but you will be made welcome. Tom can sleep in the stable and you can stop the night in his room. We've plenty of food, so we will not see you going hungry.' Reuben noticed that Tom was waiting for them both to start walking behind the horses and cart, on the long walk down the toll road to the village of Langthwaite a few miles down the dale.

'I'll be alright coming back here by myself – I'll have to get used to it sometime,' Ruby said as she walked over to the back of the cart and laid her hands on the oak coffin that held Martha.

'Nay, lass, come home with me, just for tonight. It'll be a hard enough day for you, without walking into the Tan Hill at evening time. I'll bring you back here myself in the morning and I'll check that all is in order before I leave. And I'm sure Tom will never be away from the place, if I let him.' Reuben smiled; he'd noticed the looks between Tom and Ruby – looks of love that had grown overnight, if his imagination was not playing tricks upon him.

They both went silent as the wagon set off on its journey, with Tom driving the two black horses, which were groomed to within an inch of their lives, walking slowly and steadily, with Reuben and Ruby following, along with the neighbours and friends who had decided to join Martha on her last trip from the Tan Hill. The road from Arkengarthdale twisted and turned and made its way down the valley, leaving the wild moorland behind, and the scarring of the lead mines down towards the broadening green fields of the valley below.

It was a sad procession that made its way down the steep road, passing many a house and farm, where people bowed their heads in respect as they made their way to the small village of Langthwaite, where the four-pointed tower of St Mary's stood. The village houses were solidly built from local stone and had been occupied since Viking raiders made their way up from the River Ure and settled there. Some of the Dales folk were descended from a Viking raider called Ark, giving Arkengarthdale its name. The villagers stood still and silent as the woman they knew as the force behind the successful pit inn entered through the church gates to receive her blessing and find her resting place, next to her late departed husband.

Ruby sobbed into her handkerchief as the coffin of Martha was laid to rest. She stood next to her father, who showed little emotion, but who did know that his daughter was hurting. Tom came and put his arm around her waist and risked Reuben's wrath as he held her tightly and whispered, 'It's alright, she's at peace now. There's nowt we can do to bring her back, but she knew she was loved.'

'I'm just going to miss her. She's always been there, and although I know she wasn't my mother, I always treated her like she was. Except when I found out the truth. And I regret what I said in anger – I should have been more caring,' Ruby sobbed. 'Martha did know that

254

I loved her, didn't she?' She looked up into Tom's eyes and searched for reassurance.

'Yes, she knew. Now, stop upsetting yourself. Come back with your father and me to Punchard. I don't want you on your own tonight, and I don't think I can stay another night.' Tom peered up at Reuben, who he knew was watching them and listening to their conversation.

'Tom's right. Now dry your tears and we will be away, as the gravediggers are waiting to fill the grave in and we need to be gone. We'll discuss what is to become of you, and the Tan Hill, once we are home. It is our business, not anybody else's, and folk have a tendency to listen in to conversations around graves,' Reuben said bluntly. He looked at Tom and Ruby as a group of locals stared at the mourners and whispered to one another about Reuben Blake attending the funeral, and why he was there between them.

Riding back in the cart, Ruby started thinking about the words her father had said. What did he mean about what was to become of her and the Tan Hill? It was clear to her what she was going to do, and what she wanted to do. She was going to stay there and run the inn, just as Martha had done; there was nothing else to be done. She sat quietly between Tom and her father and felt the summer's sun on her face. It was a beautiful day, but in her heart it was dark and broken, as she had lost the one woman who had truly loved her.

Ruby looked around her father's new home. He'd been right: he and Tom were no housekeepers, and it seemed more like the stable than a home, she thought, as he stirred the embers of the fire and put the kettle on to boil. Saddles and horse tack were everywhere, and the remains of the breakfast were still on the table. She wanted to offer to tidy everything away for them, but Tom, seeing her face, quickly stepped in front of her and started to clear the table. He put all the dirty plates into the earthenware sink that stood under the window, which looked out across the yard and down the dale.

'Your father would set off early this morning – he's never time to get all tidy,' Tom said shamefacedly as Ruby's father looked up at them.

'We need a woman to keep us straight. That's why I think you'd be better selling the Tan Hill and moving in with us. I've thought about it ever since you found out that Martha had left you her money and the inn. The Tan Hill is not the right place to be run by a slip of a lass. Just think what that Richard Baxter could have done to you, if I'd not been there. You'd be better off here with us – that's my way of thinking.' Reuben looked at his daughter and could instantly tell that was not what Ruby herself thought.

'You should advertise for a maid, because I'm not about to leave the Tan Hill. It is my home, and always will be. Richard Baxter has not frightened me from running the inn. Somebody would have come to my aid, of that I'm sure. I'm used to men being full of drink and blethering rubbish, and I can look after myself,' Ruby said and stood defiant; but deep down, she knew that her father was right, and she wasn't going to relish running the inn herself.

'I'm telling you that you are better off here. This is not like when you and my mother didn't see eye-to-eye; this is a matter of keeping you safe. Anyone could take advantage of you, and nobody would ever know,' Reuben said sternly. 'It's the roughest, wildest place this side of the Pennines, and in winter you are always cut off from everybody. What are you going to do then, perhaps with no food and no heat? You are best selling it, my girl, and becoming a dutiful daughter to your father – and perhaps a wife to Tom here, if that's what you both want.' Reuben scowled.

'I don't want to do either,' Ruby said in a temper. She looked at Tom and his face said exactly how much her words had hurt. 'I'm not ready for marriage and I certainly don't want to keep house, not when I could be keeping my own business at Tan Hill. I love you, Father; and Tom, you know how fond I am of you, but I'll not give up on a place and a job that I am happy in.'

'You stubborn she-devil. Why is your head so bloody hard and set in its ways? Your life would be such a grand one here; you'd want for nothing, with the money from the sale of Tan Hill Inn in your bank, and Tom and myself to look after you. Instead you prefer the company of miners and drunks, freezing on the top of a fell. By God, you are your mother's daughter. She might not have brought you up, but she's in you good and proper.' Reuben cursed and looked at his headstrong daughter.

Tom sniggered and couldn't resist adding, 'Aye, and she's not so different from her father, either. He lives like a gypsy when he needn't.'

257

'You hold your tongue, else I'll give you a good hiding, because if you think I believed you both behaved yourselves last night, then you must think I was born yesterday. I never thought being a father would be such hard work. Why wasn't I blessed with a sweet, demure young daughter, one who did as she was told?' Reuben cursed and stood by his chair, ignoring the kettle, which was coming to the boil.

'You should never have sought me out, if that's what you think, and then you'd have been no wiser, and I'd have been left running the Tan Hill as I wish. Perhaps you should wash your hands of me. Surely that would not be hard to do; after all, you never knew I existed until this spring,' Ruby said, as she tried to fight back the tears that were starting to well in her eyes as words were said in anger on both sides.

Reuben shook his head. 'You know how to hurt my heart. I know you think me hard and uncaring, with a temper from the devil himself, but it is only because I don't want you hurt in any way, now that I have finally found you.' He sighed. 'Do whatever you wish. I'll be here when you want me, and I know Tom will. He's lost his heart to you – any fool can see that.' Reuben turned to the boiling kettle as Ruby wiped her nose on her sleeve.

'I'm like your father, Ruby, I only want what is best for you. I know you love the Tan Hill, but it is a wild place – perhaps too wild for you to be on your own?' Tom said and took her hand.

'I'm sorry, but it is my home, and it took me some time

away from it to realize quite how much I loved the ramshackle place, and the people who need it, to get through their lives. Besides, I can't let Martha down. She'd want me to stay there; it had been in her family for so long. I love you both, you should know that. But yes, I am pig-headed – how could I not be, with such parents as I have?' Ruby broke into a grin as she looked at her father and wiped away a tear that was running down her cheek.

'Aye, you are your father's daughter alright. I should know, I put up with both of you.' Tom glanced at Reuben, waiting to be rebuffed.

'And you are bloody lucky as well. I should kick your arse many a time, Tom Adams. Just go out to the well and get those plates washed, because it doesn't look like we have a woman to care for us – not now and maybe never, the way we two are shaping.' Reuben decided that it was best nothing more was said about Ruby and the Tan Hill Inn. He didn't want to lose her love now that he had it. Besides, he'd always be there to make sure no one touched a hair upon her head. His name alone would make men wary of the landlady at Tan Hill.

Ruby plated the freshly fried mushrooms that Tom had picked from the fields that morning, and which were now lusciously covered in butter and in need of being eaten with some freshly made bread, which Ruby had made as soon as she had woken. It was her way of apologizing to her father and Tom, along with a quick tidy of their living rooms and Tom's bedroom before she returned to Tan Hill.

259

'I could get used to this: fresh bread and a tidy house,' Reuben said as he soaked the black butter liquor left by the field mushrooms off his plate with a slice of bread.

'Aye, I could too. My nose couldn't believe the smell that was coming out of the kitchen when I walked in with these mushrooms. Not only had I had a lovely walk through the dew-filled pastures to gather them, but I came home to find all this was tidy and there was fresh bread on the table. I never thought I'd say it, but I miss your mother, Reuben. She kept us well fed, even though she was never off my back,' Tom said as he ate his last mushroom and looked across at Ruby.

'Well, I've been thinking. I realize now that you are in need of a woman's touch about the place. What if I were to come and clean and see to things on a Wednesday? I can stay closed on a Wednesday, as usual, as it's always a quiet day, and I can bring you some fresh baking. I can't see you two making a cake or pasty, let alone bread. But only until you get yourselves a maid or housekeeper,' Ruby said and noticed the smiles appearing on her father's and Tom's faces.

'I could come and pick you up – save you the walk down here. And in return, if your father lets me, I could help on your busiest nights at the Tan Hill?' Tom glanced across at Reuben, looking for confirmation of his suggestion. 'At least you'd know Ruby would be safe if I was there.'

Reuben smiled. 'It would be like inviting the fox into the hen house – you'd both be free to do whatever your passions stirred you to do. But, aye, perhaps it is a way

260

around all our needs. I see you looking at one another. You forget that I was young myself once, and I remember how it feels to be that lost in love.' Reuben grinned. 'You both could do a lot worse. Despite Tom here being only my stable lad, I know he's kind of heart, and that is all that matters. If you are both willing, then we will do just that, as it suits me well. I couldn't be doing with a maid prying into my business and being in my house. She'd tidy and fuss around.'

'But you will employ one eventually?' Ruby asked, and urged Tom to make Reuben realize that the arrangement was not permanent.

'Aye, in my own time, when the right one comes along. You never know: come winter, you might not be so keen on living at the Tan Hill on your own and want our company – that is, if there are no unplanned surprises before then.' Reuben looked across at both Tom and Ruby as they blushed and hung their heads. 'Now, am I to take you back to Tan Hill in my horse and cart or are you taking her, Tom? There will be two horses needing feeding in that stable, if nothing else, when you get home, and either Tom or I can see to them while you see to your affairs.'

'I'll take her. There's nothing afire with our horses – I've already checked them all,' Tom said quickly and pushed his chair back.

'Hmm . . . Then I'll let you go, and I'll get on with the job of breaking in that young filly that I've been working on for a few days. It'll be Brough Hill Fair before I know it, and I want to sell her there,' Reuben said and watched as Ruby tidied the table before she left them. 'You take care of yourself. I'll come up and see you most days, and I dare say I'll have to fight Tom to keep him away.'

'I will, Father. I'll be alright – don't worry.' Ruby quickly washed the dirty pots, before grabbing her shawl. She watched Tom walk out into the bright morning's sunshine that filled the yard, as he went to the home field's gate and stood at it to whistle for the horse that would take them back to Tan Hill. She felt her stomach churning as she thought about walking into the inn without Martha being there to welcome her. It would never have the same feeling, without Martha's love. A love that had never been spoken of, but was automatic, with every glance and deed done by the caring soul. It had been a love that she had taken for granted and now that it was no longer there, she longed to tell Martha how much she had loved her and appreciated the care that had been given to her.

Ruby watched as Tom led the horse into the yard and placed the harness on it, then hitched the cart, ready for their journey. She watched as he patted the horse's head and talked gently to it, and stood looking down the dale. She knew that she was starting to love Tom; he was gentle and reliable. But he was the first lad she had felt this way about, and in fact was the first lad she had truly courted. She knew that not all men were as kind and considerate and that she was lucky to have him in her life, even though he was classed as a 'steady' lad, in her eyes.

Ruby smiled as Tom yelled to ask if she was ready, and dismissed her feelings of doubt. Of course he was the right lad for her. He was everything any decent lass could wish for: dependable, kind and loving, and a hard worker – what more could she ask for? And her father approved of their dalliance, which was something to be grateful for.

'Coming,' she replied as she pulled the worn kitchen door to and ran across the yard to join him, feeling reassured as Tom quickly kissed her on the cheek while he helped her onto the seat next to him on the cart.

'Are you alright, my love?' Tom asked as he flicked the reins over the back of his favourite horse and urged it on its way down the farm track.

'Aye, I'm grand. I'm feeling a bit upset about walking back into the Tan Hill without Martha being there, but I'll get used to it.' She looked at Tom and kissed him gently, feeling guilty at even questioning her love for him.

She stared around her. The dale was alive with the sound of the lead miners on the high fells above, and the meadows in the valley bottom were being harvested of the grass that had been mown and was now being made into hay, filling the air with its sweetness. Summer was nearing its end. Martha had been right; she had not lived to see winter return to the dale. Now it was Ruby's turn to conquer the hardness of winter at the remote inn and see if it made her or broke her.

Chapter 19

Too soon summer was on its way out on the wild moorland, the swallows were making ready to depart for warmer climes as they prepared their young for the epic journey over the world's oceans, and Ruby was making herself ready for her first winter alone. Beetroot and onions were picked and stored in jars on the many shelves of the inn's larder; and a slaughtered pig, reared by one of the miners, had been salted and hung from the bacon hooks dangling from the low beams of the inn. Black pudding had been made from the blood by Ruby, as Martha had shown her, and had been served up for supper on a regular basis while it was fresh.

Ruby had also kept to her word and had devoted Wednesdays to visiting her father and Tom at Punchard Farm, cleaning and cooking and making sure they kept themselves as tidy as two horse-loving men could, without a woman to square them up. Tom also kept his word and joined her behind the bar on a Friday and Saturday evening, although most of his time he spent too long gossiping with the local farmers and miners when he served them their ale. This made Ruby wonder why he bothered coming, but when the locals had stopped drinking and gone home to their beds, it was then that she shared intimate moments with him. Their love was growing and blossoming, even though Ruby sometimes questioned herself for loving the first man who had walked into her life. She loved lying in Tom's arms and hearing of his childhood days, and of the day he went to work for her father when she had just turned eleven. Tom was everything a woman could need in a man, and Ruby knew she had been lucky to find him.

Meanwhile Reuben wheeled and dealt in the horse world, enjoying getting a good price for his horses and watching every foal grow into a fit and healthy beast of which he was proud. His heart still yearned for his Vadoma, and his hopes of finding her at the fast-approaching Brough Hill Fair were being raised yet again, although he knew they would only be dashed when yet again she was nowhere to be found.

The cottage rented from the colliery that Richard Baxter had once occupied was standing empty, but as Ruby served Jake and the collier Rob, she heard them discussing the fact that it had been taken by a new miner from Gunnerside, and that he would soon be joining them at the open pit.

'Well, anybody is better than Richard Baxter. As long as he pulls his weight, he'll do for me,' Rob said and drank back his pint.

'I've never heard of him and I reckon to know every-body in these dales. James Robinson, you say his name is? Can't say I've ever heard of him.' Jake shook his head and took another drink.

'Aye, that's him, and he's from Gunnerside. Other than that, I know nowt about him. He could be the devil himself, for all I know,' Rob laughed.

'Nay, that's Reuben Blake – we already have him,' Jake whispered and glanced over at Ruby, hoping that she hadn't heard, then grinned.

'I heard that, Jake Hartley. You be careful, or the devil's daughter will not be serving you again,' Ruby said, then filled his tankard up with beer, seeing that it was nearly empty. 'This new fella will be alright as long as he likes a drink here. You can tell him I serve good beer and food, and if he doesn't want either from me, then he needn't show his face at my door,' she went on, looking at the gossipers.

'Sorry, Ruby, but you know what the locals say about your father. Sometimes he is driven by the devil, but he's a good man most of the time.' Jake knew that only he could get away with telling the truth. 'Like, he seems to have quietened down a bit since he found you. I've not heard his name connected to anything lately,' Jake said and looked up at the lass who always treated him well.

'I'll forgive you, but only because I know it's true, and because I know my father is more content at the moment, although he's still making tracks at the end of October to Brough Hill Fair with his horses. He will never calm down and stop dealing with the gypsies and travellers

266

until he's found my mother. And I doubt that will ever happen.' Ruby sighed.

'Well, something good came out of his dalliance with your mother. We have you to keep us fed and watered here at the Tan Hill. It's a good job Martha took you in, and I couldn't see this place without an inn. I see that Tom is getting his feet more and more under the table – is there to be a wedding soon?' Jake asked with a sparkle in his eye.

'Not yet, Jake – not if I have my own way. I enjoy my freedom, and I don't want to be reliant on any man,' Ruby replied and winked at Rob, then walked off behind the bar.

'She's a feisty one, that 'un, and it'll take someone stronger than Tom to tame her. She's her father's daughter alright: every bit as sultry and hard-headed. But she's a fair lass, and she's running this place just as good as it's ever been run. That's a credit to old Martha.' Jake looked at Rob.

'Aye, she's a good catch to the man who can handle her, and they are few and far between,' Rob said. He stared at the woman he'd known since she was a child. Whoever won the heart of Ruby was a lucky man, in his eyes, and he only wished he was thirty years younger and unmarried.

Ruby stood with her piebald horse Thistle and patted her neck as she tethered her out on the fell, next to the inn's old workhorse. She stroked the horse's mane and talked to her quietly, as Thistle looked at her, snorted and lifted her head up and down as Ruby sought her affection.

'By, I wish somebody would show me as much care and love.'

Ruby turned and sought whoever was watching her while she petted her horse. 'Perhaps they would, if you were a horse,' she replied tartly and stared at the tall, dark-haired man who had obviously been watching her for some time.

'Aye, perhaps they might. Happen that's where I've gone wrong all my life.' The man laughed and walked nearer to Ruby. 'Are they yours then, or do you just make a fuss of them?'

'No, they are mine. I tether them here on the moorland across from the inn nearly every day and take them into the stable of an evening. And you needn't think of thieving them, else my father would soon catch you up and skin you alive,' Ruby replied and glanced at the man, who was paying a little too much interest in her Thistle as he patted the horse's neck and looked her up and down.

She's a grand horse, but the other one is a bit long in the tooth. But I've no desire or need of either. I just thought I'd make myself known to you. I'm James Robinson, and I've moved into the empty miner's cottage. I start at the pit tomorrow. And you, I take it, are Ruby. Rob told me all about you when I met him the other day, and he told me you run a tidy inn with good food, if ever I'm hungry.' James looked at her over the horse's withers and smiled.

'Rob and his mate Jake are always yacking. I hope whatever he said you took with a pinch of salt, as they can both tell some fair tales.' Ruby glanced across at

268

James and thought how good-looking her new neighbour was. He was the opposite of Tom, being dark-haired and with sharp features, compared to Tom's sandy hair and round face. She found herself strangely attracted to him, as James stared at her with a twinkle in his eye.

'It's the same with all these miners – they have not much else in their lives, just like me. That's why you can expect me to come along for a drink and perhaps a meal, as I've no wife here with me,' James said. He looked at Ruby and thought how beautiful she was.

'You are not married then?' Ruby asked and patted her horse, trying not to show too much interest in her new neighbour.

'Er . . . no, I'm here by myself. As I say, nobody has given me any of their time to show me care and love,' James replied and watched as Ruby started to walk back to the inn. He stepped out quickly to walk by her side. 'Are you going in? What are you making for supper tonight? I might treat myself, seeing as I've not quite settled in yet.' James watched her as she climbed the few steps up to the inn.

'It's rabbit pie tonight. My beau trapped them and cleaned them for me yesterday, and now they are simmering in the pot with some fresh thyme, onions and carrots. I'll put a pastry lid on them later this afternoon,' Ruby said. She stopped for a minute to look at the man she knew was going to come in for his supper, regardless of what was cooking.

'You are courting? You can tell him he's a lucky fella to have a bonny lass like you on his arm. I'll be in later

269

for something to eat and a gill or two, and to admire the view.' James winked.

'You are very forward, do you know that?' Ruby said and watched as he turned to walk to his cottage.

'Aye, I know. But somewhere I heard that a faint heart never won a fair lady, so you can't blame me for trying my luck. See you later, Ruby.' James grinned, leaving Ruby watching him.

Her heart was fluttering like a trapped butterfly and her conscience was telling her not to be so stupid. That James Robinson was full of blarney, and he doubtless talked to every woman the way he had done to her. She smiled to herself and broke into a song, the first time she had done since Martha had died. It had been nice to be looked at in such a way, and to be told you were a fair lady. If it were not for Tom, James could have her heart any day, she thought, as she added a little more salt and a measure of love and lust to the rabbit stewing over the fire. This supper time there would be a customer she would definitely look forward to serving. She only hoped that Tom would not visit this evening, else she would be torn between which man to entertain. She tried to keep her flights of fancy at bay. James Robinson was no match for her Tom, and she should know better than even to be thinking about him. Still, she enjoyed his flirting ways and there was no harm in that, as long as she kept them at a distance.

'Now, that was rabbit stew to die for. You are not just a bonny face!' James said and sat back in his chair and looked at Ruby, as she removed his plate, which only had the bones of the deceased rabbit left on it.

'I'll take that as a compliment, but like I said, I think you very forward,' Ruby replied and took the plate from under his nose, feeling all of a flutter as James gazed at her with his ice-blue eyes.

'Well, it's no good wasting time when you've seen something, or someone, that takes your fancy – and you definitely take my fancy.' James looked Ruby up and down and grinned.

'I think my Tom would have something to say to you, if he found out about your conduct,' Ruby said, but she lingered with her hands full of plates as James replied.

'He's too busy catching rabbits, while I'm intent on catching the bonny creature in front of me. What do you say to that? Now it's the Harvest Supper dance at Kirkby Stephen in a fortnight: how about you and I go? There's no need for lover boy to know. We could go together and get to know one another a bit better, and I could show you a real good time,' James suggested and looked at the surprise on Ruby's face.

'I think not, Mr Robinson. I hardly know you, let alone I'm practically betrothed to my Tom and will always be true to him.' Ruby felt a flush come to her face and turned to leave her new admirer. 'Besides, I hardly ever visit Kirkby. It's always too busy, and it's full of traders and fine folk who look at me as if I don't belong mixing with them.'

'Then I'll have to come in for my supper every night until you get to know me better, and we can soon amend that,' James shouted at her as Ruby pretended not to hear.

She smiled and tried to cool down her cheeks, so that nobody could see what she truly thought of the outspoken James Robinson and his invitation to the Harvest Supper dance at Kirkby Stephen. She had always wanted to attend, but nobody had ever asked her; and in past years she had had nothing to wear, as she knew it was a grand affair. Now she was not only being asked, but she had a wardrobe of the finest clothes, thanks to the generosity of Jane Verity. But she couldn't possibly say yes to the outrageous flirt. After all, she had to be faithful to Tom.

Ruby looked over at him as he talked to Jake and Rob, and tried to think straight while she poured beer for a table of rowdy lead miners who had just eaten their supper in the corner of the inn. No, she thought, she couldn't cheat Tom – or could she? James winked at her as she put one of the lead miners in his place when he grabbed her waist. After all, James Robinson had only been cheeky, nothing more. She'd see how she felt by the end of the week. As he had said, Tom need never know and, if he did find out, then she'd say they were lifelong friends.

Ruby tried to ignore James for the rest of the evening, and said a casual goodnight to him as he left with Rob and Jake. Perhaps he had changed his mind, she thought, as she tidied the main room and blew out the oil lamps, before carrying one up to her bedroom. Part of her hoped that he had, while the other part of her longed to see James the following evening and hoped that the invitation was still on offer. Once washed and undressed, she lay in her bed and thought about Tom, and James – the new man in her life, a known flirt. She did love Tom, but he never suggested attending dances and the like; all he ever talked about was horses and walks on the moors. She thought about the dark hair and ice-blue eyes of James; he was striking, truly striking, she thought as she quenched the wick of the lamp and tried to sleep.

'So are you going to come with me or not? It'll be a good night; there's always plenty to eat and a good fiddle player that comes from Brough. Your feet can't keep still when she starts playing,' James said. He leaned over the bar and grinned at Ruby as she looked at him and was tempted. He'd been visiting her most evenings and had never stopped asking her to join him, when he was out of earshot of the locals and Tom. And now the weekend of the Harvest Supper was nearly upon them.

'I can't – I've to be true to Tom,' Ruby said as she wiped some glasses and made herself busy.

'Just because we are going to a dance together doesn't mean we are courting, although I might sneak a quick kiss, if you let me.' James winked at her, knowing that his persistence was beginning to pay off.

'And what do I do here? I can't simply close my doors, and Tom will wonder why I don't need him that night. I can't.' Ruby shook her head and tried not to look at the ice-blue eyes that made her lose her senses.

'You can. It's the same night as Brough Hill Fair and a lot of your drinkers will be there filling their bellies.

273

Tell Tom you need a night off and that it is not worth opening. He'll not know any different if you don't say owt,' James egged her on.

'This inn closes on a Wednesday and a Sunday – it never closes any other night. Folk would think there was something amiss, especially with it being a Saturday night. I can't. Martha would be turning in her grave.' Ruby tried to shake the thought of dancing with James all night out of her head.

'Well, it's your loss. A reason to dress up and eat well, and dance the night away, traded for a night with perhaps four old miners drowning their sorrows in drink. Sounds like a bad deal to me, but what do I know?' James said. He went to sit at his usual seat and look at Ruby all night until she changed her mind.

Ruby sat down beside Tom on their usual seat at the edge of the moor, gazing down and across into Stainmore.

'Would you not rather be back at Banksgill, where at least my grandmother kept you fed and you were looked after?' Ruby asked Tom as he put his arm around her. 'My father just does things that suit himself, and it must be hard for you to put up with his ways.'

'No, I respect your father. He's a good man, and what he doesn't know about horses is not worth knowing. I'm content with my lot. How could I want more? I enjoy my work, live in one of the grandest dales and have a bonny lass on my arm. I might not have a lot of money, but I'm content. Speaking of your father, I can't come

274

and help you at the inn this weekend as he has asked me to stay at home and keep an eye on the horses. He says he doesn't think you'll mind because he knows that a lot of your drinkers will be at Brough Hill Fair, as he will be. I'm sorry.' Tom took Ruby's hand and kissed her gently.

'Oh no, that's alright. In fact I thought of closing the inn on Saturday night because it will be so quiet and I could do with a night to myself, so don't feel guilty about not helping me. It works out well.' Ruby smiled and pondered which dress she was going to wear at the thought of dancing in James Robinson's arms. He had said that nobody need know about their antics together and, if anyone did find out, they were just good friends, that's all.

'I'll meet you at the crossroads, and then nobody will suspect anything,' James whispered to Ruby over the bar. 'Tomorrow night at six. Your horse can take two of us, can't it? It's not too far to Kirkby.'

'Right. I thought we'd be going by buggy, not on the back of my horse?' Ruby said and looked at James.

'What, and let all the world know that we are going together? No, it is best you ride Thistle, then nobody will think anything other than that you are going for a ride on your night off. You don't want Jake telling Tom he saw you riding out with me, now do you?' James hissed.

'No, of course I don't. I just didn't want my dress to smell of horse.' Ruby sighed as she watched James go

275

out of the inn, leaving her to the guilt she was feeling for going to a dance with a man she hardly knew.

Ruby looked at herself in the mirror. She'd chosen a plain-cut red dress to wear at the Harvest Supper dance. It was not too frivolous, but it was made of the richest velvet, and the deep plush-red showed off her skin and her dark hair, making her appear sultry and daring. Which was just how she felt as she went down the stairs of the inn and locked the door behind her.

A pang of guilt assailed her as she thought of poor Tom, sitting at home looking after her father's horses, blissfully unaware of her cheating. There had been plenty of moans from her local drinkers when they had been told the inn would not be open on Saturday night, and she would not be popular with anyone if the truth was to come out – especially with her father. He seemed to think she would be marrying Tom in the coming months, no matter what she desired.

With Thistle already saddled and waiting, Ruby mounted him and made her way quietly out of the inn's yard, glancing quickly behind her to make sure nobody from the miners' cottages had seen her. Once clear out of sight of the inn, she urged Thistle into a gallop, stopping only when she saw James standing at the edge of the crossroads, dressed in his Sunday best with a smile on his face.

'I thought you weren't going to come. Thank heavens it's a grand night, and warm for the time of year – a real harvest evening.' James held his hand out to be pulled up behind Ruby, and she felt him warm and close to her, as he placed his arms around her waist and they started to ride from the top of the bleak moors down into the lusher valley bottom. 'Are you regretting coming with me?' James whispered in her ear.

'No, but I do feel guilty. I don't want to hurt anybody, for the sake of going to a dance,' Ruby said as she urged Thistle on, hoping to reach the busy market town of Kirkby Stephen before sunset.

'You'll not hurt anybody. We are not doing anybody any harm, so enjoy yourself.' James took advantage of kissing Ruby on her neck as she held the horse's reins.

'Stop it – we are just friends, remember?' Ruby said, suddenly regretting her decision to attend the dance with a man she hardly knew. James could do anything to her and nobody would know.

'Alright, I'll behave. The night's young, but relax – I mean you no harm. I simply want us both to enjoy ourselves, and I will be proud to have such a beautiful woman on my arm when I'm dancing around the market hall tonight.'

James relaxed his grip, but squeezed up closer to Ruby as she rode Thistle into Kirkby Stephen and she felt glad to be back in civilization. Her experience with Richard Baxter had made her a little wary, but she thought herself foolish for feeling threatened as they reached the livery stable. James dismounted and offered her his hand as he held Thistle, before passing the reins of the horse to the stable lad.

The couple walked down the busy town's streets, filled with people talking and finishing their business before the end of the day. Kirkby Stephen was a busy market town set at the edge of the Yorkshire Dales leading to the fertile Eden Valley, which led to the Scottish Borders, and it was always thronged with folk of all kinds. That night it seemed exceptionally so, and Ruby was conscious of people staring at her as she walked quickly beside James.

'You look wonderful,' James said as they made their way along the cobbled street to the grand hall in the centre of the town.

'Thank you. I didn't know what to wear.' Ruby blushed as she saw James gazing at her as they queued up next to the sturdy stone pillars of the market hall and waited to gain entrance into it. People from Kirkby Stephen and the surrounding Dales were dressed in their finest, and a happy buzz filled the late-October evening, along with the sound of the fiddle band, which was making everybody's feet tap as they waited to enter the hall. Once inside, Ruby looked around her: at one side of the hall there was a long trestle table filled with delicacies – pies, cakes, dishes of steaming potatoes and soup, anything that anyone could wish to eat, along with a huge serving dish filled with punch, with a ladle and small glasses hanging from its side.

'Are we dancing or are we eating first? Whatever we do, make sure you get your fill, because these tickets cost me enough,' James said as he showed Ruby the tickets that he had bought, expecting to get good value for his money.

'Let's eat and watch who's dancing first,' Ruby said

278

and pulled on James's arm, urging him to take a plate and join her as he looked along the table at all the food the people of Kirkby Stephen had made to celebrate their harvest time. She was just helping herself to a piece of pork pie when the woman behind the trestle spotted James, recognizing him as he whispered to Ruby that it would make her fat, and grabbing her waist.

'James, what a surprise! I didn't expect you here. Where's Liza – back at home with the children, I expect? Who's this you are with? I hope your Liza knows you are here,' she said flippantly, then realized that James had not told Ruby he was married as she saw the look of horror on her face. 'Oh, I'm sorry,' she cried as Ruby dropped her full supper plate and stared at James in dismay before fleeing from the hall, as people shook their heads, thinking that a gypsy girl had obviously been routed from their harvest celebrations. As she left the hall Ruby heard their whisperings about the disgrace of inviting such people to their celebrations, not realizing that it was James who was the disgrace – that he had not told the innocent lass on his arm that he was already married with children, and that she was simply being used.

'Ruby! Ruby, come back,' James yelled as he followed her down the streets.

She was in tears when she got to the livery stable and, instead of asking the stable boy to saddle Thistle, she reached for the saddle herself and placed it and the bridle on her horse, while she battled with her tears and feelings of foolishness.

'Please, I didn't mean to upset you. My wife and I have had our day – that's why I'm at the Tan Hill. She's thrown me out. Please listen to me, Ruby. She means nothing to me,' James pleaded as she tightened the girth strap and pulled on the bridle over Thistle's head.

'You have children as well as a wife! You've treated me like a fool. Go back to your Harvest Supper dance and pick on some other idiot. I'll not be a party to children not having a father. I should never have agreed to come with you. I should have stayed home with Tom and been faithful.' Ruby pummelled his chest and pushed him back as she mounted Thistle and kicked her sides, making the horse leave the stable sharply.

'Ruby! Ruby, I'm sorry,' James wailed, but it was too late. Ruby was galloping down the street of the town, glad to get away and be on the wild moors again. The full moon beamed down upon her as she trotted slowly up the moorland road back to the Tan Hill Inn. The clouds around the moon played hide-and-seek with the beams and she sat on the back of Thistle, glad that the horse knew its way home, as she sobbed and cursed herself for being so stupid. It was her own fault; she should have been true to Tom, and she should never have gone to the supper. Folk hadn't wanted her there anyway; she'd heard them whisper and call her a gypsy as she left. As for James Robinson, he'd be making his own suppers from now on, and she never wanted to see him in the Tan Hill Inn ever again.

Chapter 20

It's an awful spot
For a roguish lot,
Is Brough Hill Fair –
An' ye'll have to leeak oot,
An' be gaily cute,
If you manidge an' keep a'square!

An' he's but a simplish sooart of a body.
At thinks theears nobbut ya' kind o' shoddy –
For whativver be t'trade
Theears tan to yan a swin'lin' blade
Wi' a ghooast of a conscience easily laid:

We went into t'Swan an' I settle wi' t'man,
Wi' a Vank of Englan', thear an' than
A fifty p'und nooat, I'd taken that day.
For coos at I'd sell't, as I com' on my way.

And he gev me change oot,
Which I didn't dispute.

An' I'd gaily good cause to gang rovin' mad
For them nooats he gev me I' change wer' bad!
Seaah twice in a day, as a body may say,
I was chisselt an' done – I' the cruellist way!

Local dialect poem, written by Jimmy Green about his
experience at Brough Hill Fair, published by the
Westmorland Gazette (1870).

Reuben made his way towards the sprawling fair, which
was heaving with travellers, gypsies, farmers, traders and
animals of every shape and size. It was a lot larger than
Appleby Fair and was more supported by folk from every
walk of life, as they traded and made their livings on the
side of Pennine Hill. Hawkers stopped him every second,
urging him to buy their matches, good-luck charms, hand-
woven blankets and anything else that they could carry
on their bodies. Half of them were warily keeping an eye
open for the peelers, knowing that they had no valid permit
for trading and that fifty shillings was the normal fine for
any offending trader, especially if the courts deemed them
to be undesirables. The gypsies were welcomed each year,
but at the same time were discriminated against for their
different looks and ways, and were obvious targets for
the law, if any crimes were committed.

Reuben pushed his way through the crowds with his
flat wagon, and the four horses that he hoped to sell

282

tethered behind it. He listened to the local accent of one farmer arguing with another over the price of his flock of that year's lambs, and watched as the deal was sealed by spitting in their hands and shaking each other's hands firmly. Deals between fellow farmers were not usually a problem; it was deals with the travellers that you had to be wary of, especially when notes were involved. There had been many a counterfeit note passed in a deal, with the unsuspecting seller walking away with nothing but a bit of printed fake paper. As long as they knew you, the deal would be sound, but if they thought of you as being wet behind the ears it was the worse for you.

Reuben made his way out of the crowds to where the tents, wagons and vardoes were parked for the two days of the fair. He found a pitch and staked his horses out, then erected a shelter over the back of his flat wagon from a sheet of tarpaulin, for somewhere to rest his head after he had done dealing, and hopefully after he had a drink at The Swan. He watched as a strong-looking gypsy boy with a halter for a bridle, and with his horse groomed, clipped and with its mane and tail braided, displayed his horsemanship, exhibiting the beast to the very best advantage as a group of interested buyers bid against one another. That was the way of Brough Hill Fair, Reuben thought – all show. It wasn't long before he was approached and asked if his horses were for sale by a traveller he had come to know over the years, one that he knew he could trust, as he took his hand and shook it warmly.

'I saw you making your way through the crowds and

I thought I'd give you time to set yourself up,' the Romany, Noah Arigho, said and looked at Reuben. 'You've fine beasts, as ever. Your young filly looks fit – is she broken in? Not that it matters, as I'd soon have her thinking my way. The piebald has got good feathering: a right handsome boyo,' Noah said.

'Aye, she's broken in – they all are, and the hard work's been done.' Reuben walked over with Noah to the four horses, where the gypsy checked their teeth and felt down their legs, then asked Reuben to run up and down the hill with each individually, to see if they moved well.

'I'm getting too old for this running with horses,' said Reuben as he bent over and caught his breath while Noah paced around the horses.

'Your dun horse is lame in the off hind leg – looks like she might be starting laminitis?' Noah said, picking up the dun's back leg and staring at its hoof. 'We'll soon cure that, but I'm not going to offer you the full price.'

'Now why aren't I surprised to hear that? Every year you tell me there's something wrong with one of my horses, and then I hear on the grapevine how much more you've made for them, after screwing me down to the lowest price.' Reuben grinned at his friend, who he knew was telling him the truth; he'd noticed the lameness, and put it down to laminitis, as he'd made his way from Arkengarthdale and had nearly thought better of selling her.

'Twenty for the three and fifteen for the dun; she might need a bit of time on her, no matter what you say. That's seventy-five pounds in your back pocket – it's not to be turned down lightly,' Noah said and held out his hand to be shaken.

'Nay, you know she's fit. Call it at least twenty for her, as she's a bonny mare and foals with no bother. It's eighty, else I walk away. There's plenty here that knows my horses are bred well, and regardless of my mare being a bit lame, they'd still give me my asking price,' Reuben said, then offered his hand to seal the deal.

'Seventy-nine, and a drink in The Swan later tonight when you are celebrating the news I've got to tell you.' Noah spat in his hand and grinned at his longtime friend.

'You drive a hard bargain, and you always end up getting the better of me. Seventy-nine it is, but I'll need more than an odd gill, at that price. At least I know your money is good, not like some of the notes being used, especially to the locals.' Reuben spat in his own hand and shook Noah's firmly, then patted him on the back. 'You take care of my horses, especially the little piebald filly, as she'll grow into a beaut.'

Reuben watched as Noah peeled seventy-nine pounds from the thickest wedge of money that he had seen in a long time and passed it to him; he quickly put it into a concealed pocket in the inside of his long coat.

'Now, what's the news that you've got to tell me? Let me guess: you've got a woman at long last, even though you smell like a rotting fish,' Reuben joked and grinned at Noah, relieved that his business had been done so easily and that he had been given a reasonable price for his horses.

'Now don't be getting hot-headed about what I'm

going to say. But I know you are still looking for the lass that has ruled your life for so long. I saw two of her brothers come to the fair – there was no mistaking them, even though I've not seen them for years. They have parked their vardo a bit away from everybody else; down under the hedge on the northern side of the ground you'll find them. But before you go off like a lurcher, take my advice: as you say, you are not in the first flush of youth, so don't take them on, no matter what they say to you. And if Vadoma is there, don't make trouble for her. She'll have had no life since you had your way with her.' Noah looked at his friend and saw the flash of wildness that always burned in Reuben's eyes and wondered if he had done right by telling him that the Faa brothers were there.

'Bloody hell, I never thought I'd hear those words, Noah, and I thought I'd lost her for ever.' Reuben grinned and patted Noah on the shoulder. 'That news is worth any payment for my horses. I'd gladly have given you them, to hear those words,' Reuben said and glanced over to where Noah had said their vardo was parked.

'Aye, don't be doing owt rash. Keep your head, else those lads will knock it from your shoulders again. I want to see you here next year for some hosses, to make me a good profit,' Noah said, but knew there would be no holding Reuben back from tackling the Faa brothers, as he untied the four horses' tethers and stood with them.

'I'll not be as brash this time. Besides, what can they do to me? They've already tried to kill me, and Vadoma might be married and might have left them. Every year

286

I have searched these fairs for her, just to get a glance of her and to know she is happy,' Reuben said. He wished Noah would get gone; he could waste no more time talking to him, when Vadoma might well be only a stone's throw away.

'Well, take care, my friend. I'll see you in The Swan tonight, unless your plans are changed – as long as I'll not be finding you dead in a ditch. I value your horses and your friendship too much.' Noah grinned and shouted, '*Dja devlesa, but baxt tuke*' – 'Goodbye and good luck' – as he walked away with the horses following him, ploughing a furrow through the crowds as he went.

Reuben didn't care that he had sold his horses cheaply. Vadoma was calling him and he would find her.

He stood for a while and watched the two brothers coming in and out of their vardo. There was no sign of anybody else, but the brothers looked tougher and larger than Reuben had remembered. He'd be a fool, he thought, if he were to pick a fight with them on his own, as he had done all those years ago. Age had made him wiser, so as he approached them while they sat on the steps of their vardo with a dish of stew in their hands, from the black pot that was cooking on an open fire in front of the van, he stepped forward with caution. He held his hands up and glanced at both brothers, who regarded him and then one another, but continued eating.

'I don't want to make any bother, but is Vadoma with you both? I need to see her, whether you wish me to or not. I need to know she's alright,' Reuben said and stared

287

at both men. The oldest brother, whom he remembered being the most violent towards him, looked up, with stew running down his chin.

'Did you not learn your lesson? We thought we had left you for dead. We should have made sure, rather than let you keep your life, with the shame that you brought to our family,' Jacob Faa growled.

'I'm not going to cause bother. I just want to know if I can see her – is she alright?' Reuben said. He still kept his distance, but felt his heart beating fast and the adrenalin pulsing through his veins.

'Well, you can't see her, as she's not with us. Now bugger off before we knock some more sense into that head of yours.' Jacob stopped eating for a moment and looked at the man he hated.

'I only want to see if Vadoma's alright – that she's well – and to give her my best,' Reuben said and moved forward towards both brothers, trying to peer into their vardo.

Jacob looked at his brother as he placed down his tin plate of stew. 'Well, she ain't. She's dead – gone out of our lives, thanks to you,' he said callously as he looked at his dish, not even glancing up at Reuben, while his brother did exactly the same.

'Dead? How and why – how long ago?' Reuben felt his heart breaking. His love was under the earth and he hadn't known. He'd never see Vadoma again. His searching was at an end, along with his will to live. 'You've got to tell me,' Reuben pleaded and watched as Jacob glanced up, stood up to his full height and looked at him.

'She's dead, and that is all you need to know. Now bugger off before I lose my temper.'

It was pointless picking a fight with the brute. His Vadoma was dead and there was nothing he could do, so Reuben walked back to his flat cart, with an ache in his heart that he had never felt so badly before.

Under the tarpaulin cover later that night he drank himself into a stupor on a bottle of whisky bought at the fair from an Irish gypsy. It warmed him and dulled the pain, as he remembered Vadoma's loving face and her kind touches. To make things worse, one of the notes that Noah had given him was a fake, when he had looked at it. 'Bloody thieving gypsies,' he swore under his breath. Hopefully he'd be able to sort the note out with Noah in the morning, but it left him thinking hard about his life. Perhaps it was time to settle down to farming Punchard like his brothers with stupid sheep, as horses and women had led him astray all his life. Well, now the love of his life had gone for ever. A light that had shone so brightly had been extinguished.

Chapter 21

'Well, I don't know why you had to close all the weekend. I could have died of thirst and nobody would have bothered,' Jake complained and looked up at Ruby as she placed his drink in front of him.

'I needed some time to myself. I've been finding it hard since Martha died, running this place on my own. Besides, everybody was at the Brough Hill Fair this weekend. I've seen many a family trundling past the inn, as well as the travellers and gypsies. So hold your noise, Jake.' Ruby looked down at the old man, who was always complaining, and wished he would shut up. Ever since Saturday night and the Harvest Supper dance at Kirkby Stephen she had been mad with herself for falling for such a trick from James, and was hoping that Tom would not hear about the stupid situation she had found herself in.

'Alright, lass, I'm just saying I've never known the Tan Hill to be closed over a weekend. It's your loss, after all.' Jake took a sip from his drink and watched as Ruby went into the kitchen without saying another word to him.

Ruby leaned over the sink. Her stomach was churning, and she put it down to the nerves she was feeling, knowing that she had nearly cheated on Tom with a man who had simply been leading her astray. She'd not slept all weekend, tossing and turning and feeling a fool, as she thought of what she had nearly thrown away, for the sake of James Robinson's good looks. It would serve her right if Tom walked in tonight and said that his love for her had gone, as she had been such a fool.

'Ruby! Ruby, pour us an ale, lass,' Rob yelled from the main room.

'Aye, I'm coming. Just give us a minute,' Ruby shouted back at him. She wiped a tear from her cheek and gave herself a good cursing for being so badly hurt by a man who was not worth the time of day.

'Are you alright, lass, you look a bit peaky?' Rob watched as she poured him his drink. 'Is that why you've had the weekend closed? You were missed.'

'She says she's tired,' Jake butted in.

'Aye, dear, you've not had any time to mourn Martha's passing. You've had it hard, and then us devils expect you to be here every minute of every day. Well, I can tell you that you'll have one less to serve of an evening, although you'll miss his brass, as he's been spending a good bit of time in here of late. James Robinson has buggered off. Foreman knocked on his cottage door and he's not to be found. He's probably realized that it's not worth his while being away from his wife and bairns,

291

and that he can make more money from lead mining for the Owd Gang – they are the biggest group of lead miners over the hill in Swaledale. Still, you'd think he'd have the manners to tell the gaffer,' Rob said and looked across at Jake.

'I never did like him – nothing but a gobby shite. You are better off without him.' Jake stared out of the window as he heard the sound of horses and the metal rims of a vardo pass by on the road and watched until it was nearly out of view. 'They are on their way back for another year. It must be back end; it'll be snowing before you know it.'

'Aye, now Brough Hill Fair's been and gone, you can say hello to winter. The gypos know when to go south, or back to Ireland and Europe. Even they don't appreciate being frozen to the sides of their wagons with their own steam. I sometimes think I should move further down the dale and take my old lass with me. The mines are nearly worked out, and who in their right mind would choose to live up here if they didn't have to?'

'I'll never leave here,' Ruby said and looked around her. 'When I went to my father's, I missed being here. I just didn't realize how attached I was to this place until I left it.' She shook her head.

'Your father will have been wheeling and dealing at Brough Hill. He seems to make his money at these fairs with his horses – the gypsies never seem to do him out of his money. My old lass always has a kind word for the one that comes around at this time every year, selling her pegs and good-luck charms and such, which you women seem to always need.' Rob went quiet, realizing that perhaps he had said too much.

'Yes, she should be coming, and I'm in need of some pegs and perhaps a bunch of white heather for a bit of good luck.' Ruby gazed out of the window at the darkening skies. She didn't know if Tom would be coming to see her or not tonight, but she hoped to see his welcoming face. No sooner had she thought of him than she saw Tom leading his horse around the back to the stable. He was with her again, she thought, as she heard the latch on the back door lift and a voice that she was so glad to hear, as she turned round and welcomed him with a kiss.

'I should happen to stay away a bit more often, if that's the welcome I get.' Tom grinned and held her tightly.

'Aye, it was a bit forward, but I wouldn't say no to being greeted like that,' Jake said, then went and sat back down with Rob. They both chuckled and whispered as they watched the young couple.

'I'm glad you are here – I've missed you,' Ruby said and caressed his jacket lapels as she looked into Tom's eyes.

'Aye, I've missed you as well. I couldn't get here fast enough. Plus, I'm glad to get out of your father's way, as he's in a right state with himself. I've never known him like he is. He's hit the bottle and won't get out of his bed, and when he is out of his bed, he's acting like a madman and he's not even bothered about his horses. I don't know what's gone on at Brough Hill Fair, but

293

something has made him change.' Tom looked at Ruby and hoped she would offer to come and see what ailed the usually active Reuben.

'He'll have had a bad deal or something. Did he return with some of his horses – could that be it?' Ruby asked.

'No, he sold them, although he was cursing over being given a fake note. Although when he'd gone and challenged the fella that had given it to him, he apologized and refunded him. But it is more than that. I'm wondering if it has something to do with your mother, as it is only her that would make him act this way. Perhaps he found her and she's rejected him. I just don't know!' Tom sighed.

'I'll come and see him first thing in the morning, before I need to open up here. I'll ride down on Thistle – it will do me and the horse good to have a ride out. Although if my father is in such a way with himself, he will not tell me anything, but I'll try and find out what is wrong with him,' Ruby said and saw the worry on Tom's face. 'It'll be something or nothing, don't worry.'

'No, I think it's something bad, as he's never taken to his bed before or drunk at home. Something has really upset him to make him turn on himself. He's usually a strong man. It will do him good to see you; it'll stop him from feeling sorry for himself, whatever the reason.' Tom looked up as a bunch of miners from the coal mine came in and wanted serving.

'I'll find out what's wrong with him in the morning. Now, don't worry – everything will be alright. Can you help me serve, do you think, and then we will talk more later?' Ruby smiled and turned to her customers.

'Aye, that's what I'm here for, as well as to see you, once everyone drinks up and goes home. I've thought of nothing else but you all weekend while your father's been away.' Tom watched Ruby blush as she thought about lying in his arms while she poured one of the miners a drink of ale.

'I'll close early if I can. I've been waiting for you as well,' she whispered as she took the miner's money and turned to her next customer. She smiled at Tom as he rolled up his sleeves to serve some of her customers.

'Now then, what's up, Father? Tom says you are not yourself,' Ruby said to Reuben as she watched him sit next to the fire and hardly bother to look at her, once Tom left him and her alone.

'He needn't have said anything to you – it's nowt to do with him,' Reuben mumbled and glanced darkly at Ruby.

'But it is, if you are not yourself. Now what's wrong? We are both worried about you.' Ruby bent down at Reuben's side and took his hand. 'This isn't you – you don't look as if you have washed or shaved this last day or two, or slept, by the look of the bags under your eyes.'

Reuben put his head in his hands and broke down. 'I've lost her – I've lost my Vadoma, your mother. She's dead; her brother said she is dead! I've searched for her all these years and now I'll never see her again, not in this world anyway.' Reuben sobbed and glanced at Ruby. 'I'm sorry, I'm being selfish. She was your mother, but you never met her, so you don't know what she was like:

295

the life she had in her, and the love she had in her. Although you have many of the same traits as her. I see it when you look at Tom, and I know how lucky he is to have you. But she's gone, lass, and my hope and searching are over.' Reuben sat back in his chair and stared at the disbelief on his daughter's face.

'I don't know what to say, as I know you are heart-broken. It must have been a shock. Were they sure? When did she die, and where is she buried at?' Ruby asked and watched her father in his grief.

'All they said was that Vadoma is dead, and I was that taken aback I didn't ask any more. When I went to find her brothers the following morning, when I'd pulled myself together, they had disappeared into the autumn mists,' Reuben said and put his head back in his hands.

Ruby looked at her father and said, 'I don't know how I feel. Am I supposed to mourn, even though I never knew her, even though everyone says that I am the image of her? I'm sorry, Father, as I know you loved her and will always love her.' Ruby stretched out and hugged her father, something she had never done before, and felt embarrassed that the hard Dalesman was sobbing into her shoulder, broken by the news that his one true love had died and his world had fallen apart.

Tom, who had stood listening quietly in the doorway, came forward. 'So your mother's passed. Sorry, I couldn't help but hear as I came in,' he said as he came and stood next to father and daughter and looked at them both with pity.

'Aye, it would seem so. That's what's been wrong with

296

my father. Vadoma's brothers told him at Brough Hill Fair,' Ruby said as she wiped a tear away, for the mother she now would never meet.

'I should have known. You should have told me what was wrong. I know how much she meant to you.' Tom stood and watched the man who had always treated him like a son, rather than a groom and stable boy.

'I'm sorry, lad, I've been lost in grief. My heart has been torn out for a second time, but now at least I have my lass to remind me of our shared love. I should be grateful for that, instead of feeling sorry for myself.' Reuben hung on to Ruby's hand as she got up from her knees, then smiled at her.

'Aye, well. I don't mind you feeling sorry for yourself, but I've never known you drink like you have this last night or two, and you aren't the pleasantest of fellas when you do. I've just kept myself clear of you, else I might have lost my head.' Tom decided to tell Reuben that he wasn't impressed with his latest behaviour, whether he liked it or not. 'If you'd said what was wrong, I'd have understood.' He looked at Ruby as she got a loaf out of the bag that she had brought with her and started to make her father some bread and cheese, along with a strong cup of tea.

'I take it that you haven't eaten, either. You get some of this inside you, and I'll see to it that you have a wash before I return home. I can still smell campfires and horses on you, and that is not you at all,' Ruby said.

She took control of the kitchen while Reuben sat and felt sorry for himself, but realized that life had to go on,

297

whether he wanted it to or not. Tom and Ruby would make sure it did, even if he didn't want it to, he thought, as he sipped his tea and took a bite of the newly baked bread that Ruby had brought him. It was just as well that he had found her when he did. What he would do now, he didn't know, but life was not as inviting as it had been when Vadoma was alive.

Ruby was late leaving her father's as she galloped back up the moorland road to the Tan Hill Inn. It was nearly one o'clock and she'd have lost dinner-time customers, but that was the last thing on her mind as she urged Thistle on. Not only had she lost Martha, but she had now lost her birth mother, and even though she had never met Vadoma, it still hurt, thinking that she now would never meet the woman who had meant the world to her father.

Reuben had been coming round as she left him, but Ruby could tell that the light that had kept his eyes burning had left him. He had loved his Vadoma deeply and true, and his world had collapsed, with the hope that he'd see her once again now banished. Ruby reined Thistle in as she neared the inn, slipping off her unsaddled back and leading her to her tethering place on the moor, leaving her to graze once she had taken the bridle off and coupled Thistle to her tether. She patted the horse on her neck and turned to make her way into the inn to start her day serving her customers, no matter whether her heart was in it or not.

The edge of the moorland was aflutter with drying clothes on washing lines. Monday was the traditional washing day for the miners' wives, and various shirts and blouses were blowing in the fresh moorland air. Just down from the clothes lines, not fifty yards away from the cottages and inn, stood a vardo with a piebald horse tethered beside it, already eating the herbs of the moorland contentedly. Ruby glanced quickly at the occupant before she opened the door to the inn; it was the usual gypsy who called every year at the inn and miners' cottages with her pegs and charms. Like the coming of the seasons, she was to be relied upon, along with the Miller family, who came a little later in the year with blankets, sheets and rugs to be haggled over.

No doubt the gypsy would be visiting her with her wares in the next few days, and Ruby would stock up on pegs and different kinds of cotton until next year, when she looked at her goods. A lot of places did not like hawkers and gypsies, but at the Tan Hill Inn they were welcome, their goods being a novelty to folk who hardly went anywhere for months on end. The gypsy would be made welcome, just as Martha had made her welcome in years past, and perhaps be offered a bowl of food, if she asked for one as she had done on previous occasions. Martha had always felt sorry for her and her ageing mother, who seemed to have no man in their lives.

Ruby looked up and smiled as the first customers came in. She couldn't show her pain at losing two mothers in a year. Life went on at the inn, whether she wanted it to or not, she thought, as she listened to the complaints about the inn not being open on time and that it would never have happened if Martha had been alive. If only they stood in her shoes for a day or two they would not complain, she thought, as she stirred the vegetable broth, bulked out with pearl barley, which she had left simmering over the open fire. Even her father could not be relied upon, now that his heart was forever broken. But at least she had her trusty Tom and she knew he loved her, and she now realized how much she loved him. He was hard-working, reliable, handsome and, most of all, true to her – and she had found out that was to be relished and not scoffed at.

Thank heavens she had learned in time about James Robinson, else her life would have taken another turn for the worse, and she would probably have ended up losing Tom and her father, if they had found out about him.

Chapter 22

Ruby took Thistle and the inn's horse a bucket of bran each, and stood and looked at them as they both buried their noses in the buckets.

'She's a grand horse, is your piebald – must have cost you a good bit of money?' The gypsy woman stood and admired the horse with Ruby as she walked, then gazed at both the horse and the young woman.

Ruby stared at the woman, whose dark hair was covered with a shawl and her face partly obscured, as she held her shawl in place. Her skirts jingled and jangled as the small circles of brass and bells adorning her garments caught the wind. Bangles and beads lay around her neck and wrist, and she leaned forward and patted Thistle as she ate her bran.

'My father gifted her to me – he loves his horses.'

'Your father, you say? I thought you lost your father a few years back, if I remember,' the gypsy woman said and looked at her, with her face still partly covered as she pulled her shawl over it.

'No, that was my adoptive father. My true father found me this winter, after not knowing my whereabouts since I was born. It was very thoughtful of him, and he is a kind person. I've grown to love him dearly since we have found one another,' Ruby said. She felt tears coming to her eyes as she stood next to her horse and the gypsy.

'I've not seen your mother – is she well?' the gypsy asked.

'No, my adoptive mother passed away this summer, and I've never known my true mother,' Ruby said quietly. 'Is your mother with you this year? She usually comes with you, and you seem to be on your own this year, like me?' Ruby took away the buckets from both horses and patted them, then looked at the gypsy.

'No, I too lost my mother. We are both on our own, it would seem. We are both adrift in the sea of life. If it would help, you could give me your hand and I will read your palm and see what your future holds. It seems to me that perhaps both of us are in need of new directions in our lives,' the gypsy said and held out her hand for Ruby to put hers into.

'I don't know – I don't believe in suchlike. How can you tell me anything about my future just by looking at my palm?' Ruby stood still and stared at the woman, who was an outcast from polite society, yet seemed so caring. Although she visited annually, Ruby realized that she had never seen the woman without the shawl covering her face, no matter what the weather, as the gypsy pulled it once again around her face and motioned for her hand.

'I can read your past and your future: both are intertwined and have been since the day you were born. Please give me your hand, and I will guide your future. I don't expect payment; this is in gratitude for you and your adoptive mother treating me right every year when I visited in the past,' the gypsy said.

She took Ruby's right hand gently in hers, as Ruby dropped the buckets she was holding.

'I see that you are happy here. You have had heartache, but you have always known love in your life, even though you ache to find your true roots.' The gypsy ran her fingers over the lines on Ruby's palm. 'There is a new love in your life, one who truly loves you, but there has also been temptation in your life. But, looking deeper, I feel that perhaps he has gone now. Which is just as well, as there is going to be much change in your life shortly.' The gypsy stared at her as Ruby pulled her hand away.

'How can you tell all this? I don't want to hear any more. You have said enough,' Ruby replied. She walked away quickly from the woman who seemed to know her inner secrets and had spoken of things that only she herself knew. She marched determinedly into the inn, leaving the two buckets outside, and sat down in one of the chairs, then watched out of the window as the gypsy woman walked back to her vardo.

She had felt something strange when the woman had taken her hand and for a second, when she had caught a full view of her face, she had seen the kindness in it – kindness and concern, which she had never seen on her face before. But more worryingly, she had seen a likeness to herself: a true reminder that she came from gypsy stock. Perhaps she was imagining things; ever since she had found out that her mother had been a gypsy she'd had a growing sympathy with the travellers and gypsies. She shook her head. The woman was playing on her feelings, that was all. She probably said the same thing to every young woman whose palm she read.

Ruby sat back in the chair as she felt her stomach churn once again. The stress and worry of running the Tan Hill Inn were playing on her mind, she thought as she closed her eyes, only to keep seeing the face of the gypsy. She opened them to find that same face looking down at her, with sympathy and softness on it.

'I'm sorry, I think I offended you – perhaps I said too much,' the gypsy said softly.

'I never heard you come in. I was resting, as I was feeling tired. No, you didn't offend me. I just don't understand how you know what I was thinking,' Ruby said and gazed at the woman who she felt she knew.

'Perhaps it is time for the truth to be told, especially as the next generation is stirring in your belly. Do you know you are with child?'

Ruby looked down at her stomach and gasped. How could she have been so stupid! Of course she was with child. She'd started feeling sick at the sight of certain things, especially in the mornings, and she was so tired. She had put it down to working so hard and all the upset in her life. But yes, now she realized that her monthly visitor had disappeared, it all made sense.

'How did you know? I didn't even realize. I thought I had been under strain lately and that was what was wrong with me,' Ruby said. She didn't know whether to laugh or cry at the predicament she found herself in. All she could think of was how thankful she was that she had not been led further astray by James Robinson, and that the baby could only be Tom's. She looked up at the gypsy's eyes. 'But you said it was perhaps time for the truth to be told – what do you mean by that?' Ruby asked.

The gypsy pulled back the scarf from her head, revealing long greying hair that had once been as black as jet, and kind eyes in a weathered face. Ruby stared at her hard: she recognized that face!

'Now that you are with child, and you have found your father, it is the right time for me to step forward and put to rest all the pain that a young couple so madly in love made, with their selfishness, before history repeats itself.' The gypsy sat down beside Ruby and looked at her, with love in her eyes. 'I am Vadoma Faa, and it is I who left you on these very steps and hoped that the woman here would be good enough to take you to your father. I'm your mother, Ruby. It was I who gave you your name and placed the bracelet that is on your arm with you, for safekeeping.' Vadoma reached out for her daughter's hands, with tears in her eyes.

'You can't be – you are dead! Your brothers told my father so.' Ruby looked at the woman, but deep down she knew she was telling the truth. Her face was the same as her own, her eyes were as dark as hers: this woman truly was her mother. 'You have called here every year for as long as I can remember. Why have you not told me this before?'

Ruby gazed at her mother and wanted to hug her, but at the same time she had to question why Vadoma had not made herself known earlier. There were so many questions she wanted to ask her. Her heart beat fast; not only had she found out that she was soon going to be a mother, but she had found the mother she had longed for, for so long. Her head spun with the news, and she felt herself standing and staring at the woman in disbelief.

'My brothers will have said that to your father because, to them, I am dead. If I had kept you, my family would never have treated you as well as the life you had here. Every year I watched the love that Martha devoted to you, and despite her not doing as I wished, I knew you'd come to no harm here at the Tan Hill. I've waited my time to be free of my brothers, who hated your father. After my mother's death this spring, they decided to abandon me, so I have set out on my own quest in life. I need to put right nearly twenty years of hurt by making myself known to you and finding your father, who I've never stopped loving.' Vadoma sighed, her eyes filling up with tears. 'Forgive me, Ruby, not a day has passed that I didn't think of you and the life I could have had with Reuben, if we had been let be.'

'I can forgive you, as you did what was best for me. But my father's heart has been broken since the day you disappeared, and he's never married. He's been trying to find you for so long, and at this moment he thinks you dead. He has been drinking himself into a stupor these last few days, since talking to your brothers at Brough

Hill.' Ruby stood up next to her mother and they looked at one another.

'My brothers are cruel men. They knew that would hurt him more than him losing his own life. I am glad I am rid of them. Now it is time for us to get to know one another. You are the image of your father – he is such a handsome man,' Vadoma said and moved forward to put her arms around the daughter she had always loved. She had watched Ruby growing up into a fine young woman every year that she had passed the inn on the busy highway between Westmorland and the North Pennines.

'He says I'm the image of you,' Ruby sobbed. 'Perhaps I'm a good mix of you both – just as it should be.' She wrapped her arms around her newly found mother and smelt the wild mountain air and the peat fires in her hair. This was her mother – her true mother, the mysterious Vadoma Faa; the woman she had always known about, but hadn't realized who she was. She'd watched her come and go every year, selling her pegs and trinkets; she'd even played with a brightly coloured peg doll that the woman had given her when she was a toddler. She'd always been there, but Martha and she had never known her identity; and, more importantly, her father had never known.

Now both her father and mother were back in her life, and she had her own family growing inside her. Telling her father that his true love was back was of the utmost importance, even before breaking the news to Tom that he was soon to become a father.

'We've got to tell my father that you have found us. He'll not know what to do with himself. He's been looking for you for so long and never found you or your family, despite going to all the places that he knew you'd be at,' Ruby said and stared at her mother.

'I love that man so much. No matter what my brothers said and did to me, I kept my love for him true. They could never take away the hope that one day I would be back in his arms. Is he still living with his mother and family at Banksgill? His mother never thought me good enough for her precious son, so I'm hoping that he has broken away from his family, seeing that he has now got you in his life.' Vadoma smiled and touched the bracelet on her daughter's arm – the bracelet that had been given with such love, despite all that had been said against their love by both sides of the family.

'He's living on his own farm, just a few miles down Arkengarthdale. We must go and see him – he'll not believe it when he sees you.' Ruby wiped her tears away, suddenly gathering her thoughts together.

'Oh, I don't know. I have loved him for so long, and I know you say that he still loves me, but I'm no longer the carefree young woman he fell in love with. He'll only be disappointed by my looks,' Vadoma said and hung her head.

'My father is not that shallow. He'd love you no matter what you looked like. It is like I say – he has never stopped loving you,' Ruby replied and hugged her mother close. 'Come, I'll saddle Thistle and we will ride to his farm together. I can't wait for him to see you. It will also

308

be welcoming news for Tom, my sweetheart. Since my father's return from Brough he's been near-impossible to work for.' Ruby laughed and wiped away yet another tear, before grabbing her shawl and pulling on her mother's hand. 'Come, we will surprise him together. I can't wait to see his face.'

Vadoma held tight to Ruby's waist as Thistle was urged on down Arkengarthdale. 'It's easy to see where you get your skills in horsemanship,' Vadoma said, as Ruby pulled on the reins to slow her steed down as they started their way up the farm track. 'So this is where your father is living. It's not as grand as Banksgill, but I can see him being happy here, surrounded by his horses and being his own boss. Oh, Ruby, perhaps I should not be here. I should have stayed out of both of your lives – it would have been for the best. The years will have changed us both. Stop and take me back to my vardo.'

But Ruby did not listen. She kicked her heels into the side of Thistle, making it impossible for Vadoma to dismount and change her mind as she entered the farm-yard, scaring the hens, which were busy going about their daily business of looking for worms amongst the chick-weed, and making them cluck in alarm.

'What on earth is going on?' Her father opened the farmhouse door and stared at his daughter and her pillion rider, as a shaft of autumn light danced – as if in joy of the moment – across the wooden floorboards of the kitchen. He watched as Ruby dismounted and helped the woman beside her off the horse's back, then he held his breath as he saw the two women embracing.

'No, no, it can't be. Vadoma! Vadoma, is that you? It can't be – I thought you were dead! You are here, with our daughter: I can't believe my eyes.' Reuben stepped quickly across the farmyard and looked at the woman he loved, and had always loved. He grabbed her and held her tightly. 'Oh, my love; my love, it has been so long. I've missed you so much.' He cupped her face and kissed her over and over again. 'And you are still as beautiful,' he whispered as he stroked her long locks.

Ruby stood back and watched as Vadoma and her father held one another and whispered, sobbing and holding each other tightly. Vadoma whispered to Reuben in a language that Ruby had never heard spoken before, but she knew it was only words of love that were coming from her mouth as Vadoma kissed him.

Reuben turned to Ruby. 'How did you find her? I thought her dead.'

'It turns out that she's never been far away – she's visited me every year. My mother has always been here, it's just that I've never known until now.' Ruby looked at the two people, who she could tell still loved one another, and noticed Tom with a pitchfork in his hand, standing in the doorway of the barn. She smiled. 'I'll leave you together for a while. I need to catch my breath and talk to Tom.'

Her mother and father embraced, still in love after all these years, as she had known they would be. It was as if they had never been apart as they walked into the farmhouse together. Now it was time to tell Tom her news and to hope that he would be as faithful as her father had been to her mother.

310

'Is that your mother? I thought her to be dead! She is a bonny woman – no wonder your father's heart belonged to her.' Tom put down his pitchfork and reached for Thistle's reins. 'You rode this poor devil hard: he'll need towelling down,' he said as Ruby pulled on his arm.

'Leave him for a minute, there's something more important I've to tell you,' Ruby said. She pulled him towards the field gate, where they both stood and stared across at the opposite fellside. 'Tom, I've not only found my mother today, but I've also got some news for you.' She looked at Tom and felt her stomach churn; would he stand by her or would he want nothing more to do with her? 'I'm having a baby, Tom – our baby.' Ruby put her hand on her stomach and gazed with love at Tom as he shook his head.

'A baby – our baby?' Tom grinned and then ran his fingers through his hair and stood back. 'Well, we'd better get a wedding planned.' He held Ruby tightly and kissed her. 'It's a hell of a day. I didn't expect this when I woke up and got cursed at by your father, because of his black mood. Oh Lord, what will your father say? He'll bloody kill me.'

Chapter 23

Ruby made her way outside the Tan Hill Inn and walked across to the vardo that had been her mother's home for so long as she travelled the roads and hedgerows of the countryside. She sat on the caravan's steps and listened to the horse munching the moorland grass, and heard the skylarks flying up above her head. She'd now found her mother and her father, and she knew her parentage good and proper; in fact she had been loved by two sets of parents all her life, but had not known it.

She put her hand on her stomach and thought about the other news. Tom had been over the moon when she had left him, despite dreading telling her father the news. A tear trickled down her cheek and she brushed it away. In truth, she was frightened. She was young to be with child, and what if her father decided Tom was not good enough for her? After all, he'd warned the two of them against being intimate with one another, and now they were in trouble, just as he had predicted.

She got to her feet and decided to quell her worries. Tom loved her, he was standing by her, and her father could not be too hard on either of them; after all, he had done the same thing, so all would be well. She looked at the open door of the vardo and climbed the wooden steps into the bow-roofed wagon, staring around her. It was dark inside, with only the main door and a small window at the back of the wagon letting in light. At the back, under the window, was a bed covered with a patchwork quilt, and on the other side was a trestle and cupboards. From the roof hung herbs drying, and the shelves of the caravan were filled with jars of potions and food. On a small table there was a wicker basket filled with the hand-carved pegs and bunches of white heather that she or Martha had bought every year from Vadoma, without realizing her true identity. This was how her birth mother had been living. Some people would look at it with a romantic eye, and others would spit at the sight of the gypsy's arrival.

Without Ruby hearing them, Vadoma and her father had arrived outside the vardo to take it back to Banksgill.

'Do you like my home?' Vadoma stood quietly on the step leading into the wagon, watching her daughter as she peered around it.

'It's very small, but you have everything you need. I'm sorry, I hope you don't mind me looking in. I've never been inside a caravan before,' Ruby said. She felt embarrassed that she had been caught being nosy.

'Oh yes, you have, but you will not remember. You were born right there, in that bed. My mother – your grandmother, Roma – helped me bring you into the world.

313

She lifted you up and slapped your pink bottom and smiled as you wailed, happy in the knowledge that your lungs worked all too well.' Vadoma smiled. 'I remember holding you close to me and wishing that your father was with me, to protect us both, and for me to be able to keep you. I didn't know that my brothers had left him for near-dead in the gutter. They told me to forget him, to get rid of you, and then we would be on our way back down the country. My heart ached as I left you for Reuben on the step of the inn, and my mother watched me for days, frightened that I would take my own life or try to return for you. She knew how much my heart ached,' Vadoma said quietly.

'I'm sorry. I know my father would have come for you if he'd been able. He's always thought of you,' Ruby said and looked at her mother as she sat down at the trestle.

'Tom has told him that you are with child. Don't be afraid, my child; he was angry at first, but now he's at peace and is urging Tom to set a date for your marriage.' Vadoma held her daughter's hand and smiled. 'I think it will be a boy – a strong, healthy boy – as good-looking as his grandfather.'

'I thought Father would be angry at first, but he always seemed to accept that Tom, his stable hand, and I are made for one another. And Tom is definitely the baby's father. Father's watched over us both the last few months, so I don't suppose it will have come as a great surprise to him to be told I'm with child. I just feel that perhaps I have disappointed him and he will be ashamed of me.' Ruby hung her head.

'Your father will never be ashamed of you. And who

314

is he to judge, when we did the same thing? Love makes you have no sense – we both know that.' Vadoma smiled. 'Not only am I to become your mother, but I am looking forward to being a grandmother, now that I know my Reuben still loves me.'

Ruby glanced at Vadoma. She knew that, given time, they would grow as close as a proper mother and daughter should be. They both left the vardo and watched Reuben unhitch Vadoma's horse and hitch it up to the caravan.

'Well, lass, tha's picked a fine time to find yourself with child. A week ago and I'd have picked up my gun and threatened to shoot that no-good Tom. As it is, and with Vadoma by my side telling me it will be a blessing, I might just forgive you both. I told him to keep it in his pocket.' Reuben scowled, then held his arms out to embrace his daughter. 'We are all here for one another now – things are right in all our lives. I wish you and that lad all the best.' He squeezed Ruby tightly and then let go of her. 'Now I've wanted to say these words all my life to you, my Vadoma. It's time you came home with me, to stay and always be here by my side.' Reuben looked at both of his women.

'And I've always wanted to walk by your side to our home together. My days of wandering are over.' Vadoma pushed her arm through Reuben's and kissed him on the cheek.

'Then let's go home, where we both belong.'

Ruby sat next to Tom and gazed at the valley below them. All around them the moorland was ablaze with the purples and reds of the blooming heather. She placed her head on his shoulder and squeezed his hand. 'I love you. We are going to be alright, aren't we?'

'Aye, of course we are. The wedding date is set, and you are keeping well. We have nothing but good things to look forward to.' Tom kissed Ruby on her forehead and put his hand on her stomach. 'I can't wait for this one to show itself. Do you think it's a boy or a girl?'

'My mother says it's a boy. She'll be right; she knew I was expecting before I had realized. She just knows things, and I don't know how. And I've never known my father so happy – it's like a huge weight has been lifted from his shoulders.' Ruby stared out across the valley as the cooling autumn winds blew through her long black hair.

'He's a different man since Vadoma came back into his life. He's been missing her all that time, and I'm glad he's found her. He gave me a good dressing-down when I told him we were to marry because he was going to be a grandfather. I thought he'd have knocked me into the other side of next week when I stood in front of him. But instead he slapped me on the back and asked when the wedding was.' Tom laughed.

'I'm glad we told him,' Ruby said and put her arm around Tom, holding him tightly to get some warmth from his body and his jacket.

'Come on, you are cold, let's get back to the inn. Warm you through and get ready for our customers,' Tom said. He stood up and pulled Ruby to her feet.

'*Our* customers, is it, Tom Adams? A few weeks ago you didn't know a jug from a gill, and now you are claiming the Tan Hill as yours.' Ruby grinned.

'Well, your mother's done me out of a job, and your father hardly knows me these days, whereas you do. We'll make a good pair running the inn together. Things had to happen as they have done. Life has a way of sorting itself out eventually.' Tom took Ruby's hand and they walked across the moorland towards the Tan Hill Inn, with the smoke coming from its chimney up into the clear blue autumn sky.

'This is our home now – a home for both of us and our child. My baby will never be a foundling. I was a foundling, and I was always loved and cared for,' Ruby said, then stood and looked at the man she loved and was about to be married to.

'Aye, and I'll always be there for you, and this one. The Tan Hill is in safe hands and will always make travellers welcome as they pass our doors,' Tom replied as they walked together into the inn.

Ruby stood for a second and gazed out across the moorland and at the busy miners' cottages. This would always be her home, and home to her family. She was no longer the foundling of Tan Hill. She was soon to be Mrs Ruby Adams, the landlady and the wife of Tom, the landlord of the inn. And all was well in her world and that of her father.

The Mistress of Windfell Manor

DIANE ALLEN

Charlotte Booth loves her father and the home they share, which is set high up in the limestone escarpments of Crummockdale. But when a new businessman in the form of Joseph Dawson enters their lives, both Charlotte and her father decide he's the man for her and, within six months, Charlotte marries the dashing mill owner from Accrington.

Then a young mill worker is found dead in the swollen River Ribble. With Joseph's business nearly bankrupt, it becomes apparent that all is not as it seems and Joseph is not the man he pretends to be. Heavily pregnant, penniless and heartbroken, Charlotte is forced to face the reality that life may never be the same again . . .

OUT NOW

The Windfell Family Secrets

DIANE ALLEN

Twenty-one years have passed since Charlotte Booth fought to keep her home at Windfell Manor, following her traumatic first marriage. Now, happily married to her childhood sweetheart, she seeks only the best for their children, Isabelle and Danny. But history has a habit of repeating itself when Danny's head is turned by a local girl of ill repute.

Meanwhile, the beautiful and secretive Isabelle shares all the undesirable traits of her biological father. And when she announces that she is to marry John Sidgwick, the owner of High Mill in Skipton, her mother quickly warns her against him. An ex-drinking mate of her late father who faces bankruptcy, Charlotte fears his interest in Isabelle is far from honourable. What she doesn't realize is how far he's willing to go to protect his future . . .

OUT NOW

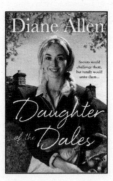

Daughter of the Dales

DIANE ALLEN

The death of Charlotte Atkinson, the family matriarch, at Windfell Manor casts a long shadow over her husband Archie and their two children, Isabelle and Danny. With big shoes to fill, Isabelle takes over the running of Atkinson's department store but her pride – and heart – is tested when her husband James brings scandal upon the family and the Atkinsons' reputation.

Danny's wife Harriet is still struggling to deal with the deaths of their first two children – deaths she blames Isabelle for. But Danny himself is grappling with his own demons when a stranger brings to light a long-forgotten secret from his past.

Meanwhile, Danny and Harriet's daughter Rosie has fallen under the spell of a local stable boy, Ethan. But will he stand by her or will he cause her heartache? And can Isabelle restore the Atkinsons' reputation and her friendship with Harriet, to unite the family once more?

OUT NOW

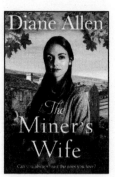

The Miner's Wife

DIANE ALLEN

Nineteen-year-old Meg Oversby often dreams of a more exciting life than the dull existence she faces at her family's farm deep in the Yorkshire Dales. Growing up, she's always sensed her father's disappointment at not having a son to help with the farm work.

So when Meg dances all night at the local market hall with Sam Alderson, a lead miner from Swaledale, a new light enters her life. Sam and his brother Jack show Meg a side to life she didn't know existed. But when her parents find out, she's forbidden from ever seeing them again.

Although where there is love, there is often a way. When Meg's uncle offers her the chance to help run the small village shop, she leaps at the opportunity, seeing it as a way to escape the oppressive family farm and see more of her beloved Sam. But as love blossoms, a darker truth emerges and Meg realizes that Sam may not be the man she thought he was . . .

OUT NOW

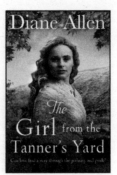

The Girl from the Tanner's Yard

DIANE ALLEN

After facing the horrors of the Crimean War, Adam Brooksbank returns to Black Moss Farm filled with regret over the path he has chosen in life. Starting anew, he decides to focus on rebuilding his family's rundown farm and making it a home again.

Lucy Bancroft lives with her parents near the local tannery, and is the most beautiful girl in the village. But unfortunately her wealth doesn't match her looks, and she soon realizes that nobody wants to court a girl from the filthy flay-pits, let alone marry her.

Yet when Lucy comes to work for Adam as his maid she finds herself falling in love with the farm, set high upon the wild moors of Haworth. Furthermore she begins to imagine a life with her new employer that goes beyond just being his maid.

As they spend more time together, their feelings develop for one another despite her parents warning her nothing good will come of it. As rumours swirl around the village, igniting jealousies and unearthing deeply buried secrets, will love find a way?

OUT NOW

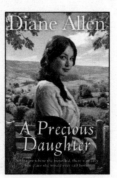

A Precious Daughter

DIANE ALLEN

When Ethan Postlethwaite, his wife Grace and their daughter Amy announce that they will be leaving the family home in the Yorkshire Dales, Grace's parents are heartbroken. Hoping for a new life prospecting for gold in the wilds of Canada, the young family say goodbye and set sail across the Atlantic in search of a brighter future.

The journey there proves hard and treacherous, however, and upon arrival it becomes apparent that the riches they had been promised in the gold fields have already been plundered. So when the family is devastated by the death of Grace, Ethan decides he must take his daughter back to England.

Arriving in Liverpool, Ethan and Amy soon find work in a dairy as cow-keepers, but Amy is restless and struggles to settle into yet another new life. And when a chance encounter at a cattle show ignites an old friendship, she must decide where her own future lies and what she must do in order to find happiness at last . . .

OUT NOW